ROGUE WOLF

PROTECTOR WOLF SHIFTER SERIES BK3

LILLIANA ROSE

To my dog
Kimba,
Miss you by my feet boy

BLURB

Tamaska is to become a wolf shifter but she might not survive the change.

If Tamaska wants to survive being hunted by vampires she must transformed into a wolf shifter. But new information brings into question if the transformation process will work or not.

Kodiak doesn't want to take any risks that might end Tamaska's life. She is his mate and he can't imagine living without her. He'd rather she is alive, protected by himself against the vampires. But the vampires capture Kodiak.

Can Tamaska find someone else in the pack to transform her into the wolf shifter? Will she find a way to rescue her wolf mate without letting the vampires capture her?

Fans of Roxie Ray, Kim Richardson, and Sarah Spade will devour Lilliana Rose's world of unexpected adventure and dark imagination.

Begin the journey in this protector turn lover and opposites attract series set in a dark, urban fantasy world.

CHAPTER 1

THE BLOOD OPAL WAS EVERYTHING.

If Tamaska kept telling herself that, then the rest of it wouldn't matter. Not the blood that had been split the night the vampires attacked...an attack that burned raw in her mind, and not Kodiak and Shota's fight to the death for the alpha position.

Kodiak had won, but at what cost?

She shivered as questions and thoughts tangled in her mind.

Because no matter how progressive Kodiak might be, so much was lost. Shota. Olcan. That horrible, bloody fight. Was that all this world had to offer now? Death and bloodshed?

And what about her? What were her options? She could turn into the thing she hated or the thing she still feared. She'd chosen to become a shifter, for Kodiak, the man she loved, but even that...that might kill her.

Yet what could she do? Not become a bloodsucker. She hated the vampires who had killed her best friend, who'd marked her; stolen the opal.

And deep down, while she could accept what Kodiak was, a wolf shifter, she still feared canines. His offer of turning her, something she'd accepted, could she do it? Really? Was it worth the risk?

She'd said yes and she did mean it. But underneath turmoil ruled.

So she clung to the mystery of the Blood Opal, their mission in finding it and unraveling whatever importance it might hold.

"Just keep it together," she muttered as she scrubbed the brush back and forth on the carpet, its bristles stained red with blood.

She dipped the brush into the hydrogen peroxide laced water, the stench one of death and crime, half hidden by the searing bite of the cleaner.

If only she could erase the memory of that bloody night from her mind as quickly as she could erase blood stains from the floor. She'd give her brain a good scrub and then get on with life.

Instead, her life had been shattered and its pieces scattered, some of them never to be found again. She'd entered an entirely new world, one full of beasts she'd always thought were only myths made up to scare children. More than that, she was about to become a monster herself.

Either way, that's what she would become. A shifter, she told herself for the millionth time, was preferable to a vampire any day.

"You don't have to do this," Ash said. The pretty female shifter cleaned nearby, moving a red-stained cloth up and down the meeting room wall at the back of the wolves' clubhouse.

"I do," Tamaska replied, her elbow aching from scrubbing.

"You look exhausted," Ash said.

Eyes dry from a lack of sleep, she dipped the brush into the bucket of cold, chemical-filled liquid. The water turned red so quickly, it needed to be replaced again.

"So do you. And I have to help." Tamaska doubled her efforts on a stubborn spot.

"No, you don't. This is pack business." Ash's jeans and shirt were stained from hours of washing every inch of the clubhouse. And she looked like Tamaska felt; tired, drawn, like she'd visited hell along with everyone else.

No, she needed to help with clean-up. If she was going to be part of the pack, then she'd pull her weight.

Even if she wasn't about to join the pack, about to be turned, she still needed to pitch in. Wolf shifters had already been killed protecting her against the vampires. She owed these people her life. Not just Kodiak, but all of them.

Her heart squeezed at the thought of his name.

"It's the least I can do." Tamaska slammed the brush into the carpet and, pressing down hard, she scrubbed.

She rinsed the brush and continued, determined to show the others she could do it. Each time she scrubbed, she removed more blood. After so long, though, it felt like with each cleaned patch, another would appear. She felt like Lady McBeth.

There was so much blood to clean up in the main building. How long would that take? The pack needed to regroup before the vampires came for her again. And so long as she was marked, they would.

There has to be an easier way.

Yes, like turning into a shifter. And, unbidden, a shudder passed through her.

What would it be like to have fur?

Tamaska swallowed, her skin prickling like a blast of cold

air hit her despite the exertion from cleaning all day. Sweat soaked into her shirt, which she'd borrowed from Kodiak.

I'm going to become a wolf. She couldn't stop the frightening, thrilling thought. And the only thrilling part was it would bring her closer to Kodiak.

These were the wrong thoughts. With the vampires declaring some kind of war and coming for her because of the Blood Opal she needed to not just up her game in scrubbing up blood. She needed to get her fight on. But as a human she was weak.

Would becoming a wolf give her those fighting skills she desperately needed?

She wasn't even sure the transformation would happen, anyway. Despite everything that had happened, the pack hadn't entirely accepted or approved her becoming one of them.

Some of them looked on her as the one that had brought dissent and trouble to their ranks. And they weren't wrong. Turning her—if she survived—wouldn't make it go away. No, it would make it worse.

The recently killed alpha, Olcan, had ruled mating with humans was forbidden. He'd reasoned that the pack needed to keep their bloodline pure; only finding and mating with other shifters from other packs.

They had a job to do, and bringing humans in would muddy their waters. After all, the wolf shifters had come from America decades ago, following vampires to Australia to help keep humans safe.

Kodiak, the new alpha, was going rogue immediately, changing pack rules and causing a stir. Ash whispered to her earlier in the day that word of his changes would spread fast and wide. After all, his first act as alpha was to officially announce he intended to take Tamaska as his mate and she'd undergo the rarely used transition of human into a shifter.

That decision had divided the pack.

Since then, tension hung heavy and thick in the air. It was her fault—that, and the Blood Opal's mystery.

She seemed to be entwined with that gem for reasons she couldn't begin to understand. The vampires had attacked the shifters because of her, the opal, and whatever they needed her for. Because they wanted her, and the pack—no matter their collective feelings on her being Kodiak's chosen mate— bore the brunt of that want.

If she went away, the pack would be safe. They all knew that.

And yet they protected her, anyway.

She owed the pack. Big time.

They had a code, though. One so ingrained and strong even she could see it. Tamaska didn't doubt for one moment the pack members would see her as weak if she didn't repay her debt—not that she didn't want to.

It was more than that. If she was going to be changed and become part of the pack, she had to work to convince them of her worthiness so they'd accept her.

That was one big reason why she cleaned alongside them beyond the point of exhaustion. Beyond her capacity for pain and death and destruction. She needed to find that inner strength, use it, push past all limitations.

If she could do that, then they'd see she could one day be the mate Kodiak needed and deserved. And that meant getting past her fears. Embracing the change to come.

At least, that's what she hoped. Of course, acceptance could only happen if she managed to survive the change.

With the mark of the vampire the change seemed so much more dangerous.

Kodiak—her heart squeezed tight at the thought of him— had instructed Ash to research ways to ensure a successful transformation.

For the last hour, all Tamaska had wanted to do was question Ash about what she'd found; more importantly, when would she be changed?

Fruitless to ask, though, so she kept scrubbing away the blood. And it seemed insane to her this was one of the last things on the clean up list. That's how deep the damage from the brutal vampire fight went.

"He'll be back, soon," Ash said.

Kodiak was off trying to shore up the barriers outside. He'd gotten up early, leaving her arms, leaving her missing that warmth of him, the heady scent that spun her head slowly, the heaviness of his limbs that felt so right.

They'd taken a dorm room for themselves, one of the few places untouched by the fighting. And for two nights, after the maelstrom of emotions that whipped up in the compound, he was hers.

They'd kissed and touched and made love. They did it like they had forever, like everything was about to be stolen from them the next second. Desperate and slow, a dichotomy of need and want and refuge.

But this morning, before dawn, she knew something was about to shift and change again. So, for a few hours, they'd been clean in each other's arms, fucking and kissing and holding each other, the nightmare around them forgotten.

She stood now, cricking her back, surveying what they'd done.

It didn't seem much.

"You smell like him," Ash said.

Tamaska turned. "Because I'm in his clothes?"

The other woman shrugged. "Because you've been laying down with him and he's somehow infused himself into you."

She must have stared because Ash offered her a small smile.

"It's a good thing, Tamaska," she said, rinsing her rag, then checking on something running on her computer. "It means you're taking him on as your mate, and he you."

"But it's not just up to him," Tamaska said, "everyone gets a say."

Ash sighed. "The old ways are deep, but if we don't change, then we stagnate and die out. The idea of keeping bloodlines pure and not mixing with humans is...antiquated. But it also makes sense because the human has to be turned and not that many want that."

The words weren't pointed at her, but it felt that way, and they weren't wrong. Her fears, all of it... Tamaska sucked in a breath. "I'll do what I can to prove my worthiness."

Ash only looked at her and went back to her task.

Tamaska sighed. It wasn't only all of that bothering her. Kodiak told her something else after the fight, and she couldn't make sense of it. He'd told her she might be more than just human.

She didn't know what the fuck that meant. Was it to do with the mark of the vampire? But she certainly wasn't one, wasn't turning. Sunlight didn't hurt her and she didn't suddenly crave blood. And hadn't he told her how the vampires and shifters hated the smell of the other? She loved Kodiak's scent.

So what the hell did he mean?

Am I some other monster?

Her mind whirled through the list of fantasy creatures she knew about.

Dragon, banshee, zombie, witch, bogeyman, goblin, golem...

She would know if she was one of those...right? None of the creatures that came to mind felt right.

Wolf shifter?

Tamaska shivered. That was impossible. She couldn't be something like a wolf and not know about it. She couldn't be discussing the dangers of turning into one if she was already one.

Were there other shifters out there? Could be be one of those? Or maybe something she hadn't thought of. Something horrible…

Again, it didn't make sense.

Then again, when she'd gone to the nightclub alone in search of the Blood Opal, it was like her senses had been on steroids. She could hear and see better than normal.

Maybe the vampire's mark and her weird link to the opal made her something else, something more?

Superhuman?

Was there even such a thing?

Or maybe she was a mishmash of vampire and shifter that was coming to life with the exposure to this dark underworld. Or the mark put on her had opened something inside her.

But that could work in her favor. If she was superhuman in some way, then her transformation into a wolf shifter might be less risky. From the very little Kodiak had told her about the process, she understood the risks. A change could go horribly wrong.

Especially since she'd been marked.

"Ash, can I ask you something?"

The shifter looked at her carefully. "You can ask anything you want, whether I answer…"

Tamaska narrowed her eyes, but took a breath. "What should I expect when I become a wolf?"

Ash dropped her rag in the bucket next to her, then she swirled it in the water, and squeezed, returning to her task. "There's nothing to tell."

"I don't believe you." She clenched the brush hard. "You might not go around turning people, but you know." Ash didn't answer. "Why won't you tell me? I have a right."

"You don't have any rights."

A lump formed in Tamaska's throat. "I've the right to know what's ahead of me."

"Look at the walls, the floors. That's what's ahead of you."

"My future is to be the house maid?"

Ash threw down the rag and glared. "I mean this life isn't made for humans, even if Kodiak's accepted you, even if I do and the rest of the pack, it's a hard road ahead. There are risks, Tamaska. Big ones that will impact others. It's not all about you." Ash growled and returned to cleaning the wall. Intense anger vibrated from her, like a hot wind.

"I don't mean to be a burden. I'm...I'm asking because I want to do right by all of you. If you think I should just go, I will."

Ash's shoulders lifted. "That isn't what I'm saying. The vampires want you, and it's...it's all a mess. But this isn't an easy life. And if you can't even take me getting annoyed then maybe you should rethink it, because you can destroy Kodiak."

Her words blindsided Tamaska and her eyes prickled with tears. She blinked quickly, pushing away the emotion. "I would never—"

"But you could. And not even on purpose. We're a closed bunch. And protective of each other. And Kodiak's never brought in an outsider." She trusted Ash more than the others and her words hurt. "You come with a unique set of problems that even if all goes well, life will be hard."

Would it always be this tough for her when it came to the pack? Would she always be an outsider?

"I just want to do what's right."

"Then clean this shit with me." Ash threw a red-stained cloth into her bucket, then rinsed it before returning to cleaning.

The shadows under Ash's eyes lay dark and heavy.

Strands of hair escaped her ponytail. She didn't look like the pack member Tamaska had first met. The pack's infighting and the loss of the alpha had burdened Ash. It burdened everyone. And she didn't know how to help them apart from cleaning up.

"I need more water." She picked up the bucket and stretching her tired muscles once more. "Ash, should I go?"

"You go and he'll tear the world apart, don't try and pretend otherwise."

"But if I'm a danger—"

For fuck's sake, Tamaska. You can't be this needy. We're wolves. Strong, interdependent, yes, but beyond strong. Find that strength. And you know you can't leave. It is what it is."

The sharp breath hurt her lungs as she dragged one in. "I guess I'll go get fresh water."

Ash didn't even glance her way.

"Do you want me to change your water?" Tamaska asked.

"I'm all right, thanks," she said sharply.

"Okay, then." Tamaska picked up the bloody bucket of water, her opposite hand outstretched to counter the bucket's weight as she carefully walked outside.

Out of all the pack members, Ash had always supported Tamaska most. To have her lash out hurt. Badly. Everything was so complicated. Because she couldn't blame Ash. They were intrinsically different beings. Human and shifter and she despaired right then of ever truly understanding.

In that short exchange she got something.

Even if she changed successfully into a shifter, she wouldn't truly ever be one of them until she understood them, down to the fibers of her soul.

Until she could do that, she was destined to be an outsider.

Tamaska understood the pressures the pack members faced. It was more than just the vampires' attack. They'd lost members, and the most prominent loss was Olcan. Then, Kodiak fought Shota for leadership and announced Tamaska as his mate.

People were angry. Hurting. Lashing out. And they were stoically doing what they needed to.

The minutia of the levels of complication were so intricate how could she find a way in.

Love wasn't enough.

Tamaska sighed heavily. The shifters had their ways and their secrets. And she was an outsider, but she had something they wanted; a connection, somehow, to the Blood Opal.

It might just be the sacrifice the vampires need to unlock whatever power it holds. She didn't know.

But the opal was the biggest and most dangerous secret of all.

She might be human, not one of them, and destined to never be one of them, even if she changed, but she vowed to do what she could to find the opal.

Find the stone, unlock its secrets and stop the vampires.

And maybe then she could find acceptance.

Maybe then she'd be worthy of Kodiak, the man she loved.

CHAPTER 2

amaska

OUTSIDE, she tipped the foul liquid near the fence marking the boundary between the pack's property and the National Park. She'd lost count of how many times she'd trekked out there to change her water.

After hooking the bucket on the top of the garden tap, she filled it halfway, then poured in a healthy slug of the hydrogen peroxide. This routine gave her a bit of a workout, though the gym would have been better.

It did soothe something in her, the mundane routine. But she wished it wasn't to do with the aftermath of violence.

She rubbed her chest between her breasts with the heel of her hand, trying to relieve the tightness and the cold heaviness there. But how could she when to her right, between the bushes, lay the graves they'd dug for the fallen?

They mocked her with their sacrifice each and every time.

Even Shota's death was her fault by proxy.

After all, if she hadn't been there, hadn't been chosen by Kodiak they wouldn't have fought for the right of alpha. They wouldn't have fought over whether to keep things the same and turf her out, or change things and make room for an interloper...worse, an interloping human.

She didn't want any more pack members to be killed, but their fates were out of her control.

Tamaska tugged up the too-big jeans she wore. She'd love to control which clothes she wore. Kodiak's were obviously too big, but he forbade her from returning to her apartment alone. Until that moment, she hadn't wanted to. But after nearly two days of cleaning up, she needed to get away from the clubhouse.

It was day, so no risk of vampire attacks. She got his protectiveness, when it made sense, but during the day she wasn't about to be taken by any blood sucking monsters. Going home, getting some clothes, her computer...it would go a long way to feeling stronger, and another laptop in the mix would help.

And...shit. She needed fresh air, a change of scenery. At least for a few hours.

She slipped the bucket's metal hook from the tap, grunting under its weight as targeted arm muscles ached from overuse. She didn't mind the hard work to gain the pack's respect, but there had to be an easier way to clean the carpets.

With each step the fumes of the hydrogen peroxide assaulted her senses as the bucket assaulted her shins.

Suddenly, Kodiak marched out of the building, the back door slamming shut behind him. She almost dropped the bucket.

The man stole her breath and made every muscle ache in an entirely different way.

Tall, muscled, arrogant and strong. Sexy as hell. And all hers.

That last thought tore through her like a bushfire. She wanted to rush up to him, throw her arms around him and kiss him.

He was an oasis of pleasure in this endless desert of pain and destruction. But Tamaska remained where she was.

Kodiak had duties now, ones that must be crushing down on him. To become the leader was burden enough, but under these circumstances... It twisted and turned with all he needed to do.

Not even the fact her man was going to be the new alpha, and if she got turned, successfully, her at his side, could lighten that burden.

A smile broke over his strained expression as he turned and looked at her. Everything lit up inside and Tamaska hurried over to him, unable to resist.

He slid his arm around her waist and pulled her against him, his mouth whispering kisses and bites against the sensitive flesh of her throat.

Her body flooded with heat and a low, sweet ache only he could ease.

He closed his fingers on her hip, slipping one beneath the loose waistband of her jeans. "You smell good enough to eat. Feel even better." He bit her earlobe making her heart flutter wildly.

"There's no one around out here," Tamaska said, the words slipping free.

He groaned.

"Any other time, and I'd be ripping you out of my clothes," said Kodiak as he embraced her. "Unwrapping you like a gift."

He sucked on her artery and she sighed, arching for him.

"Any other time, and I'd stick a bow on and say have at it."

She looked up at him and curled her hand against his cheek. "But there's so much work to do and I can't have them thinking you're playing favorites."

"But I am…"

"Kodiak," she whispered.

He pressed his nose to hers and sighed.

"Yeah, I know. I've got so much fucking shit to do. This… this is all bad, Tamaska." He sighed heavily, his stress visible in the thick lines on his forehead.

She smoothed the lines away with her fingers. "I know. But you can do it. I have faith."

"It's gonna take more than faith," he said, kissing her cheek.

She reluctantly stepped out of his embrace. "Can I help, though?"

"No." He ran his thumb over her lips as he looked her up and down. "You don't have to do this."

Tamaska smiled. "You're the second person to tell me that. Yes, I do. Otherwise, I'll never be accepted."

A darkness entered his eyes. "Tamaska…"

"What is it?" A sharp pain lanced her. "Did you learn something about my transformation?"

"No, we have to finish cleaning up this place before we do anything else. It's too risky to leave it looking like this." He swallowed hard, as if pushing away emotion. "If the cops come…"

But she didn't need to say even if they got it spotless, nothing they did could hold up to modern forensics or even a bit of a dig around in the garden.

She placed her hand on his throat, like she could comfort him from that. The heaviness of his pulse slowed under her palm as she tried to think of something.

Actually…

"I've got an idea to help with that," she said. "I—"

"No." Kodiak took her hands in his, lifting them from his chest and squeezing them tight. "Leave it all to me."

"I can't. You know the saying… A burden shared is a burden eased. And I can help."

But he shook his head. "It's pack business."

"Then make me a part of the pack, Kodiak."

"Tamaska…"

But she shook her head. "Don't you want me to be changed *now*? Don't you want me to be part of the pack?"

Tamaska tried to pull her hands away from his, but he tightened his grip. "I didn't mean it like that," he said.

"What did you fucking mean, then? Because I've had enough of you all keeping outside the loop when you're risking everything for me."

"We're not."

"You are," she said lifting her chin. "You're all keeping secrets from me."

"We're doing it to protect you."

"That line's wearing thin."

"It's not a line. Turning you now is dangerous, and there's so much for you to lear. Too much to learn all at once. Until we get things sorted here, you have to wait."

"Fuck that." She managed to get her hands away from his.

"Tamaska." He eased her close and nudged her cheek with his nose. "Please. We need to deal with the vampires and the opal and maybe the police. You here, wanting this change to be with me…it's more than enough and it means everything to me."

Crap, her heart started to melt right away.

Fuck it. Tamaska fought and held on to her rising anger. She wasn't about to let him get away with this. Yes, she believed him but he was also putting her in her place. Treating her as the little human. And she might be weak, but she wasn't weak of mind or will.

And perhaps they were noble and true as per their nature, but the tricky, fickle parts of humanity they didn't like, along with the greed and meanness, well…those faults could all be manipulated.

By her. The weak little human burden.

"Keys to your car." Tamaska, put out her hand.

His eyes narrowed into glittering slits. "No one drives my car. You know that." Kodiak's voice took on an edge.

"Then, drive me. We need to get industrial carpet cleaners, like the stuff the crime scene cleaners use and I know where to get them."

His brows rose. "Is there something you need to tell me about, Tamaska?"

"No. But the places that people hold openings and galas to show off things like that bloody opal sometimes need a forensic clean down. One we did was at a grisly murder scene. Very Goth, but it needed to also be free of anything disgusting. People like the idea of crime scenes but not anything remotely linked to the reality. Of course, other places have just been plain derelict and filthy." She sighed. "I can help us not only speed up the cleaning, but make it look like nothing happened and we decided to burn old furniture for a bonfire."

Kodiak looked at her like she'd just sprouted another head. "You didn't think of it earlier?"

"No." Tamaska snapped the word. "I was too busy dealing with what happened. But now I've had a chance to think… I just want to fit in, do my part. Prove myself, Kodiak."

He rubbed a hand over his chin. "And where do you get this stuff."

"I can talk to the crew we hire, back when…" When she had a job. "I did that stuff. I've got a good relationship with them, I bet I can get them cheap."

"No way. It's too risky," said Kodiak.

Tamaska nodded. "Okay, I understand the risks. But if we can't get outside help, because any human would take one look at the place and call the police, then what if I bring the chemicals and machines here. They have enough, and I've helped them clean places before. If I can use them, so can everyone else. No one will know what happened here."

No way Tamaska was letting go of her brilliant idea.

"Kodiak, we need your help. More carpets need to be removed," Onai called from the back door.

"Fuck! I'm coming." Kodiak over his shoulder at his pack-mate and then back at Tamaska.

Her heart jumped at the intensity in his eyes burned deep into her. He might be the alpha, but she'd prove worthy of being his mate. To him and everyone else.

And he'd have to learn to accept her help from time to time.

"Keys." Tamaska wriggled her fingers.

Kodiak growled under his breath. "No."

This was clearly a hill he was ready to die on. Men and their cars, she thought. Some things didn't change no matter whether they were shifter or human. Their cars mattered.

"I mean it," she said. "And you know making this place as clean as possible makes sense. Cleaner than we can make it as is."

For a second she thought he would dismiss her but then he sighed.

"You can take Olcan's car. And I don't want you going alone."

She shrugged off his words. "It's daytime. I'll be fine."

"No." He caught her arm and held her there.

Tamaska blew out a breath. "Everyone's busy. If someone comes with me, it'll only hold up the cleaning process, and you've already said it needs to be done quickly."

Kodiak muttered something then pulled her in against

him, holding her, biting at her throat and tiny thrills of delight raced through her flesh. "Anyone tell you you're a stubborn woman?"

"You? And you need that. Because how else am I going to get you to respect me as much as you want to fuck me?"

"Goddamn it, woman." He smiled against her, she could feel the shift of his lips. "Go, get what you need, and get the fuck back here, or I'll make you pay for your disobedience."

"Now that's tempting."

He tightened his embrace and she moaned softly, wanting to burrow deep into him and forget everything in the world but him. "You might not like what I have in mind."

"I'll find out, then." She rose on her toes and kissed his lips. "Maybe take my time, earn my punishment."

"No, you'll go and come straight back. You will *not* go anywhere else. Promise me."

It wasn't a question.

"I don't know what I would do if something happened to you," he added.

Her heart softened. "I'll come straight back."

The back door to the club house slammed shut, the noise shattering the moment.

And he sighed, stepping away from her. "What the fuck is it?"

"Kodiak, Moki thinks he should be in charge of the computers and he's fucking it up," called Channing.

Other members of the pack had come into the clubhouse and she was still learning who was who outside the core few she'd met when that fateful night threw her and Kodiak together and on this path.

Kodiak growled. "I should rip their throats out."

He didn't mean it but she still shuddered because beneath his words lay the hard and dark center of what they were facing. And she'd seen how things could escalate.

"They sound like children," Tamaska said, trying to lighten the mood.

He glanced at her, letting his guard down momentarily as he dropped his voice to a mere whisper. "This is a lot for the pack to recover from. There's going to be rifts for a while, and it's up to me to bring them all together."

"You will." And she believed that. No matter what the future held for her, she knew this man was a true leader, who, given the chance, could make great changes and strides for his pack and his kind.

"Kodiak, quickly, you have no idea what a fucking mess he's making," Channing yelled. "I'm going to fucking break his neck if you don't come!"

"Ash'll show you where the keys are. Straight to the equipment, and straight back." He pressed his nose against hers once more.

"I will."

He kissed her hard, a short, hot, wild ride of a kiss, then hurried over to Channing, who held the door open.

"I told him I was getting you, but he didn't care," said Channing.

According to Kodiak, Channing was one of the youngest pack members, and also one who had specifically been assigned to his team during previous investigations and attacks.

"I'll sort him out," Kodiak said as he strode quickly to the back door.

At the door, he paused, looking back at her and everything in her flared into needful heat. Then he slipped inside and she found herself mising Kodiak already.

She marveled at how he could do that to her when he'd only just stepped inside. Was this how it would be? Bonded so tight that even a second apart was too long?

Or maybe she just wanted to cling to the only familiar

thing here. Because they weren't bonded. She hadn't changed so all she had was a burning need for him and a chance at a life.

With him.

The door banged closed and Tamaska brushed her hands, straightened her clothes, glad to be done hauling the damned bucket around. Permission to go and get industrial carpet cleaners was a small win, but a smart one and for her, that made it so much bigger.

The quicker the place was cleaned the faster they could track the opal and make the vampires pay for what they'd done to the pack.

And hopefully no one else would have to die in the process.

CHAPTER 3

 *odiak*

GODDAMN IT ALL to fucking hell. The latest squabble was one Kodiak didn't need. One he knew was happening because people were stretching and testing boundaries. Times were uncertain and apart from the bloody vampire attack, he'd thrown one hell of a wrench into the works regarding wanting to mate with and change a human.

This might be something the others could all get behind if he were nothing more than an underling, a shifter lacking in importance.

And, of course, if things weren't so insane.

The change in power, the attacks, the opal that somehow threatened their safety and the world around them.

If the vampires were to take Sydney, Australia's official capital, what was to stop them from moving up and on?

He didn't know and he had no intentions of finding out. The goal was to nip it all in the bud.

But first things first.

Kodiak growled sharply at the shifters who opened their mouths to make their cases as he entered the computer room in the concealed bunker under the clubhouse, where the surveillance gear was assembled.

Right now their cases could fuck themselves. Their system had failed.

This room was the brain of the compound, but its failure had let the enemy inside. They didn't need arguments. They needed cohesion, ideas and ways to not only shore up the problem but also fix it. Kodiak wouldn't allow the vampires to destroy his pack, not while he was in charge.

He looked around. Everything seemed in one piece.

Fortunately, the vampires hadn't made it into the computer room. He'd assigned Channing and Ash to update the security system, to prevent what had happened the other night from happening again.

Yet Moki sat at a computer, just like Channing said and from the guy's energy, he clearly was claiming his spot, whether given to him or not.

And that didn't fly with Kodiak. It had nothing to do with who was best, there were ways and means to state a case and he'd listen. But just upending everything and steaming ahead simply didn't work.

"What are you doing?" Kodiak asked, firm and loud. His arms loose by his side, hands closing into light fists.

It should have told the kid Kodiak wasn't there to play. And he'd fight if necessary."

Moki didn't even glance up from the computer as he typed. "Fixing it."

"This is Channing's job. He knows computers, and you don't." Kodiak stepped forward.

"Yeah? Well I know humans and you don't and yet you brought one back here."

He considered Moki. "I get it. You hate the fact I'm with a human. And you're what? Blaming her for this attack?"

And yeah, it was her fault, by proxy. But she hadn't deliberately sought out the bloodsuckers and led them here to sabotage us on some fucked up Trojan Horse mission.

"It is her fault."

Argue that and he'd lose face, respect, and the kneejerk shit never worked. So he just nodded. "Just say it is her fault. She did all this deliberately. Stupid fucking human, right? Don't know any better than to bring about trouble."

"Yeah."

"But Moki, have you and the pack forgotten our purpose to protect humans from vampires?" he asked softly.

Moki snorted. "Whatever, dude. I actually do know computers." Moki's hands flew over the keyboard.

Kodiak kicked the chair out from under Moki, who tumbled to the floor. "I'm not dude. I'm Alpha. And you'll learn respect, the chain of command and the power of talking things through, or I'll fucking turf you out of the damn pack. You got me?"

Moki pushed to his feet, glaring.

"What's going on with the computers, Channing?" Kodiak asked.

"Shit."

Save him from juvenile wolves. "Can you be more specific?"

"Boss, this is going to take me hours to fix," said Channing, looking at the screen. It flashed with green numbers and letters. The pup ran his hands through his hair and made distressed noises as if in physical pain.

Kodiak strode forward, picked Moki up by the back of his shirt so his feet dangled above the floor, and hauled him up and against the wall.

He looked at Channing, who slipped in front of the

computer and began typing, undoing what Moki had done. While tutting disapprovingly. "It's not done that way anymore, Moki. There are better ways…you have no fucking idea."

"You were told to stop." Kodiak turned back to Moki who he still held up above the ground. "What, are you working with the vampires or something?"

"Of course not," stammered Moki. He turned a little green at the edges. "I wouldn't work for them, ever."

Kodiak narrowed his eyes and tightened his grip. "Trying to ruin things for me so I'll lose my place as alpha, then?"

"No…" Moki looked at the ground.

"Should we fight over who's in charge?" He came in close to Moki's ear and growled low.

"N-no need for that."

Kodiak grinned. "Because you'd lose."

"I can fight."

Oh fucking hell, he didn't need a wet-behind-the-ears pup thinking he was king of the heap. Or maybe this was just pure and deliberate distraction. He didn't know, but he was going to find out.

"Really? You're a champion, are you?" He growled again then said, "Why not openly challenge me, get your little show on the road, prove your worth? Or are you not worth anything at all and you cover that up by making noise and causing disruption?"

"I don't want your position."

Kodiak looked him up and down. "I don't believe you. Maybe we should fight to the death?" He let go of Moki's shirt, and the shifter fell hard onto the concrete floor.

"My leg," groaned Moki, rolling side-to-side on his back and clutching it.

Channing made a sound but didn't dare speak up. He knew what the pup wanted to say, that surely there'd been enough bloodshed. For all his bravery, Channing hadn't ever dealt with anything so destructive, not on this scale and not so close to home.

Close?

It had invaded their home.

He didn't want a fight and neither did Moki. But Moki needed to learn a lesson.

"Get up and stop faking it." Kodiak didn't give him a choice. He grabbed Moki by the arm and pulled him off the floor.

"Let me go!" yelled Moki, trying to break free.

Fucking childish pup. Kodiak needed to push it, so he did.

"Let you go? No. Not until you kneel and pledge yourself to me. Do that, or I won't bother with a fight. I'll rip your head off your shoulders right now and feed your remains to the crows."

"I can't. You're not sworn in as our alpha," Moki said.

"Can't? Or is that won't?" Kodiak punched Moki, sending him stumbling backwards into the panelled wall.

But the kid stood there, and Kodiak knew he was either looking at a future leader or a future Brutus. Or maybe a vampire's lunch. This kind of foolish bravery could go any of those ways.

If he learned wisdom, it would be the first; cunning the second; and just thoughtless chest puffing bravery? The third.

"Let's try this again, Moki. Kneel." Kodiak held up his fists, ready to strike.

"No."

He didn't hit the idiot. Instead, he insulted him by unfurling his hand and giving him a powerful shove.

Moki's face turned a ruddy red. But he didn't raise his fist to Kodiak.

"That's why you're in this mess." Kodiak stepped up to

him. "You're useless to me if you can't follow my instructions."

The kid scowled. "I'm better suited to work here than where you put me."

Kodiak's anger got the better of him, and this time he punched Moki, hard. But then he dropped his hand. His anger wasn't going to help. He needed to try and stay on top of it, to manipulate it into something constructive. "You. Stay there and don't move.

He turned from Moki to Channing. "Kid, tell me what he was doing."

"Hooking up the system to his phone so he had special access," said Channing, typing quickly.

"Is that so, Moki?" Kodiak spoke slow and deep. "So, I'm thinking sabotage?"

Moki's eyes widened with fear.

"You need to prove that you deserve to stay in the pack," said Kodiak.

Moki lifted a shaking hand and pointed a finger at him. "The only one who should leave is that human of yours."

Kodiak punched him again. Time to cut that negativity towards Tamaska out. He wasn't unreasonable. He got it, but this really wasn't about her and he knew it. This was anger, fear, and frustration. This was trying to get a handle on the change in power and the changes set to roll in.

No one knew how to change a human into a shifter. They had once, but that knowledge was buried in history. Kodiak needed to check on Ash and see if she'd learned anything about how to do that. And do it safely.

He wouldn't attempt to change Tamaska if the process put her life at risk, no matter how much she claimed she wanted it.

To take a risk on something she said she wanted wasn't

worth it. Not that he thought she was lying. It was more…he didn't know if she understood what it meant.

It wasn't just a chance to be with him. It was everything. And he didn't know what that damn vampire marking might have done on a molecular level to her. Or how well a human would handle it. They were complicated compared to shifters. They were both less and more than shifters. Lines weren't delineated like for him and his kind.

And his Tamaska…only a few days ago she feared and hated dogs and now she wanted to be a canine shifter. For him.

Right now he couldn't start to unpack it all. He'd only been at the top for a day, and he already had his hands full of problems, one thing on top of another.

The Tamaska thing of what, exactly, she was beyond human needed to wait.

So far, Ash hadn't found any evidence that Tamaska was anything but human. Kodiak was sure that Tamaska had some supernatural abilities. But, so far, proof had eluded them. And now they had so many other things to deal with.

Correction. He did. Her change, if they did it, couldn't be a top priority right now, even though he knew she wanted just to get it over and done with.

You'll understand what it feels like to juggle when you're in charge. Olcan's words echoed in Kodiak's mind, a sentence from one of the few conversations when the previous alpha had opened up to him.

You're laughing at me, aren't you, Olcan? Wherever you are.

Right now, he had a very particular problem to deal with and aggression was the only way.

"You're going in chains," Kodiak said, pulling Moki up from the ground, ignoring his bleeding nose and swollen eye. "For treason."

"Controlling the cameras with my phone is easier than

relying on the system here," said Moki, pointing to the desk's three computers. , a big screen showed Ash cleaning the meeting room by herself.

An unpleasant thought came to him. Had Moki been watching Tamaska?

His stomach lurched with regret. He shouldn't have let her get the carpet cleaners by herself. Then again, she wasn't any safer among his own pack members. Not until they got the systems back up and running, patched and improved.

Besides, it was broad daylight, where the sun was strongest. She'd be okay. Still... He wished he was with her.

"Yeah, but you were only setting it up so you could watch Tamaska," said Channing, goading the other pup.

"I was going to fix the system. I just needed more time," said Moki in the same tone.

Kodiak's gut told him he shouldn't trust Moki. Even his head agreed, but he had to consider the pack's code.

None of them would follow him if he simply killed another member. He had to prove his strength, forgiveness, and intelligence to bring the pack together. Putting Moki in chains would do that, but giving him a second chance would still be better.

Kodiak's gratitude to Channing, who had let him know about Moki's disobedience, eased the new alpha's stress a little. At least there were a few wolves who still supported him. Kodiak hoped that would be enough to pull them all together.

Just like he hoped Moki would come around. They didn't need more in-pack fighting. They needed unity.

"You want the chains or are you going to obey?"

I don't want the chains," he said.

"Are you going to obey?"

Moki took a beat too long to respond. "Yes."

So Kodiak gave him another hard shake.

"Let me go," growled Moki, blood dribbling from his nose to mouth.

"I catch you doing this again, and you're out of the pack." Kodiak looked him up and down. "We work as a team, always."

"Fine."

"I mean it." Kodiak said.

"So do I." Moki cast his eyes down.

Kodiak growled. He didn't want to let Moki go, but he needed to give him another chance. A brutal reign wouldn't go down well with the rest of the pack.

And brutal was the last way he wanted to rule.

"Go to the meeting room and wash the walls." Kodiak released Moki, then pushed him towards the door.

Moki stopped short of growling at Kodiak as he left. And inside, something dark stirred for the other wolf. Fuck, he hoped it wasn't a twisted version of stupid bravery that took him out. Morals and self-righteousness had a habit of biting the dust hard when it mixed in with all the wrong things masquerading in an upstart's head as right.

Kodiak stared after the other wolf. "What's the damage?"

"With what he did? I can't believe he tried this," said Channing, shaking his head.

"So he lied?" asked Kodiak, shifting to a position behind Channing to get a better look at the screen. He knew a bit about coding and hardware, but he wasn't an expert.

"See for yourself." Channing flipped between screens to bring up the code, then scrolled slowly.

Kodiak scanned the information onscreen. "Would it be a good system to control security from our phones?"

"No, at least not if we did things Moki's way. It would take up too much memory on the phone." Channing thinned his lips.

He looked at the pup.

"But you could do it, right?" While he couldn't afford to jump to conclusions and get it wrong, he also couldn't dismiss something that might be innovative.

Channing shifted a little as the back of his ears turned red. Shit. The kid was young and could be hot-headed at times, he had something to prove, too, and he protected his space fiercely.

Still, what counted was his loyalty to Kodiak, and Channing had that in spades. He guessed the trick was to find the right balance between hot headed loyalty and territoriality and hot headed got-something-to-prove shit that might help them. And he had to do that, not the two wolves.

"Channing?"

The pup sighed. "Of course, boss."

"So, really, the issue was that he was touching your computers." Kodiak folded his arms over his chest.

"No, boss, I wouldn't bother you with that. I know you're busy." Channing's ears turned a brighter red as he leaned closer to the screen, turning his face away from his alpha.

Kodiak growled softly. "I'm counting on you to be the bigger shifter here, just as much as I'm counting on you to fix the system by tonight. If what Moki was doing works, those upgrades can be done later."

He didn't speak for a beat. "Moki wasn't technically doing an upgrade. He was fucking up my system."

Kodiak almost smiled. A tiny bit of stress eased away from his muscles. "It's good to see you stepping up to take over the computer system and defend your territory from Moki. But something must be said for being open to new ideas."

"Yes, Alpha."

The gentle pride in the pup's voice warmed him. He liked the kid. It would be good for Channing to make his mark on the pack, raise his status and expand his skillset. Channing had the potential to be one of the strongest members of the pack someday.

Kodiak had to make sure he nurtured Channing's potential. He was intelligent, brave and he listened. He also had heart and loyalty. He'd make a fine Alpha in the future.

The thought struck him hard. The weight of that responsibility nearly crushed Kodiak's chest. Is this how Olcan had felt about him?

"Next time, sort it out with him before you get me," said Kodiak. "Even if you have to break his fucking neck."

"Got it, boss," said Channing, typing on the keyboard.

"Good." He paused. "Don't actually break his neck. Talk it out, find a way."

"I know what you meant."

Kodiak left Channing to work his computer magic and went to find Onai. The carpets they'd ripped out would be burned later with the wrecked furniture behind the clubhouse. That stuff was too ruined even to begin to try and save. He'd never realized how much carpet existed in the building until they'd been forced to rip most of it out and clean the floors beneath.

Kodiak ran his hand through his hair, striding down the hallway. He felt Onai through their pack connection. The shifter worked on the side room, a space no larger than a small study. An easy room to forget about, which annoyed Kodiak. For every step they'd taken forward in cleaning up the house, it felt like they'd taken two steps backwards.

"How bad?" asked Kodiak, stepping into the room.

"See for yourself."

He investigated the space and shook his head. "Let's get this done. Then you can start the fire so we can destroy the carpets and broken furniture."

"Consider it done," said Onai.

Together they made light work of rolling up the bloodied

and torn carpet and carrying it out to the pile behind the clubhouse.

Kodiak's fists tightened. This should never have happened. It was all because of some power within the Blood Opal...and Tamaska.

He made the connection, a realization that hit him as hard as a sucker punch.

There was something special about her blood.

She had to be more than human. He just needed to find proof, and then he could work out exactly what the vampires were up to.

What powers could the vampires gain from combining the Blood Opal with Tamaska's blood?

Whatever it was, it was beyond bad.

odiak

HOLLOW PAIN FOLLOWED by bubbling anger filled Kodiak at the sight of the discarded, ruined carpets. The loss of life that pile represented was deep and jagged. He clenched his fist, wishing for a vampire that he could make pay right now for the destruction of his pack.

No. Not destructed. Attempted destruction. They were stronger than that, they had to be. And he could never let the vampires win.

"Yeah." Onai looked at the pile, picking up Kodiak's thoughts. 'It's a lot, but you're right. We are stronger."

"I worry about the upheavals on top of the attack," he said softly. "But we'll get through this.

"We always do. I'll start the fire," said Onai.

"Thanks." Kodiak put his hand on the other shifter's shoulder. "Loyal members will keep the pack alive."

Onai patted his hand and nodded. "We're packmates, in life and in death."

"You're a good second," he said, right as his phone beeped, and his stress spiked, like he was being torn in a hundred different directions.

He glanced at the screen. "Pain delivery is here, at the gate. Bubblegum pick okay with you?"

Onai laughed. "Always."

"A fresh coat of paint's going to go a long way," said Kodiak, slipping his phone into his pocket.

Neither of them mentioned it was nothing more than a Band Aid. But sometimes, they needed a sticking plaster in metaphor to push off in the right direction. Dig down and find that extra fuel to get to the other side.

And time for a shower and clean clothes. He didn't think he could stomach food yet. First the paint, and then he would unleash hell on the vampires.

"When you're done lighting the fire," Kodiak said softly, "can you get the paint from the front gate? Moki can help you."

And give the upstart something to do.

Onai nodded his head, eyes shadowed once more with grief.

Kodiak headed inside the clubhouse. His shower could wait. He wanted to speak with Ash in private about Tamaska's change.

He stopped inside the door and took in the scene. Everyone was doing their bit in getting things sorted. They'd rearrange furniture later, but for now the repetitive task of cleaning helped soothe souls.

It pleased Kodiak to see Moki working hard with Ash, cleaning on the other side of the room. He still didn't entirely trust Moki, but for now at least he was pulling his weight.

Couches in the center of the room would need to join the

carpets on the fire. Those were ruined, their fabric covered with bloodstains, claw scratches. Even their stuffing oozed out. Every little detail reminded Kodiak of what had happened. The other couches were salvageable for now. Still beaten up and destined for the tip or a fire, but those could be covered with a sheet or two for now.

"Moki, help take these ruined couches out and then join Onai in burning the carpets. Afterwards, help bring in the paint. Start painting in the front rooms and work your way back here," said Kodiak. "Others will help."

"Yes, boss," he said, forcefully throwing his now-red cloth into a bucket of water.

Kodiak glared at him. Moki kept his eyes cast down as he left the room. For now, he was obedient.

"You think we'll get this place cleaned up today?" asked Ash, climbing down from the stepladder.

"We have to. There's no more time. The vampires could come back."

"So why bother cleaning, then?"

He cut her a look. "You know why, Ash. Morale is part of it, as is order."

"Yes, but are we really sitting about waiting?" She breathed out. "We should find them and crush them."

"Opal first, and we need to know what it does."

"How? Throw your girl at them and see what happens?" She stopped at his dark expression he shot her way. Ash held up her hands. "I like Tamaska. I'm just saying sitting about isn't a plan."

He ran a hand over his face and leaned against one of the ruined couches. "No, it isn't. But I don't think they're coming back in a hurry. They'll be hurting, too. But they'll be back and we should be ready."

She crossed her arms. "Again, Kodiak. We don't sit around."

He knew what she was asking; had he gone soft because of Tamaska. It was something he privately asked himself. Because she made him vulnerable. And he fucking hated that.

However…

"We're running out of time to putter about. We need to be ready this evening for them. I know they'll attack again because we have Tamaska, but there's nothing to stop us from attacking them." He paused. "After we get the opal. And change Tamaska. If we can."

One more thing needed to happen today—the ceremony to anoint him as alpha of the pack. Kodiak wanted to complete that tonight. They needed to be as cohesive as possible before they launched whatever they were going to launch of the blood suckers.

"I've never done so much cleaning in my life." Ash dumped her cloth in the bucket, rested her hands on her lower back and stretched backwards. Like the rest of the pack members, she'd pushed her grief aside and tried to put their clubhouse back together.

But she'd also neatly side-stepped the Tamaska issue. So he straightened and went up to her. "Ash?"

"Kodiak—"

"Did you learn anything about changing her?" He lowered his voice. He didn't want to let anyone else overhear.

"She's been asking me about it," said Ash, moving to Kodiak. "I'm not sure what to say."

Kodiak went still. "Does that mean you found something?" Ash was great at finding information quickly.

"It's not that simple."

"Can she be changed, or not?" asked Kodiak. "It's the only way Tamaska will be accepted into the pack, and you know it. Maybe if I wasn't to become Alpha…"

Her eyes widened. "You can't turn it down. Not after Shota."

Not after he'd killed Shota she meant. But it was fair. "No, I'm not going to do that. We can't afford more upheaval even if I wanted to do that. Which I don't. Okay? I just want to smooth things and that's the best way, her becoming one of us."

If she didin't die in the process. If that wasn't a risk on the table. If it was, he'd…what? Let her go? Find a way.

"Ash. Can she be changed? Without risk." \

"Yes and no." Ash pursed her lips, her eyes meeting his.

"Out with it." Quickly losing patience, he struggled to keep his temper in check. And he needed to. As a leader, he needed to do that. Picking and choosing when to hold it in and unleash was a huge part, and Ash didn't deserve his wrath, no matter how much he wanted to lash out.

"A bite from anyone in the pack can change her." Ash looked down at her hands a second.

"I guessed that. So I can do it. Right? There better not be some fucking clause about her not being bitten by her future mate." It had to be him. He knew that in his bones. If he bit her, then there would be that undefinable bond. "I won't let anyone in the pack bite her, not even you. And I trust you." Kodiak pointed at her.

"It's not that simple, anyway." She addressed him with a firm stance.

"So it's dangerous?"

Ash half shrugged.

"Tell me."

"As I said, it's not that simple. She must be bitten at a full moon," said Ash slowly.

"And…?" Kodiak asked.

"By an alpha."

Kodiak pressed his lips together tightly. He was the alpha, but not officially. The ceremony needed to happen to seal his new status. He would make that a priority if it would help change Tamaska. And he was going to do that, anyway. "I'm planning on the ceremony tonight if we can. So we make it happen."

"Kodiak."

"Is there something else?" he asked.

"Yes, because she's human, she'll only change when it's a full moon."

"Do you mean every time?" Shit. His brain raced. "Can that be fixed if that's the case? Could she learn to control it, to change whenever she wants?"

"No."

He nodded. "We could work around it, right? It's not altogether bad." Then he stopped, sensing Ash was still holding back.

"What else?" he asked.

"She could die if she's not strong enough to endure the change. Humans don't have the genetics for it. So there's always a risk."

"I'm not risking her. It's off the table."

"Kodiak," Ash said, "I don't think we should rush there. I know you care about her, but the vampires want her, that's why they attacked. And it's got to do with that stupid Blood Opal. Isn't it a bigger risk to not change her? What if they get her, turn her themselves? Use her for whatever the opal does?" She took hold of him."What if they kill her?"

"That's a fuck load of what ifs." Kodiak breathed out and pulled away, pacing the room and finally returning to Ash. "But if we take the risk, she'll be strong at the full moon."

"I wish that were true. But she won't regain her strength for months after the change." The words rushed from Ash.

"You sure?" They didn't have months to wait. The vampires wanted her now.

What the fuck was he meant to do? Change her, risk her

life, or leave her human and risk the vampires taking her? He folded his arms. "How big is this risk?

"I don't know. There's not much written about it but I think the risk is enough to tell you all of that. But I can do more research."

"We don't have time." He wanted to punch a vampire just to release his anger. "So what the fuck do we do?"

"Are there anti-human sprays to hide her scent out there because if so, we could use that," said Ash.

"Not funny. And they marked her."

"Then even if we turn her and she survives she'll still be marked, so…"

Kodiak turned and punched the couch. "Fuck. I don't know what to do. She wants to change, and it's the smartest thing to do, but I also can't risk her life."

"She's strong, boss."

"I'm aware," he snapped. "She's the strongest human I've ever known. Look at what she's been through already. But I can't risk her."

And yet how could he not? He was risking her leaving her human. At least if she smelled like a shifter—not of a human hanging with shifters—she's have a better chance when she got her powers. If she survived.

"Kodiak, there's a full moon next week if you and Tamaska decide to take the risk. Change her then and hopefully that will make her stronger immediately."

He growled under his breath. They were clutching at fucking straws on a windy day. They didn't know and if he asked Tamaska she'd take the risk. He knew it.

"You know what she'll do, Ash."

"It's her decision, not yours."

He laughed and shook his head. "No, it's mine. I'm the only alpha she knows."

"Kodiak…" His name was a warning. "At the very least it needs to be a decision made by both of you."

Ash was right. This change needed to be decided by both of them. Not just her. Or him. If Tamaska couldn't shift forms like the rest of the pack, then the change wouldn't guarantee her acceptance, anyway. Even without the vampiric danger.

But something else came to him.

"Have you found anything about humans with repressed or hidden supernatural abilities?" he asked.

"No, nothing. And trust me, I've been looking into the main bloodlines here in Australia."

He finally said it out loud, the thing that had been haunting the corners of his mind. "I think she's more than human, but we need to know for sure. That could affect her change."

"How? She's still essentially human so if we do this, we complete the change on the full moon."

"But if she has some sort of blocked ability, could that interfere negatively with the process?"

"Mights and maybes." She breathed out. "But yes, that's possible. Or it could enhance it."

Those fucking straws again.

"Keep researching. There has to be another way," said Kodiak.

"I will."

"For now top priority is to keep her away from the vampires. I have a theory that they want her blood to bring out some power in the Blood Opal, to benefit themselves."

"Good theory." Ash's eyes widened. "I'll see what I can find, though there's not much written about the Blood Opal."

"You're doing great uncovering all this information. You'll find what we need to help us change Tamaska and defeat the vampires," Kodiak said.

But he wasn't sure if he was convincing her or himself.

"And what should I tell her?" asked Ash.

"Nothing. Maybe try and find something that could help reassure her, something to give her hope that the change will be successful."

"I'll try."

He took a breath. "Tonight, at the hut in the Blue Mountains, we'll have the ceremony."

A smile broke out, the first genuine one from Ash he'd seen since this started the other night. "You'll make a good alpha."

"Only with pack members like you supporting me. I'll let everyone know."

"Where's Tamaska, by the way?" asked Ash, looking about like she just realized the woman in question wasn't there.

He rolled his eyes. "Getting industrial carpet cleaner supplies."

"By herself?" Ash's panic didn't sit well with him. After all, it had raced through him earlier.

"It's daytime." He'd let Tamaska go off alone. He'd regretted the decision since the minute he made it. "Daytime, Ash."

"I know." She didn't need to explain, he got it. She looks at the floor. "We should really replace all the carpets," said Ash, rubbing her boot into a stain.

"We don't have the time or money for that," Kodiak said. "We need to make this look normal."

"If someone comes knocking there's no reason to get into it?"

"Something like that."

It was too risky to leave the carpets and too risky to rip them all out. There would be stains on the floor beneath. And he wouldn't put it past the vampires to tip off the police and encourage them to snoop around.

Hopefully Tamaska's idea would remove evidence of bloodshed and they could focus on sorting out their vampire problem.

Kodiak glanced out the front window, looking down the driveway. There was no sign of the van. Tamaska's absence weighed on him, she should have been back by now.

Where the fuck was she?

CHAPTER 5

TAMASKA SQUEEZED the oversized carpet cleaner onto the backseat of Onai's car, then angled it so she could get the door closed. She stepped back, admiring her work. The chemicals were packed and the three carpet cleaners she'd crammed in meant cleaning up the clubhouse could be done within hours.

Hopefully her idea would win brownie points—not with Kodiak, but with the other pack members. Being seen as a useful team player could bring her even closer to getting accepted into the pack.

Sweaty from rushing through the physical work, Tamaska wiped her forehead as she slipped into the driver's seat. What she wouldn't do for a shower and clean clothes.

Tamaska didn't care about the odd looks she got from people while collecting the carpet cleaners. Kodiak's clothes didn't suit her at all. They were baggy in all the wrong places, but at least they smelled like him. The scent of his musky testosterone had kept her motivated to get back to the clubhouse.

And even if she didn't want to admit it, smelling like him gave her a feel of safety, like he somehow protected her, even though he wasn't here.

There was also something sexy about the scent of her man on her.

The sweat, on the other hand, that wasn't nice at all. The clamminess was uncomfortable. Kodiak's shirt clung to her damp back, and she felt like she'd just finished a high-intensity workout at the gym. She needed a shower.

Tamaska started up the car, ready to drive back to the pack. She'd promised Kodiak she wouldn't return to her apartment, but it was the middle of the day, when vampires slumbered or whatever they did…hung upside down like bats? She was safe in any case and the chance to shower, to wash away the past few days and grab some clean clothes was too tempting.

What's the worst thing Kodiak could do to me?

The thought opened all sorts of delicious possibilities that she shut down.

It wouldn't take long. She'd just grab some of her clothes and toiletries, a few things that would make the clubhouse more like home for her.

"But he said to head right back."

Tamaska drove the car through the crazy Sydney traffic, heading back to Kodiak.

Home called just as strongly as doing what she was ordered to do. She was sick of wearing sweaty, stinky clothes stained with blood.

It reminded her of the vampires, the fight, and the death she'd witnessed.

Tamaska gripped the steering wheel tightly, as if that action could push away the images burned in her mind.

A horn blasted from behind, and her attention crashed back into reality.

The lights ahead were green, and the cars behind were impatient for her to drive on. Tamaska took her foot off the brake too quickly and lurched forward.

Another blast from a car behind her set Tamaska on edge.

If she was careless and caused an accident, the pack members likely wouldn't be so forgiving—especially Onai, since Tamaska drove his car. She needed brownie points, not black crosses against her. She couldn't keep messing up and doing the wrong thing.

Kodiak wouldn't need to know.

And he wouldn't, not if she was quick. He was too busy with his new role, leading the pack. He wouldn't even notice, never mind be angry at her.

All she had to do was to get to her apartment, then get back with the carpet cleaners.

Easy.

Tamaska parked in front of her apartment.

It's close to the clubhouse, anyway.

Without another thought, she got out of her car and hurried inside the apartment building. After being transformed, she would never need to go back again. It made sense for her to get some of her things now rather than later.

Excuse after excuse for this disobedience filled her head.

The sun shone warm on her skin—another excuse…it was too early for the vampires to out hunt her.

Returning to the apartment might be a sightly risky detour, but if she skipped the shower it wouldn't count. She's just go in, grab some things and leave. Easy.

The elevator ride to her floor was slow, and she had to stop herself from pacing the small space. Fortunately, none of her neighbors seemed to be around, and she hurried to her apartment before anyone saw her and started asking questions.

Tamaska took the hidden spare key out of the lockbox, unlocked the door, and swung it open. She's just do a grab and dash so—

She gasped. Her hand covered her mouth as she stared, horrified, at the sight.

Her neat apartment was torn apart.

Tamaska stood frozen in the doorway. The words *who did this* filled her brain, but she knew. Of course, she knew.

Vampires.

If she'd been in her home when they'd come... She swallowed, a wave of nausea hitting her. Lucky to be alive didn't even come close and the wait for what could have happened crushed her. If Kodiak hadn't taken her from Sydney, she may have fallen into the vampires' hands. Maybe she would have already been dead by now, like her friend.

Or worse.

With vampires, there most definitely was a worse.

Her pulse drummed a panicked beat. A sound behind Tamaska made her jump and she whirled around. Her neighbour, Angela, stood there, keys in her hand at her door opposite and she started to crane to look inside the ravaged apartment.

Tamaska slammed the door shut.

She refused to give into the shaking. Or the urge to run. The sun hadn't set. The vampires couldn't be here now. This had happened earlier, probably on the night of the vampires' assault.

Besides, she was already here. It would take mere minutes to grab some shit and run.

A thought hit her as she started for the bathroom. Did Kodiak know? She had alarms. The attack on the clubhouse must have kept Kodiak distracted from her alarms that would have been triggered when the vampires tore her place apart to look for her.

Or he just didn't tell me.

No. She couldn't give in to the rising anger. It was counterproductive. Nothing more than a kneejerk reaction to discovering this. She grabbed a travel bag on a shelf in the bathroom and filled it with what she could salvage.

Then Tamaska moved into the living room and she looked about in despair. Even if she had wanted to keep some of her furniture, or other belongings, most of them were too damaged to go anywhere but the dump.

She couldn't comprehend why the vampires wanted her so badly. All she had wanted to do was sell the Blood Opal. It's not like she had any kind of special connection with it. Kodiak seemed to think her blood wasn't human, that it could combine with the opal to produce some special power. But that ide didn't resonate with Tamaska.

Then again, what did these days? Everything was the wrong way up and her only anchor was a man who happened to be a wolf.

A man she loved.

And even then, she didn't know if love was enough.

She rushed into her bedroom, and the sight nearly broke her heart. The bed where she'd had a spicy time getting to know Kodiak had been pulled apart. Tufts of filling poured out of tears in the mattress. It was hard to imagine the fun she'd had with him in this moment, and she longed for a more peaceful time, for more time to get hot and heavy with him.

Without all the complications that surrounded them.

Her body ached for his touch, to have his hands slipping over her skin, massaging the sweet spot between her legs. If only it could be that simple for them to be together intimately, exploring each other and doing what all couples wanted to do early in their relationship. No new couple dreamed of fighting for their lives against a foe that shouldn't exist.

Tamaska grabbed an overnight bag that had been tossed out of her wardrobe and threw the travel bag in there. Nothing in the apartment had been left unscathed, but her bedroom was especially damaged. It looked as if whoever had done this had exploded in a blind rage, tearing apart anything they could touch.

She swallowed hard, a lump of fear filling her throat. She snatched up clothes lying around and pushed them into the bag. Panties, jeans, tops—all crumpled, some torn—went into the bag. She hoped she could scavenge a few pieces of her former life to take with her into the future.

Tamaska's instincts screamed at her to leave, but she couldn't. She was stuck filling up the bag until nothing more would fit. Then she zipped it up, slung it over her shoulder, and started towards the living room and the front door.

A movement within the kitchen made her yelp. She dropped the bag, her pulse pounding frantically, telling her to run.

Instead, she froze.

"So," a dark, cultured voice said, oozing like oil, "we finally meet."

Out from the shadows of the kitchen stepped a man, dressed all in black. His skin was ghostly pale, his eyes dark.

"Get out of here," she spat at the vampire. Kodiak was going to kill her—-if she managed to survive this encounter.

"I'm rather comfortable here, Tamaska."

The way he pronounced her name sent bile burning up her throat.

"You shouldn't be here."

"Why not?" He shrugged an elegant shoulder. "You're the one I want. So much blood was spilled because of you."

"Stay away from me." She struggled to breathe in, to keep the guilt at bay.

He laughed. "Don't you want to know what I want first?"

"I mean it." Tamaska didn't want to know what he wanted.

The vampire stepped forward, and Tamaska automatically moved backwards into the open living room. Her eyes fixed on him, ready to make a run for it if he attacked her.

"I'm Amdis, the leader of the vampires."

A sick sensation slowly spread through Tamaska. Her vision wavered. He was the vampire who wanted her.

What the fuck had she done by coming here?

"Doesn't mean anything to me." Her voice lacked confidence.

"You're not a very good liar." He smirked, moving closer to her.

"Get out." Panic rose within her. She kept her eyes on the vampire, suspicious that he hadn't rushed towards her yet. "You shouldn't be here."

She had to get away from him.

This time, she wasn't so sure Kodiak would get there in time to help her.

If only she's been smart, obeyed, even though obedience wasn't a natural state for her. Kodiak was right. There were so many things about the world of shifters and vampires that she didn't know, that she had no idea about. Her ignorance and stupid decisions were going to get her killed.

Maybe today.

Amdis smiled slowly, coldly. "I can be anywhere I fucking choose. And what better place to be than here with you."

He held out his hand and for a moment she wanted to put her hand in his.

She snatched her hand to her side and, stepping back collided with something hard and she wobbled, stumbling over the broken coffee table. Pain shot through her leg as she hit the floor.

Tamaska struggled to get up from the ground. She turned over and pushed broken pieces of furniture away as she pushed up, collapsing again as her foot hit something and shot out from under her.

At any moment, she expected the vampire to grab hold of her and break her neck or something.

She had to get on her feet and be ready to fight.

She steadied her hands on the ground and pushed up, wincing as broken glass cut into her palms.

She wobbled but stood, her leg throbbing with pain. Her eyes locked on the vampire.

A chill went through her, freezing her blood.

Amdis licked his lips slowly.

The stickiness on her palms along with the coppery smell warned her to get out of there immediately.

"Don't you want to know what it is like?" he asked, his voice mesmerizing. "To be powerful, to feed on the essence of life itself?"

"No." But to her surprise, curiosity welled within her as her brain grew fuzzy at the edges.

What's wrong with me?

"It won't hurt," he said softly, beguilingly. "It's not so different from having sex."

"As if."

He seemed to get bigger, to steal her space and air and she wanted to step into his arms, let him lick her skin, clean up the blood...

"There's a moment of afterglow like nothing you've ever felt before." That cold smile appeared again as he voice weaved around her.

51

"So what?" Oh, fuck. It was almost as if she could taste the thrill and knew it would be better than anything she'd ever felt.

She wanted…she wanted…

"Don't you want to know what that would feel like?" His voice caressed her. "I'll show you a first time you'll never forget."

Her mind grew fuzzier. Was he doing something to her? It was getting harder to move, as if he'd placed a spell on her. She couldn't flee.

But she fought it, gathering all her strength and she pushed out, "Get out."

"Not without you." he crooned. "I want you to come with me."

"That's never going to happen." She clenched her fists, as if that would stop the scent of her blood from wafting towards Amdis' greedy fangs.

"Why not?"

"You're not my type."

The spell snapped. "Like them furry, do you?"

"Fuck off." She narrowed her eyes, trying to work out her best plan of action.

Amdis sighed. "Of course, you like him. Big and hand-some if you like that animalistic roughness. You could like my kind too, you know. You could become one of us." He leaned against the doorframe of the bedroom. "You want to change into one of his kind? That's basic. Change into one of us and understand true beauty and sophistication."

Her gut churned, and she fought not to double over. Did he really know she wanted to be changed and become one of the pack, or was he simply guessing?

"The change to become a vampire isn't as intense as the transformation into a wolf shifter, and you don't have to keep switching between forms. As I said, shifters are basic, we are not. You'd still know exactly who you are," Amdis said.

"What do you want? You've already got the Blood Opal." She shuffled back cautiously, careful not to trip again.

"I was wondering when you would bring up the gem."

"I want it back. It's not yours."

"It is now. If you want it, then you need to come with me. I can tell you all about it and what it can do." He lifted his nose in the air, inhaling slowly. His gesture repulsed her. "Mmm, delicious. You're delicious beyond the vile stench of shifter. Come with me, Tamaska."

"Like hell."

"I could simply take you," he said. "I don't mind tying you up to take you with me."

"I'm not going with you."

Tamaska glanced at the camera concealed in the corner of the room. Was it still working?

She didn't think she'd fare too well in a fight against Amdis.

Please, see. Check the cameras, Kodiak.

He would go feral on her for disobeying him, but she'd rather face Kodiak than get killed. Death—in the form of Amdis—was looking at her, and she didn't like it.

Tamaska moved back further, stepping into a pool of golden sunlight. Amdis didn't follow her.

Why isn't he following?

The last of the day's rays spread in through her apartment window. This used to be her favorite time to spend at home.

Then, she understood why he couldn't follow her. Not until the sun set.

She went to make a run for the door. She didn't see the object hurtling towards her. Pain exploded in her head, and she stumbled. Her vision blurred, and a bottle of hot sauce rolled across the floor.

He threw that? At her?

"I told you, Tamaska, you aren't going anywhere unless it's with me," Amdis said from across the room.

She wanted to mouth the words 'Come and get me,' but her head pounded. He had a hell of an aim and a fierce throw. She tried to straighten up, but the room swayed from side to side, and she collapsed on the floor.

"See? You're not leaving without me."

Tamaska looked at the column of light spreading from the window in front of the bedroom door. The beam was too wide for Amdis to jump across. But he didn't need to. In less than an hour, it would be dark, and she would be at his mercy.

Kodiak, can you see me?

Kodiak could very well be her only chance of getting out alive.

odiak

KODIAK DIPPED the roller into the off-white paint again, the work taking his mind off Tamaska and the fact that she hadn't returned.

I should never have let her go by herself.

I should've been firmer with her.

Yeah, should've. But there was something that made him weak when he was with her, the need to give her everything she wanted and to see her happy. To make it up to her for the things she'd witnessed, things she never should have seen.

For a human, she was holding up incredibly well, which only added to his theory that she was more than human. He desperately wanted to take her as his own. Secretly, he was glad she wanted to change for him, no matter if there still lurked a place in her that wasn't entirely sure.

She cared for him enough to override fears and misgivings and become a wolf.

That meant the world.

But at the same time he couldn't allow her such a risk if it wouldn't work. If it might harm her.

Kodiak's phone beeped. Sick of answering a million questions, he ignored it, pushing the roller up and down the wall, removing the last hint of blood. It was already beginning to look less like a crime scene now the painting was well under way.

Erasing the horrors and loss of that night from his memory wouldn't be so easy.

He'd taken stock of the damage. A few rooms needed new carpet. For the rest, he hoped that Tamaska's industrial-grade cleaning would work. But the sun was sinking fast, and the pack needed to get on the road to begin his initiation as alpha.

What if she'd left? For good?

But no, she'd never do that.

He saw her commitment in the way she spoke, in how she'd helped with the gruesome cleanup.

He didn't need to check a watch or phone to know something was wrong. It had been too long.

Something had happened.

Something bad.

Kodiak pushed down the sudden fear as he returned the roller to the pan of water to soak. The beat was in his blood now. The beat something was wrong.

He should go and find her and— Go where? Her phone sat on a broken table near where she's been working. He didn't even fucking know where she'd gone to get the carpet cleaning shit. It could be way out in the industrial suburbs.

He didn't fucking know.

That was his problem.

Ash stood on a stepladder, painting, and Moki rolled fresh paint over the ceiling with an extended pole, the air of resentment hung heavy, giving the room a sour smell. He'd be having it out again with Moki

Ash kept slipping him glances, worry all over her face. And he...shit. He needed to get the fuck out there to find her.

As alpha he needed to be here. He had duties.

His woman was smart and resourceful, and the sun had just started to sink. The panic, he told himself, came from the recent troubles. Nothing more.

Tamaska knew better than to veer off her mission. He didn't know how long it took to get the cleaning supplies and Sydney traffic could be an utter nightmare, sometimes tripling the time a trip took.

Especially at rush hour.

Ash turned to him and raised an eyebrow. He knew exactly what she was going to say and glared at her. He didn't need another reminder to never let Tamaska go off alone.

"It's nearly dark," said Ash, stepping down from the ladder her gaze moving from where he's put the roller to his empty bunched hand.

Kodiak met her gaze. "I'm aware."

"Maybe we should—"

"Send a search party? We're already stretched. I'll go soon."

"You can't," she said. "You're Alpha."

As Alpha he should be able to do anything he wanted. And he wanted to find her, have her safe in his arms. He wanted to tear the world apart.

He was troubled out of his mind over Tamaska and desperately trying not to show it.

And he couldn't go anywhere. He had to prove to his pack that he was a leader worthy of respect, not go running off after a human. Especially not the one whom the others blamed for the vampire attack and Olcan's death, one he never should have let go.

"She's strong." He squeezed the water from the roller and dipped it into the paint, applying it once more to the wall.

The movement of rolling paint soothed him, releasing some of his tension. If she was going to be so fucking stubborn, then why should he risk his pack for her?

Because that's what he did. Because she was his world.

Because he had feelings for her.

"I don't know how you're being so chill about this," said Ash, refilling the tray of off-white paint.

"Because I'm damned if I do and damned if I don't."

"And here you wanted to be leader of a new era."

"Gotta do the ceremony first, Ash," he said, "you know that."

"I do and I wish I didn't. She's human and they want her." Then, she climbed back up the stepladder with her tray and brush in hand. "Maybe we shake shit up, Kodiak."

"She has to learn what it means to be part of a pack," he said. "And that means we don't babysit. They'll never accept her if that's the only job."

"And yet it is. We have to protect her. So, what are we going to do?" She started to paint again. "Because it's getting late."

Kodiak didn't respond, he knew that. All of it. And it might be getting dark, but there was still daylight, so Tamaska would be all right. They still had about an hour before it would be truly dark.

She has until then.

And then he'd probably fuck over his position and try and find her.

"Hey Kodiak, it's getting late," said Onai, coming into the room.

Kodiak threw the paint brush into the pot, then glared at Onai, who stopped in his tracks. Tiredness weighed on his shoulders and fogged his mind. "I'm aware."

"I mean, shouldn't we go to the hut now?" asked Onai. He stood firm, maintaining eye contact for a moment before showing his submission to the alpha-to-be.

The anger that burned within Kodiak morphed into a tightness in his chest. It was time for the ceremony that would mark him as the new pack leader. And Tamaska wasn't there.

"Where's your would-be mate? " Onai asked softly.

"With your car," he said.

Kodiak's phone beeped again, but he ignored it. Tamaska had left her phone behind, so it wasn't her. He didn't have time to answer messages. Everyone had received their instructions, and they just had to get on with it.

If he stuck to routine, then things would calm.

"She's not back with my car?"

Kodiak growled under his breath. "No," he said.

"But we need it to get to the ceremony."

"Onai, she'll be back. Grab a brush and help finish painting," Kodiak said.

His phone beeped again as Onai nodded. "I'll start in the front room. It won't take us long."

"Kodiak, where are you?" Channing burst into the room looking about frantically.

"What the fuck now?" Kodiak asked.

"Didn't you get the notifications on your phone?" asked Channing, nearly knocking Onai over.

"What are you talking about?" Kodiak ran his hand through his hair, unease spreading through his bones. "What's wrong?"

"It's Tamaska...apartment...phone...images." Channing breathed quickly, his words jumbling.

"Slow down," said Onai.

"She's getting carpet cleaners for us. She's not at her apartment," said Kodiak, relaxing a little. Fuck, he needed a shower. He needed not to worry. She...she wouldn't fucking defy him would she?

His pulse increased. It was Tamaska. Of course she fucking would.

"No, she's in her apartment." Channing's breath slowed, but the panic remained in his eyes. "I saw. I think she's in trouble."

The worst-case scenario played out in Kodiak's head. "Vampires?"

Kodiak snatched his phone from his pocket, fingers shaking as he flipped to the latest footage.

The bottom dropped out of his world at the image. Nothing moved. But there, on the floor, lay Tamaska.

"Fuck."

The place had been torn apart. And she— He had to go, now. But he stopped himself. This could have been hours ago or minutes. He needed information, so he forced himself to calm.

"The footage stops there. I don't...I don't know if she's still there, Kodiak," Channing said.

"When did they first go to her apartment?" asked Kodiak, his throat constricting. "And I don't see a time stamp on this footage."

"The vampires went there on the night of the attack, before they came here. And it has the date, not the time stamp."

He gritted his teeth. "Why didn't I see it?"

"You were at the hut, right?" asked Channing.

"Yeah."

What he needed was a weapon. What he needed was fucking information. What he needed was her. Here. Now. In one piece.

"Then you would've been out of range, maybe." Channing

raised a shaking hand. "Plus, I only just upgraded the system to alert you if the cameras get triggered."

"That's thanks to me, right?" interrupted Moki, smirking.

Channing shot a stormy look towards Moki. "It's thanks to my work, not your bloody hack job…"

"Focus." Kodiak put a hand on Channing's shoulder. They didn't need another fight between members. The vampires were their enemy, not their packmates.

And Tamaska… He needed a plan.

"Kodiak… There's more. I think there's a vampire there. Hard to tell, you know, since they don't show up on camera," said Channing, stress clouding his eyes. "But if there is…"

"Then she's still there."

And the vampire was trapped, until full dark. Shit.

"Shouldn't have let a human into the pack. It will only cause us constant trouble," said Moki, still painting the last section of the wall.

"Shut up, Moki. You're out of line again, and I'm ready to break bones right now. I don't care whose," Kodiak growled as he started for the door, the others following close.

Moki clamped his mouth shut, and the glimmer of fear in his eyes satisfied Kodiak. Moki wouldn't cause any more trouble for him, at least not at the moment.

"How much time do I have before dark?" asked Kodiak, turning to Channing.

"Less than half an hour."

"I'll come, too," Onai said.

Channing nodded. "Me too."

"No." They jumped at Kodiak's sharp tone. "I do this alone."

"We can't lose you, too," said Ash, coming up from behind. "We're a pack. And you're the alpha."

"You don't know how many there are," added Channing. "It's nuts for you to go by yourself."

Kodiak held up his hand when Onai opened his mouth to speak.

"You've got your jobs to do. So, let's get on with it."

Ash moved to speak.

"No, I don't want to hear it," he said. I'm going to get Tamaska. I'll be back within the hour. If not, you can come and get me."

"I'm setting my timer," said Ash, getting her phone out. "If you're not back in an hour and a half, I'm bringing Onai with me."

"You won't need to do that," answered Kodiak. "I'll be back by then. You just ensure that the painting gets done and everyone is ready to go to the hut for the ceremony."

"We will," said Ash. "You just get back in one piece, and hurry."

Half an hour. He got in his car and roared off. That was more than enough time. He could get to her.

He hoped.

CHAPTER 7

 amaska

TAMASKA'S HEAD POUNDED, stars sparkled in her vision despite her closed eyes. She lay on the floor, trying not to move. Her palms throbbed from where new scabs formed along her cuts from the glass.

She sensed Amdis watching her, hunger radiating from him. It turned her stomach.

The sight of him would make her even sicker, so she kept her eyes closed. The darkness helped to slow the spinning in her head and kept her from watching the sunlight on her floor disappear. The light acted as a timer that crept ever closer to the moment when Amdis would close the last of the distance between them.

Would he sink his teeth into her neck?

Tamaska shivered involuntarily. The adrenalin had worn off, leaving her cold and in shock. She didn't know why she couldn't leave, only that every time she thought it or made a move to the door her head wanted to explode.

What if this was her body somehow wanting the offer he made to make her like him? She almost gagged, even as it wound through her, pulling her to go to him. Maybe it would be better, maybe— How could she entertain such sickening thoughts?

It wasn't so long ago that she was horrified by the sight of the blood-drinking vampires in the nightclub. Now, she was fantasizing about it.

Kodiak, please look at the security footage.

She'd been reluctant to allow the security system installation, but now she was glad to have it. The cameras were her only chance to get out alive.

That is, unless she managed to get control of her aching body. All she had to do was to get up, rush to the door, and get the fuck out of there.

The thumping in her head surged at the thought. The sickening nausea settled only if she didn't move.

But she couldn't stay. She had to push through the pain and nausea.

Tamaska pressed her palms against the floor, trying to push up from the ground and get on all fours.

"Don't even think about leaving," Amdis hissed.

Shivers ran through her, as if thousands of ants had been let loose to carry goosebumps across her skin.

Automatically, she glanced at the sunlight marking the boundary between her and Amdis. It was only just wide enough to keep her safe.

It would only be a matter of minutes before he could get to her.

Tamaska pushed up from the floor again. The room spun, and bile rose to her mouth.

I have to get out.

Kodiak wasn't coming to save her. He didn't know she was here. For all she knew the feed back at the clubhouse had been damaged. If she didn't pull herself together, then she could end up dead—or worse, a vampire.

"Not long now, Tamaska. Then you'll be mine."

It sounded so good, like falling asleep, like— No. He was doing this to her, somehow, putting these thoughts in her. Making it almost impossible to leave.

But almost meant there was a possibility of escape, so she focused on that.

"I'll never be yours." She collapsed back onto the floor, panting from the exertion. Darkness clouded the edges of her mind, threatening to take her consciousness once more.

She gritted her teeth, forcing her eyes open. She could do this.

"You will be. You're the perfect way to activate the Blood Opal."

She latched on to that. If she focused on the opal and what it could do maybe she'd learn something and find the strength to run. Tamaska licked her dry lips. "What do you mean?"

"Curious now, are you?" He laughed. "The Blood Opal will rejuvenate my kind, make us stronger. Your blood will enable it."

"I don't see how my blood is different from anyone else's. Maybe what you're trying to do with the Opal is just a fantasy, a waste of time."

"You don't know, then?"

"Know what? That you're an idiot for trying something like this?" There was no way she would ever let him have her blood.

"You don't know about your ancestors? Though, I suppose that's why you're attracted to him. Maybe part of you remembers."

Everything in her started to vibrate. Her ancestors? What…" Drawing a breath, she pressed for more. "Remembers what?"

"I know what you're doing, having a little fishing expedition." But he laughed again. "It's too delicious. I can't tell you right now. No, I'm going to have fun making you guess."

"I'm not playing that game."

"You will, if you want to find out."

"Whatever it is, my life has been just fine without knowing it," she said. "The knowledge means nothing to me."

"Ignorance is bliss. But you're not so ignorant anymore."

She closed her eyes, summoning inner strength. His words had planted a seed in her mind, and it grew with every passing second.

What secret about her ancestors could possibly be relevant to her now? Her parents had never mentioned any unusual ancestry, and her grandparents seemed as normal as anyone else in her younger years.

Or maybe it was something else. Then again, he could be fucking with her. "You're lying. You want me to want you."

"Nope."

Tamaska shifted her body weight and pushed up onto her elbows. This time, she made it into a kneeling position.

"Getting brave, aren't we?" Amdis asked, pacing a little.

Her dizziness had subsided enough to give Tamaska the courage to try and escape. All she needed to do was get to her feet, and race out the door. Push through the pain. And run like hell. Take the stairs and not the lift.

She mentally rehearsed the plan. Thank goodness she'd parked the car nearby.

Let's do this.

She moved to get up.

"You've forgotten something," said Amdis.

She froze at his tone, then looked in his direction. Emptiness filled her. The strip of sunlight in front of her was almost gone.

She'd waited too long.

Fuck. Her muscles tensed as she readied to run, anyway.

Then, the door flew open. A wolf bounded in, growling and snapping its teeth. And her heart sang.

In wolf form, Kodiak crossed the room so fast that he was a blur of fur. He launched himself at Amdis, swiping at the vampire's chest with one deadly paw, his claws sharp.

The vampire ducked and slipped out of the way at the last minute, super fast.

And she thought she'd have been able to outrun Amdis.

The wolf growled, an angry vibration that raised the hairs on the back of Tamaska's neck.

Kodiak rushed after the vampire. Keeping himself between it and her. He stayed close behind it, snapping at it and narrowly missing each time.

Tamaska wasn't going to stand and watch this unnatural fight. She'd seen enough of the vampires' lethal power during the clubhouse attack.

She struggled to her feet, needing to do something that would help. She wasn't strong enough or fast enough to fight the vampire. And she's only get in the way. But...

She stumbled over to the glass balcony doors. She pushed the curtain back, allowing the last of the sun's rays to flood the apartment.

But would that be enough? She moved out of the way, to minimize blocking the light.

Kodiak switched tactics, his attacks pushing Amdis closer to the sunlit balcony.

Tamaska pulled the curtains back even further, sending the last of the day's light straight into the vampire's path.

Amdis screamed as if being pierced with a knife. He stumbled, struggling to move as the light hit his body.

Kodiak sprang into the air, aiming a powerful swipe of his paws directly at Admis and preparing to sink his teeth into the vampire.

Instead, Admis rolled out of the way. He howled in pain as his exposed skin sizzled bright red in the sunlight.

The vampire threw himself against Tamaska and grabbed her.

"You're coming with me," he said, rushing to the door. He pushed it open, dragging her behind him.

"I said no!" Tamaska pulled hard against Amdis' grasp, trapping him in the sun's rays as Kodiak shoved him further into the light.

"You're mine," hissed the vampire.

"No, I'm not." She twisted her arm, trying to find a weakness in his grip.

He only pulled harder, and she stumbled toward him as Kodiak snapped at her shirt to pull her back.

Her wolf wasn't attacking, and she realized it was because Admis was too close.

"Don't worry about me, Kodiak!"

"Because she's mine," snarled the vampire, hauling her against him again and edging for the shadows.

"Do it," she whispered.

Kodiak growled beside her. His muscles tensed as he prepared to attack the vampire.

Amdis hissed at Tamaska as Kodiak swiped his arm with sharp claws, "I'll be back for you." Then, he let her go.

He rushed out into the fading sunlight. His inhuman speed and agility allowed him to climb quickly around the building, clambering out of the light and away from Tamaska.

She turned back. Kodiak stood naked in front of her. She wanted to rush to him, to be in his arms, but the stormy look on his face stilled her.

"What are you doing here?" he asked, voice cold.

She swallowed sharply. "Getting some things."

"After I told you not to."

"I'm sorry, I didn't mean this to happen." She held out her hands that shook. "I thought—"

"I'm starting to think you don't think. Or maybe that you'd rather be with the vampires than me." He raised his arms in exasperation.

"That's not true." Moisture pricked at her eyes.

"Your life is more important than your things."

"I didn't think they'd be here during the day," she said. "And I needed clothes. I needed…"

"What?"

How could she explain she needed some things of her own. That it was important to her. So she just said, "I didn't think they'd be here."

"Why not? It's you they want." The anger and coldness hurt. "Why wouldn't they be here? Even worse, it was Amdis. You're lucky to be alive."

"All thanks to you." It was getting harder to stand, her head injury a constant and painful reminder of her stupidity. "I'm an idiot."

He didn't refute her. "What would have happened to you if I didn't come?"

Amdis' words echoed through Tamaska's entire being.

Your blood… activation… Blood Opal… ancestors.

What the fuck had he been going on about?

It made Tamaska sick to her stomach that he might know more about her life than she did. She placed a hand on her belly, swallowing hard against the bile rising in her throat.

"That's why you have to do what I say. You have no idea what type of world I live in."

"You think I'm a problem?" Tamaska squared her shoulders and faced Kodiak, ignoring the nausea building in her gut.

"Yes." His eyes flashed and softened a small bit. "You won't let me protect you."

"I just came for some clothes and toiletries."

"You want to be part of the pack, you need to behave like a pack member."

"What the fuck do you mean by that?"

"You don't know how to function in a pack."

"Because you don't fucking tell me." She stumbled, her knees giving way.

She couldn't stop herself from falling, but Kodiak caught her in his strong arms and drew her against him.

"You drive me crazy, Tamaska. I need to protect you, and you need to obey. The pack is struggling just to stay together. You have to trust me. Is that so hard?"

Tamaska buried her head in his chest, his musky testosterone scent soothing.

It was so hard to trust him—not because he was a wolf shifter, but because she was so used to being independent. She had put up more walls around herself than she realized. If she didn't take control of a situation, she felt weak.

He stroked her head. "You haven't answered me."

Tamaska nuzzled closer against his chest, trying to avoid the question.

"Tamaska, if you can't trust me, and if you can't let me guide you through how to behave in a pack, then they *will* reject you."

"I'm trying, but it's hard. I keep making mistakes with the pack, with you. It was day so I thought it would be fine. A few minutes and…and I fucked up. Maybe if we change me things'll improve."

"That won't help, not unless you start understanding

things now. Changing you won't guarantee that you'll be accepted into the pack."

"What about all the hard work I've done cleaning up the clubhouse?" She closed her eyes as memories of the bloody mess filled her mind.

"You should've stayed in my room like I told you to. You should have stayed out of it. That was too horrific for you to experience, to process, especially since you're new to this life." He kissed the top of her head. "They'll accept you if you're obedient to me. I can't protect you if you don't listen to me. And if the others see you defy me, that puts my position in jeopardy, which in turn puts you at risk."

"I messed up.." She just wasn't the submissive type. Maybe in bed, being tied up in the name of pleasure, sure—but in day-to-day life, she wasn't one to acquiesce. And he didn't bend.

"Do you have a death wish or something?"

"No," she said, her voice muffled against his bare chest. She hadn't even gone through with the change, and her life was already so much more difficult than anticipated.

"Tamaska." He eased her back a little to look at her. "The ceremony is tonight, and I need you by my side."

Anticipation fluttered in Tamaska's stomach as his words sank in. She wanted to be by his side, showing her support.

"I really was trying to help," she added again.

Kodiak squeezed her. "All you need to do is to listen to me."

"I am."

"No, you're not. You're being stubborn, and I love it under normal circumstance, but right now it could get you killed."

"I'm not submissive."

"Jesus you don't need to be" Then he chuckled softly. "Well, only when I fuck you."

Her pussy contracted and her clit throbbed as need thundered through her. Fuck, if only he would take her now. But that was the last thing they needed to do now.

"Come on, we need to get back before Amdis decides to return with friends. There's a lot to do at the clubhouse before we head to the hut in the Blue Mountains for the ceremony."

Tamaska inhaled slowly, allowing his scent to fill her lungs. She held her breath for a moment to savor the delightful sensation, then exhaled. That was as much pleasure as she was going to get for now, and she would enjoy it.

"First, do you have some clothes I can wear?" he asked.

Tamaska nodded. "I think you left some things."

As she picked her way back to her room, the enormity, the reality of what she planned to give up set in. Before, she'd been gung ho, ready to change for Kodiak. Now...she still wanted to be changed, but it was all more complicated than she'd realized it would be.

Tamaska pushed through the pounding in her head as she searched for his clothes.

"Yes," she whispered, pulling out a pair of jeans and light blue T-shirt.

"Here." She left the bedroom, enjoying the sight of Kodiak's naked body.

He brushed her fingers as he took the clothes from her, sending a shiver of pleasure through her body and the sweet sensation pooled low in her abdomen.

Kodiak dressed quickly, but she couldn't take her eyes off his perfect form. She could look at his naked body forever. He zipped his jeans, and they both looked at his feet.

"I don't have any shoes that will fit you."

"That's fine, I'm used to walking around without shoes. It happens way too often."

Tamaska couldn't imagine experiencing that, not even after she changed.

"Let's go. You're not coming back here," said Kodiak, moving toward the door.

"I should grab a few…" Tamaska let the unspoken words evaporate from her mouth. The look Kodiak gave her chilled her to the bone.

"We go now. It's getting dark. You're coming with me now. I'm not letting you out of my sight."

So much for my plan to help.

Tamaska grabbed the bag she'd packed and followed him to the door. "What about the car?"

"I'll send someone back for it. We need it to get us all to the hut."

Then the others would know she'd rebelled against him.

"I'll drive back." Driving would be dangerous after her head injury. But it wasn't far to the clubhouse, and she didn't want the others to find out what she'd done. Once more, she'd put them all at risk.

What if Kodiak had been hurt in the fight with Amdis? More than ever, she needed him to protect her. He obviously couldn't do that if he was injured, or worse.

"Like hell, you will," growled Kodiak as they left the apartment, he sent a text, then locked the door behind them. "You're hurt and in no condition to drive."

"I'll be fine." She bumped into him accidentally, and her vision blurred from the sudden movement.

"In a few days, maybe." He took the bag and wrapped his arm around her, guiding her to the elevator. "Someone's already on their way, they'll be here before the sun sets."

She'd really fucked up this time. Would the pack hold it against her? Would this be the reason they'd been looking for, the thing that would stop her from becoming one of them?

CHAPTER 8

 odiak

THE PACK WAS EVEN MORE vulnerable after Tamaska's act of defiance. Kodiak's muscles were permanently tense, and his head throbbed.

Tamaska had been sent to his room to rest in disgrace. He hated doing that, treating her like a child, but it showed the others that even if she became his mate, he wasn't playing favorites.

Roan who had some medical experience, was assigned to check on her. Kodiak also sent Ash to keep watch. He couldn't trust Tamaska not to do something impetuous and hot-headed.

She was human. Even if there was more to her, she was essentially human, it's how she thought, how she'd been brought up, so he couldn't expect her to magically obey unspoken shifter laws and rules.

But sending Ash served another purpose; it would give

her extra time to continue researching the Blood Opal and Tamaska's transformation.

The pack needed to get on the road, and they would, as soon as Fern returned with Onai's car.

They'd have to clean the carpets tomorrow. Anger still beat in his veins, whispering it was a waste of time to bother with the carpet cleaners.

Tamaska's recklessness put her at risk, as well as her being accepted by the pack.

Now would be the perfect time for the vampires to attack, even with clubhouse security up and running, thanks to Channing's hard work, and the fencing electrified, if enough came, if they managed to overrun their system, it could well mean the end of the pack. The pack remained vulnerable as long as their enemies had the Blood Opal.

Kodiak couldn't wait to get away from the clubhouse, the constant reminder of how the vampires had defeated them.

But it wouldn't be any easier at the hut, not when they were going there to bury the dead.

Kodiak glanced out of the living room window.

"Again, why can't we go?" asked Moki, still painting. The pack members had done what Kodiak had asked, and they were nearly finished with the final coat.

Kodiak let the curtain fall back over the window. "We need the car. Or do you want to stay here on vampire watch?"

"I'd like to pay my respects to the dead and you as the new alpha."

"Good." He didn't entirely believe Moki. But, so far, Moki was toeing the line, which was good enough for now.

The young shifter held Kodiak's gaze before turning back to his painting. He might be a pain but he wasn't the only one who'd voiced discontent over the fact that Tamaska needed to be rescued from yet another vampire.

The pack didn't want her around, especially if she wouldn't obey the pack rules and follow him—the alpha. He heard their whispers. She was putting his leadership at risk.

Even as she didn't mean to.

Kodiak would have to think of something smart to convince the others of her value to the pack. Fuck, he was going to have to convince himself.

It wasn't just the anger or the fact she'd got herself into trouble. And for him it wasn't value. She had great value in many areas, but packlife might not be for her. It even happened for shifters who took off to integrate into the human world or just roam. Some weren't born for the pack.

And Tamaska… His worry was borne of his being the next Alpha; of the unknown risks of the change; of whether, deep down, she truly wanted it.

Once she changed that was it. She couldn't ask for a refund.

Worse she didn't understand the obedience that was ingrained in them. She's asked him to explain but he couldn't, not when it either was or wasn't.

He could tell her it didn't mean lack of independence or weakness. He could tell her it wasn't submission.

Everyone and everything had its place and she…she didn't.

She'd either get it or not. It was how things worked in his world. The pack would force her into exile if she couldn't obey when asked. He couldn't allow that to happen. Even though their bond existed, always growing stronger, he would ignore it and push Tamaska away if she couldn't she was capable of working as a team, of following their rules.

And pushing her away when this was done—not before—meant he needed to decide soon. Because once changed he might as well kill her if the pack rejected her.

Pushing her away was the only way to keep her safe and alive and with hope for a future without him.

If it came to that.

If, if, fucking if.

Kodiak turned back to the window. He shifted the heavy curtain to the side. His superhuman sight allowed him to see clearly despite the dark. He watched for Fern's return, and for any sign of vampires.

If anything happened to Fern, Tamaska would have no chance in hell of ever being accepted into the pack. Then Kodiak would have to make that hard decision now. No change and as soon as it was safe, Tamaska would need to leave.

The thought almost killed him.

Fern, are you nearly back? Kodiak reached out through their pack connection, hoping she was close enough to sense him.

No answer.

He didn't like that. He also didn't like how quiet it was in the clubhouse. Moki was finishing the last of the painting in the living room while the others prepared for the trip to the hut in the Blue Mountains.

Ordinarily, the clubhouse would be alive with banter, pool competitions, darts, drinking, training, and sparring. Not heavy with this silence that got under his skin, tightening his anxiety like a screw into his chest.

It was too soon to go out and check on Fern, but Kodiak considered it anyway. Right now, he couldn't be too careful. Too much was riding on her return.

Headlights appeared, and Kodiak exhaled slowly.

"Get ready to leave," he said to Moki, leaving the room without waiting for an answer.

Kodiak strode out to meet Fern. "No problems?"

Fern got out of the car with blood trickling down her face.

Fuck. Whatever had happened wouldn't help Tamaska become part of the pack.

"What happened?" asked Kodiak.

"The usual. Vampire attack." Fern slammed the vehicle's door. "Happens a lot, now that *she's* around."

"It's our duty, remember?" Kodiak inspected Fern's face. A gash near her hairline needed patching up.

"Like hell it is." Fern pushed his hand away.

"It's more about the Blood Opal than anything. And if it weren't for Tamaska, then we wouldn't know that the vampires want it. They're up to something."

"Bullshit. Look at what's in the car! Nothing there is going to help us. All she's done is make more work for us."

Kodiak growled under his breath. "Taking this out on her doesn't help."

Fern shot him a dark glare.

"Watch it," warned Kodiak.

Anger burned in her eyes, and he sensed her wolf form pushing to get out. But, to her credit, Fern remained in control. She was still loyal to him. Just barely.

"Where were you attacked?" asked Kodiak.

"There were two," said Fern. "At the car. They were lying in wait from the looks of it. Because they attacked—on the street—the moment I unlocked the car."

"Fuck," responded Kodiak. Fern had been lucky to get away alive.

"The thing is, while there was barely any sunlight, it should have been enough to stop them. Vampires don't like even a touch of sun." Fear flashed in Fern's eyes. "Kodiak, they shouldn't have been able to walk around, like the sun didn't bother them.

Kodiak put his hands on his hips and kicked at the stones

on the ground. Fern was right, and he had no answers as to why they could endure sunlight like never before.

Even Amdis, while he's sizzled seemed to grow used to the brighter sun at the window. But, Tamaska had told him when it was much stronger, he couldn't cross it.

Could it have something to do with the Blood Opal? Or could it be a natural evolution of their species?

It all seemed impossible—yet it was happening.

Whatever it was, it was fucking bad.

Even if they could only now stand weak sunlight, Amdis still couldn't tolerate stronger levels, which gave Kodiak hope that the anomaly wasn't a species-wide change. He could still smell the leader's burning skin, a stench that turned Kodiak's stomach.

"Were they in pain?" asked Kodiak.

"Too busy defending myself to find out."

"Do you think they were new vampires?" Maybe Amdis had turned some humans and made them fight in the fading sunlight, apathetic about whether they died.

But it didn't explain how Amdis seemed to tolerate the weak sunlight without worse damage.

"Possibly. Again, busy fighting for my life."

"What happened to them?" It was arrogant for them to attack like that, in a busy city with humans watching. Maybe the vampires were moving toward total domination.

Fern shrugged. "I managed to get in the car and take off. I hit one, and the other ran away, I suppose."

"Change the license plate before you go," Kodiak said.

"I will. But is that enough?"

"Tomorrow, sell the vehicle—cash only—and then see what you can pick up for a replacement." Kodiak didn't need the police turning up at the clubhouse, asking questions about a vehicle involved in a hit-and-run.

"Sure thing," answered Fern. "Onai will be furious."

Kodiak put a hand on Fern's shoulder. "I'll get to the bottom of this. The vampires won't get away with the things they've done. And don't worry about Onai."

Fern nodded with a sigh as tension and aching left over from the fight leaked out of her.

"Go to my room. Roan is there, he'll attend to your wound. Then we'll get going to the hut." Kodiak stopped short of announcing Tamaska's presence in his room, in case that prevented Fern from getting medical help.

"I'll help you get the carpet cleaners out first," said Fern.

"Like hell. you will. Go, I've got this. We need to get moving." Best they got out of there and over to the hut. They needed to give themselves space to properly rally the troops before another encounter.

Kodiak pushed Fern towards the dormitories on the left side of the clubhouse.

"Go," he instructed.

Kodiak carried the carpet cleaners inside, marveling at the fact that Tamaska had managed to get them in the car by herself. She was strong and independent, qualities worthy of a place in the pack. If only she could work on her obedience.

Was it that hard for her to submit to him?

He left the carpet cleaners in the foyer. There wasn't anything else to do in the clubhouse. It was time to go.

Kodiak went through each room to ensure the windows were locked and secured. He noted the new security cameras in each room. Channing had done his job well.

"We're going now," he said to Jaha, one of the pack's younger males who was cleaning up in the kitchen.

The place looked almost back to normal, yet the scent of blood remained heavy on Kodiak's senses.

"You want me to drive?" asked Jaha, his expression full of hope.

"Go with Fern, she might let you drive," Kodiak said biting down a smile.

Jaha sighed, hope fleeing from his eyes. "Sure thing, boss."

"If not, you make sure she's awake and alert. Otherwise, you can tell her I ordered you to drive."

"Really?" Hope burst back into life.

"Yes, if you can stand up to her should the need arise." It was a test for both Jaha and Fern.

Kodiak trusted Fern to drive, but why not give Jaha a chance to drive for a change, remind him that he has a purpose in the pack?

"Thanks! I'll go find her now." Jaha rushed past Kodiak.

Kodiak used the pack connection to find Fern.

"She's changing the plates," Kodiak said as he pointed Jaha toward the back door. Hope pulsed through the young pup at the chance to drive to the hut, alleviating some of the stress Kodiak carried.

To be young again...with no responsibilities.

Kodiak felt as if he'd aged at least a decade in the last few days, now that the responsibility of being alpha rested firmly on his shoulders.

He locked the back door, then headed for his room instructing everyone he passed along the way to meet out front. Once everyone gathered, they could form a convoy to the hut.

Tamaska sat on Kodiak's queen-sized bed, wearing clean clothes that she'd borrowed from one of the pack's females. The scent told Kodiak that the jeans and top belonged to Ash. Her bag sat untouched, like she was too shamed to open it.

Tamaska's eyes lit up as soon as they locked on his. He wanted to scoop her into his arms to hold her tight, but there wasn't time, and he had to be careful going forward, until things were sorted one way or the other.

"Are you all right?" he asked, standing in front of her. His temperature spiked from the proximity.

"I'm fine. I haven't caused any problems." Her eyes flashed with a defiance that simultaneously got under his skin and turned him on.

"She's concussed. She'll need a night watch." Roan packed up his first-aid kit.

"No, that's not necessary," said Tamaska. "I'll be fine. I'm ready to help out."

Roan shook his head, snapping his bag shut. "Concussions are serious. You need to be careful, like I told you. This isn't something you can just brush off."

That wasn't the news Kodiak wanted to hear. He didn't have time to watch Tamaska, not with the upcoming funeral and the Alpha ceremony. And he wanted her safe. Under his watch, his care.

"Are you good to go?" he asked Tamaska.

"Yes." She stood up quickly, swayed, and started to fall to the side.

Automatically, Kodiak caught her, wrapping his arms tight around her. Kodiak felt her sigh into his embrace, as if giving herself over to him. But then she stiffened, sensing his distance.

He couldn't help it. There was too much for him to juggle right now, and she was just another ball. That wasn't fair. Or true. But right now he had to think of her like that, no matter how much he just wanted to hold and soothe her.

"Tamaska—"

"Don't I deserve you pulling away, I know that." She pushed his hands away from her.

He half reached out then let his hands drop. "It's not like that."

"It is. We both know it. It has to be." Her voice was a little broken and it killed him.

He missed holding her, and wished he could given her more reassurance. But she was right. couldn't right now, not so quickly after she'd defied him. Things needed to be done a certain way.

"I'll lock up. Go with Roan, and meet me out front," he said.

Sadness clouded her eyes. She lifted her chin, and he braced for an argument.

"Fine," She said tightly. "I'm here. Obeying."

Fucking Tamaska, and a part of him wanted to smile even as it irked her. Defiant in her obedience. What else would she do but that? She got it, but not deep down. Not in the soul of things.

Not yet.

But…she tried.

She stalked out of his bedroom. He punched the air and growled softly. Time wasn't on his side. He had to get moving. He quickly but systematically moved through the living quarters, ensuring all the windows and doors were locked.

Camera lights winked red at him as he walked from room to room. The security system was working better than ever.

Satisfied that everything was locked up, Kodiak went to the front of the clubhouse, where the others waited.

They all looked at him as he approached the pack. Tamaska stood to the side of the group with her arms folded over her chest, lines of exhaustion circling her eyes. It didn't bode well that she wasn't mingling with any of the pack.

"Ready?" asked Kodiak.

A few nodded. Some met his gaze, their eyes full of grief. A reverent silence lay heavy in the early night air.

Kodiak scanned the group, taking note of their number and planning who would travel with whom in the few vehicles they had available. Fern looked grumpy, even more so every time Jaha inched closer to her. She wouldn't like it if Jaha had to drive.

Ash leaned against Onai's car, which was equipped with its new plates. She held her laptop in one hand while typing with the other.

"Ash, you're with me, Tamaska, and Roan," announced Kodiak. He trusted those two the most with Tamaska right now. Plus, he hoped Ash might've found something important in her research. A few hours of driving together in the car would be the perfect time to debrief.

Ash looked up and nodded, snapping the laptop shut, and walked over to Kodiak's car.

"The rest of you, follow behind. And Fern—" He paused until she turned and looked at him. "You listen to Jaha."

The look of pride on Jaha's face made Kodiak's comment worthwhile.

Kodiak grinned, then strode to his car. At least driving would help to ease the tension he carried.

"I'm riding shotgun." Roan got into the front passenger-side seat.

Kodiak didn't correct Roan. Tamaska got in the backseat with Ash.

"Sorry," added Roan as he put on his seat belt. "I get carsick easily. Best for everyone if I'm in the front."

"Fine with me," Tamaska said. Kodiak detected an edge in her voice. He sensed she wanted to be with him, alone, but once more the pack's needs were placed above their relationship.

She has to get used to this if she's going to be my mate.

More than that, Kodiak needed to find a way to explain what seemed unexplainable, this unfamiliar world, to Tamaska before she did something else to put all of their lives at risk.

CHAPTER 9

 odiak

FOOT HARD ON THE GAS, Kodiak sped away from Sydney down the Great Western Highway. The city lights blurred behind him as the scent of death faded. He longed for the fresh air and open space at the hut. His wolf pushed hard at the surface, begging for the chance to be free and enjoy nature.

Driving ordinarily helped Kodiak relax. Not tonight, not when the risk of a vampire attack still remained.

Then, there was Tamaska.

He could smell her, feel her, and the force of their bond unnerved him. How had such a strong bond formed between him and a human? It didn't help that every time he looked in the rearview mirror, he saw her looking at him with an expression of confusion and hurt on her face.

Tamaska didn't say a word—though, from time to time, her mouth would open as if to speak. Instead, she would sigh.

It's her own fault. He had every right to be angry at her. And he tried to hold onto the anger as it gave him distance.

But his anger cooled too quickly with her, just like he knew it wasn't entirely true, that it was all her fault.

Kodiak needed to tell her more about the pack, about the bond between them that she couldn't ignore. Then, he needed to explain the details of the change. Bring her into that ultimate decision, just as Ash had said.

But not before I have more information. I don't want her risking her life if it's too dangerous.

He adjusted the rearview mirror, glancing at the backseat instead of scanning for any traffic coming from behind. Tamaska's gaze sent a ripple of pleasure through him. He quickly looked at Ash, who was busy on her laptop.

You found anything? He asked Ash through the pack connection, searching for a distraction from the things Tamaska stirred within him.

Fuck, Kodiak. It's only been a few minutes, Ash answered without looking up from the screen. Her fingers didn't even slow as they typed.

It's been the better part of an hour.

I'm not that good.

You are.

She harrumphed.

Tamaska glanced between them, trying to work out what they were communicating.

Another thing he had to explain to her. Another thing to add to his ever-growing list of burdens.

Leave me alone. I need to concentrate.

Kodiak withdrew, not wanting to further disturb Ash.

"What was that about?" asked Tamaska, a soft pleading in her tired voice.

Even without seeing her, Kodiak felt her glare burn into

him and it set off the familiar heat inside him that both pulled him to her and turned him on, and riled him. Jesus. The others had to be picking up on that. Something he didn't need.

Kodiak pressed harder on the gas instead of answering her. The sooner they reached their destination the better. He swerved around a vehicle going a little too slow, the driver honking, and he cut the corner too fast, and he narrowly missed hitting another car.

"Fuck," he muttered.

Roan paled, still next to Kodiak in the passenger's seat.

"Don't you go puking in my car, Roan," warned Kodiak.

Roan inhaled, then held his breath and clutched at the door handle.

"It wouldn't be a problem if you knew how to drive," said Tamaska.

Kodiak shot her a dark stare. "Don't comment on things you don't understand."

"I understand the concept of driving. And you're doing a bad job. Both Roan and Ash would tell you if they weren't so bogged down in pack rules of never calling you out on something. They should be able to." Her hand flew to her head.

"Not this again," Kodiak said. His foot remained heavy on the accelerator. "You don't understand."

"Fuck you, Kodiak. I understand that dictatorships don't work. I get there are rules. And maybe because I'm human I see it differently, but I don't think so. You wanted to argue with Olcan all the time. So—"

"This isn't the time, Tamaska," Ash said. "Everyone's stressed, including you."

"Maybe I can't ever fit in. Maybe you don't want me to," she said to him. "You were so angry with me and adamant about me obeying you never let me tell you what happened."

"I know what happened. You fucked up."

"Both of you," Ash said, "stop it."

"Ash…" He gripped the wheel hard and swerved around another car, ignoring Roan's soft sounds of protest.

Ash half closed her computer. "She has a point. We're a cohesive group with delineated places, but it's not a dictatorship and Olcan wanted you precisely because you poked and prodded and annoyed him. You made it fairer and gave us room to speak, so how—"

"Not the time, Ash."

"And me?" Tamska asked. "Maybe you just don't want me." He could hear the pain in her voice. "I got more information out of Amdis than you, and that's really saying something. Maybe I've chosen the wrong side."

His blood turned cold at her last words but she was clearly just trying to rile him, right?

"What the fuck are you talking about?" Kodiak asked. A low, heavy growl erupted from him. How could she fucking get under his skin like that with just a few sentences? "You want to be with that bloodsucker, be my guess."

"She didn't mean it, Kodiak," interjected Ash. "Did you?"

"I did, too."

"Tamaska…" Ash shut her mouth, took a breath and opened her laptop. "You're both ridiculous. Work it out yourselves or I swear I'll challenge for Alpha." The sound of the typing filled the car again.

"I can stop and leave you for the vampires right here," said Kodiak, taking his foot off the gas. "If you want."

"I didn't mean it, I'm sorry." Tamaska shifted in her seat, moaning.

Kodiak could feel emotion vibrating within her. Her pulse quickened, and fear flooded her body, he smelled that. Did she mean what she'd said? Did that fucker do something to her? Or was she pushing his buttons. He gritted his teeth.

"Don't say anything like that again, or I'll deliver you to Amdis myself," he growled.

"Because he told me things?"

"No. Because you claim you chose the wrong side." Then he paused. "What the fuck are you talking about?"

"I didn't...I didn't mean that. You should know that. But he said some things and you never let me tell you. Just shoved me away in your room under watch."

Kodiak hit the brakes. Tires screeched as he rolled onto the side of the road. Loose stones spun beneath rubber and flicked the underside of the car.

Tamaska screamed, grabbing the door to steady and brace herself as she flung forward. The seatbelt snapping her back as the car abruptly stopped.

"Fuck, Kodiak. That wasn't necessary," said Ash, readjusting her laptop.

Roan opened the door and stumbled out to throw up.

Kodiak turned and glared at Tamaska. "You want me to listen? I'm fucking listening now. This isn't a game. So, spill." It took all his self-control to remain in his seat.

"Okay, just..." She took a shuddering breath as she massaged her temple and his heart both ached and raged. How she could pull him in so many directions at the same time baffled. "He...he said something about the opal."

"Got that."

"He said the Blood Opal gives the vampires power. It rejuvenates them, makes them stronger."

"And allows them to walk in the light," said Kodiak softly. Shit. Maybe she had a point about his hard ass stance but he needed to while they all transitioned into the new pack order. And with the fucking vampires...

Vampires who could walk in light. "Weak light. It's why Amdis didn't burn up into dust, isn't it?" And they had the opal.

Worse, it looked like they needed Tamaska for something to do with it. Did that mean if they got her, really got her, their powers would increase more?

"Fuck, if the opal comes to full power, could they walk in full daylight?"

"I don't know. He didn't mention that."

Frustration bit Kodiak like a swarm of angry ants. He had to prepare for the worst, whether Tamaska could confirm it or not.

But he kept circling back to the importance of Tamaska to the bloodsuckers.

"And your blood will activate the Blood Opal, or something like that?"

She closed her eyes a long moment and nodded. "Something like that."

"Fuck, we have to get the gem back." It wouldn't be enough just to protect Tamaska. But then, he had always known that.

"Amdis said there was something about my blood…"

"What about it?" If Amdis had told Tamaska something that might help, Kodiak had to know.

"That my blood is the reason why I'm attracted to you…I don't know what that means." She looked at him, misery bright. "Maybe that means it's why you want me. It's just blood, not because…not…"

Not because he loved her.

She thought that?

She thought her worth to him was nothing more than a trick of fucking blood?

"If that were true I wouldn't have disliked you when we met."

Her lip trembled. "B-but there's something weird about my blood. Am I some kind of freak, Kodiak? It's not enough to be a freak for being human to your pack, I have to be a freak to the world because there's something wrong with my blood?"

Damn, Kodiak. Do something... Ash's thought hit him full on.

He didn't even spare her a glance. She was right. But this wasn't in his set of skills. How the fuck was he meant to soothe a human female. It wasn't like he could just have sex with her here, in front of the others.

"Tamaska... No. You're not a freak."

Kodiak softened a little toward Tamaska. The world she knew had been shattered, and he needed to help her. But there was so much to teach in so little time that he didn't know where to start.

He ran his hand through his hair, shaking his head. Thoughts surfaced like young pups, all demanding attention.

She nodded and rubbed her temple again. "Amdis said it has to do with my ancestry, but I have no idea what he's talking about. My parents and grandparents, who immigrated to Australia, were normal."

Kodiak's eyes widened. "They did. Why didn't you tell me?"

"This is Australia. Most of us have immigrant ancestors."

He glanced at Ash now, "Do you think this could help us? Now we know."

"Not sure," she said, looking over at Tamaska. "But the things she's said about Amdis might be helpful. I'll look into everything."

"Another mistake I've made," his woman said.

"No. Just..." He paused. "Make sure you tell me, or Ash, or someone in the pack if you get information like that again, or anything that comes to mind, really."

"I didn't think you'd believe it, coming from me." She

turned and stared out the window at the night and the passing cars. "I have nothing to add to the pack, nothing but trouble, do I?"

"You do have a lot to add to the pack," said Kodiak. "It might not seem like it now, but that's just because we're in the early days. The others will adjust. Just hang in there."

"He gets there eventually," Ash said, so he could hear.

Kodiak gripped the steering wheel tightly. It was even more important now to get to the hut, complete the ceremony, and officially step into his role as alpha.

His theory must be correct. Tamaska was superhuman. Even more, it seemed like she might have wolf shifter genes. Some shifters had dormant genes, allowing their human half to dominate their wolf side.

She was too vulnerable to hear that right now; Tamaska would take it as proof he didn't care. But if it was true and she had those genes, then maybe the risk for change would turn out non existent.

"Got all that, Ash?" asked Kodiak. Through the pack connection, he sensed Ash wanted to speak to him.

He knew her well enough that she was giving him the necessary space to talk to Tamaska. "What else do you need to know, Ash?"

"Got it. What's your last name, Tamaska?" asked Ash. "When did your grandparents come to Australia, and what city did they travel from?"

"Lane. They came to Australia in 1921 from Seattle."

"Unusual." Ash struck the keyboard hard and fast to enter the new information. "Most migrants came during the goldrush and after the second world war. Mostly from China and then Europe respectively. So this might make finding something easier."

Roan slipped back into the car. "What did I miss?"

Kodiak revved the car, the sound powerful and strong. He ignored Roan, who closed the passenger door.

"Don't keep information from me again," he said firmly.

She nodded. "I won't."

"Make sure you don't, Tamaska." He flashed a smile into the rearview mirror. I want you with me. We're a team."

A real one, where we share things?" Her voice was soft. "Like about what I am?"

A heavy pause weighed in the air as Kodiak reentered the highway.

"After the ceremony, if there's anything Ash has found. We'll talk then—but only if there's enough time."

"Promise?" she asked.

The word twisted in him, unravelling parts of him and he hated the way she undermined him so easily without meaning to.

"Only if you promise to obey me, like we talked about."

She quirked her lips in an almost smile. "Promise. Master."

"Then I promise, too."

"See, that wasn't so hard, you two. You've got your first lovers' fight behind you. Now it's just smooth sailing ahead," said Ash.

Kodiak growled a warning.

"Not seeing the humor, then?"

He growled louder. Ash put her head down, returning to her research on the laptop.

"You know, Tamaska, everything I've done has been to protect you," said Kodiak.

"I know."

"Then we understand each other better now," said Kodiak. "We do."

If Tamaska had wolf shifter genes, everything would

make more sense. What excited him more than anything was that he'd no longer be bringing a human into the pack.

Her ancestry would give her the right to be there, and she'd be more likely survive the change.

Things were starting to look brighter for the pack. But how long would that last?

CHAPTER 10

amaska

NIGHT WRAPPED around the car as they continued driving along the highway. The odd flashes of headlights and red taillights made Tamaska feel more alone than if they were the only ones out here.

Like normalcy could now only be experienced through a window.

An uneasy silence settled over the car after her altercation with Kodiak. But Tamaska hoped things would improve now they'd made their mutual promises. And he was right, this was huge for them. So many changes and losses it hurt thinking about it.

Her heart ached for him. For the burden that lay on him, not just with her and keeping her safe but with the pack, with taking on leadership.

She rubbed her aching head. The pain seemed to get

worse, not better and she put it down to the stress of everything.

Because understanding the heaviness of his burdens, of pack structure as much as she could, it was still difficult for her to accept, her being shoved into a passive role.

It was hard not to make suggestions and take the lead. She was so used to running a team herself from her job organizing marketing events that being bossed around was new.

Though that wasn't entirely true. She's had bosses to answer to. She'd worked well enough with them, but she'd had a team to command, responsibilities and if she was brutally honest, her goal had never been to sit on her laurels.

She'd planned on being her own boss. Not part of some shifter commune. Again, not fair, but that's how it felt. And she felt...utterly useless. A burden herself.

Somehow, she needed to change her ways. She had to get used to being told what to do and become part of a team in a very different way than she was used to.

I can do this.

At least she was still in the car with Kodiak, and he hadn't pushed her away like she'd done to him. He certainly had every right to, after the huge mistakes she'd made.

Pushing him away wasn't her goal. It never had been since she accepted him for what he was. And yet that's what she did.

And Kodiak? Under all the hard edges and uncompromising air he had a softness for her she loved.

Even if he didn't he was a decent man. He's never abandon her to the vampires because she hadn't followed his orders.

No, but he just might lock her away somewhere.

The thought made her almost smile and she would have except her head hurt.

She looked up and her heart lurched. For the thousandth

time, she caught his fleeting glance in the rearview mirror before looking away.

Tamaska didn't trust herself to hold his stare for long because of the desires it stirred within her. They needed a lot of time to talk and to, well, fuck.

Instinctively she knew sex was a big part of expression for him.

And she... She needed to stop. She couldn't indulge in hot daydreams and fantasies, not even to pass the time in the car. It distracted her, and what...what if they noticed?

Besides, vampires were out there wanting her blood, and she wasn't about to let them have any—not even a drop. She would not be responsible for helping them evolve into something even stronger.

Ash muttered to herself and Tamaska eyed the computer, trying to discern what she was researching. That took her mind off how fast Kodiak was driving and how carsick Roan still looked.

The female shifter typed fast, and the screen shone dimly, even in the dark car. The light wasn't enough for her to glean any information before her efforts worsened her headache. Still, Tamaska kept trying to read the words Ash typed and the information flashing on the screen.

"Don't be so nosey," muttered Ash. She angled the laptop away from Tamaska.

This is about me. I have a right to know.

Tamaska didn't speak the words out loud, hard as that was. She'd caused enough ripples in the pack after letting Amdis corner her. She needed to think long-term, to get on better with the pack members—even if it meant being silent, being less domineering.

Still, that didn't mean she would give up on trying to find more information. Instead, she would simply go about it more subtly.

Tamaska pretended to look out the window until Ash moved back to her original position, which made it easier to type. Once more, Tamaska tried to read the screen through her peripheral vision.

Wolf genes...ancestry...family tree...Lane...

None of the information she gleaned gave her any further insight. What it did give her was a more intense headache and increased nausea.

"Are you doing all right?" asked Roan from the front passenger seat.

"Yeah," she lied, resting her head against the cool window glass and closing her eyes. There was nothing to be done for her medically. She had to endure the side effects of a blow to the head and suffer the consequences of a stupid decision.

"You know, you can ask me some questions," offered Roan.

"About what? Transforming into a shifter?"

"No." Roan paused, inhaling slowly. "General questions about wolf shifters and vampires."

Tamaska's eyes flicked open, immediately locking with Kodiak's in the mirror. He nodded, giving his approval.

"Are they sworn enemies?" This could be a good time for her to see if there was any truth to the stories she'd seen in fantasy books, TV series, and movies. "Or is it just this particular lot with your pack?"

"Enemies all over. We want different thing to them." Roan laughed weakly and she knew he was fighting the nausea. She felt it too, but for different reasons. "We want to be left alone, they want destruction. And they're arrogant, they think they should rule, so we keep them from taking over the human world."

"I thought so." Tamaska fired off the next question. "How long can you be in human form?"

This she really wanted to know. All the questions about shifters pushed at her, wanting to be asked.

If they could control it, then maybe after she changed she could too. Maybe she could—

"As long as we want, depending on how disciplined we are," Roan said. "Our wolf side gets more restless the longer we leave it, but it can be managed for months at a time if necessary."

"What about your wolf form? How long?"

"A night, a day, a few days, max. Otherwise the wolf form will dominate, and the human will be lost. It's also dangerous to be in our wolf form too long, because humans will kill us if they see us."

"But you protect humans." She already knew that basic information, but repeating it helped ease the restlessness rippling through her.

"Yes," Kodiak muttered, "because we know how to kill vampires. It's our duty."

"How do you do that? Garlic? Holy water?"

Kodiak said softly, "If only. You know how, you've seen it. It's as bloody as all get out, ripping them apart with our teeth or claws. Or you can stake them through the heart."

"Exactly that," said Roan. "Never think about it, really. It just is."

It just is. She rolled his words around her head. Maybe that's why Kodiak found it hard to tell her the information she craved.

"Like in the movies, I guess," Roan said. "Truth morphed into fiction once supernaturals were forced away from humans and into the shadows centuries ago. They think they forgot us, but they remember us in movies. They think it's all fiction, but it's not."

She nodded. "So, no special way to kill them?"

"Not really...sounds like you're keen to kill one," he said.

"Of course. Aren't you?" She looked at him in surprise. If she was going to kill Amdis, then she needed all the information she could get.

"Yes, but only on a need-to-kill basis. I don't go around hunting them. No one in the pack does."

"Apart from pups with something to prove," Ash said.

Kodiak laughed. "Pups always have something to prove."

She wanted to laugh with them, but somehow it make her feel more of an outsider than before.

"Don't get me wrong," Roan said, "we need to stop them from doing whatever they're doing, and we'll fight them to the death."

Tamaska had fought vampires herself with the few karate moves she'd remembered. But as she went over all they were saying she wasn't sure if she meant it about killing one. She hated them yes. Hated them for killing her friend. But maybe her knee jerk reaction of death and destruction just made things worse.

Or maybe it just showed the wide gap between her and shifters yet again. Even if she did have shifter blood, she'd been brought up human. Thought human. Shifter ways still seemed alien.

And really, would she be able to do that? To kill like the wolves did on the night of the attack?

Pain shot through Tamaska's head, and she inhaled sharply. She was overthinking. There was so much to process, and she'd barely scratched the surface. If only her headache would go away so she could keep questioning Roan.

Another bolt of pain cut through her head, and she winced.

"Here, I have something for the pain," said Roan. He rummaged through the medical bag, which rested on the floor between his feet.

Roan passed a blister pack back to Tamaska. "They'll help."

"What is it?" She turned the foil package over in her hands, noticing two tablets inside but no writing on the outside.

"An old herbal blend I put into tablet form."

"Not anything illegal?"

"No!" he exclaimed. "For that, you need to go to Moki."

"Is that right?" Kodiak didn't sound happy.

"I don't want those kind of drugs," she said.

Tamaska didn't take recreational drugs these days, not since she'd decided to grow up and work to having her own business. Not that that would be happening.

Did shifters even have regular jobs? They had a security business, but just normal jobs? And then would she be allowed to get or start her own business if they did all work?

It seemed unlikely. Her kind of job meant attention, they operated in the shadows. The other side to the vampire coin, she supposed. Security gigs were always less is more in the being seen department. What would her role in the pack even be?

"I'm going to have to talk to that idiot. Drugs. Since when do we dabble in fucking drugs? Evey pack member needs to be ready to fight vampires. We can't afford to be under the influence at any time," said Kodiak firmly. "And, like Olcan, I will enforce that. Or if he's been doing that under Olcan's nose, step hard on his stupid neck and stop the pup."

"As expected," said Roan. "I think Olcan had other worries. Not that you don't."

Tamaska popped the tablets out of their pack before dry-swallowing them. "Will these work?" She closing her eyes to endure more shooting pain in her head. The increased throbbing ripped the rest of her questions to shreds. Tiredness weighed on her, and she fought to keep herself alert. She wanted to witness Kodiak become the alpha.

"Hell, yes," said Roan. "But you're still going to have to take it easy for a few days, at least."

Tamaska didn't need to be told that her injury would prevent her long-awaited transformation for the next few days, that was clear without him saying it. The waiting and sitting about annoyed her, but she wouldn't say anything. If keeping her mouth shut would help speed things up, then she would gladly oblige. For now.

Within a few minutes, the effects of the tablets started to ease her head. "For herbs, this stuff is powerful."

"We wolves know a few of nature's tricks," said Roan proudly.

Curiosity, jealousy, and the longing to be included stirred something else deep within Tamaska, as if a part of herself was only just beginning to wake up. That part was impatient and desired freedom. She'd never felt anything like that before.

It was as if her brain was opening up and soaking in all the things in the air in the car.

Should I tell Kodiak about this?

But he had enough to deal with and it was just the herbs. Besides, she wanted to hold on to this strange awakening as her secret, even for now. Surely even the closest of pack-mates didn't share every single detail with each other?

Tamaska was about to ask Roan another question when Kodiak slowed and turned off the highway. They had nearly arrived. Tamaska sensed that somehow, even though it was black outside with no streetlights or cars around.

Was it just the tablets that heightened her awareness?

Or was something else happening to her?

Maybe learning about wolf shifters and vampires opened something in her and these crazy new sensations were to do with her potential shifter ancestry. Maybe she was finally reacting to the horrors she'd witnessed during the vampire attack.

Then again, maybe her new awareness was just a side effect of this new world she'd been thrust into. Maybe she was simply adapting, finally noticing things that had always been in plain sight but beyond her understanding.

Tamaska shifted in the seat, waiting to get out and stretch her legs. After the long car ride, she longed to fill her lungs with fresh country air.

The car bumped, sending Tamaska bouncing around the backseat. She scrambled for something to hold on to before slamming into Ash.

"Geez, Kodiak, this is the last time I'm riding with you," said Roan.

The wheels rumbled across gravel, announcing they were close to the hut. He kept driving, down a curving drive until a glowing light appeared.

Kodiak ignored Roan, his concentrated gaze set straight ahead. Despite their bond, Kodiak felt more distant than ever in that moment.

Tamaska's pulse increased. She needed to be fully prepared for the events that lay ahead. No matter what. Her gut tightened, convincing her there would be more to Kodiak's ceremony than she'd been told.

CHAPTER 11

amaska

SHE PRESSED her nose against the glass of the car window. The clearing in front of the hut had been transformed into something fascinating.

Bamboo torches protruded from the earth at regular intervals to form a semi-circle, their flames bright against the darkness of night. Shadows danced from the fire flickering on the ground. The surrounding dirt had been raked smooth, all its rocks and plants removed.

The sacred feel immediately struck her, like she was about to witness something extraordinary, and her gut churned with excitement and trepidation.

Regardless of the fact they were protecting her, she was aware of the privilege of being here. One she didn't take lightly.

Tamaska shivered as Kodiak parked the car somewhere out of the way.

"Come on, we have a ceremony to start," said Kodiak, getting out of the car and stretching.

Ash finished typing, snapped the laptop shut, and rushed out. Roan, too, was out in a flash, taking deep breaths. His skin had finally started to lose its sickly pallor from the journey.

Tamaska struggled with the seat belt. Those tablets must have slowed her down. Ash stood nearby beside Kodiak, their heads bent close as they whispered.

Her heart squeezed. What had Ash learned? Tamaska was desperate to find out. But she stopped herself from overreacting. They had a lot on their plates and maybe this wasn't about her. She needed to calm.

She finally got the seatbelt off and stumbled out of the vehicle, the cool night air she inhaled making her lungs ache. The sharp scent of the eucalyptus trees surrounding them cleared her mind, but that wasn't enough to help her make out a single word from Kodiak and Ash's conversation.

Tamaska pressed one hand against the car to steady herself. The concussion still held her back, adding to her frustration. She picked her way around the back of the car, heading for Kodiak and Ash.

Now would be a good time for some magical super-hearing to kick in. Didn't wolves have sharper hearing, or something like that?

Then again, even if she had magical super-hearing, the thumping ache in her head and the effect of the tablets would probably dampen her abilities.

Christ she was a mess.

Kodiak stood with his back to Tamaska, and Ash refused to even look in her direction.

"Hey, slow down." Roan grabbed her arm, simultaneously steadying her and moving her away from Kodiak. "You know, you're supposed to take it easy," he added.

"I was."

"Typical human wanting to rush ahead. We're like that, too. But we heal faster. Come on." Roan steered Tamaska away from Kodiak, toward the other side of the clearing in front of the hut. Heat from the flickering torches warmed her as they passed.

"You know, it isn't always about you," said Roan.

"What do you mean?" she asked.

"Give him some space. He needs to be ready for the ceremony," said Roan softly. They approached some other pack members, who waited outside the fiery semi-circle of light. "It's hard, I know, but it won't always be. These are unusual circumstances."

"But what am I supposed to do?" she asked. "I want to help, be proactive. And if there's something about me—"

"We'll find out. Until then, you're supposed to wait." He shrugged. "Be what he aaks."

Tamaska sighed heavily, and Roan chuckled. "It's hard."

"I know, but it's like I said. He's got a lot to deal with right now," said Roan, "and he needs you to be there for him. The best way to do that is to wait for him and do everything he asks of you."

"Sounds easy when you say it," said Tamaska, but his words just didn't sit right in her belly. "But I want to do more. I'm not some meek little wallflower."

"No, you're not, and he knows that."

Did he, though? Roan's reassurance eased the frustration cutting through her chest and soothed the strange sensations that had stirred within her since riding in the car.

She was being unreasonable, but nothing seemed to work no matter how hard she tried. "Sitting about is counterproductive."

"It feels like that but it's not. It's showing respect."

The word how rose but she swallowed it down.

Roan put his arm around her shoulders and squeezed. "You're an outsider to the pack. But patience and strength will lead to acceptance. If you put your mind to it, I believe you can show the pack that you possess those valuable qualities."

Tamaska's chest tightened, his words striking home in her heart. Still, those words would have been so much more special if Kodiak had spoken them. Even though she knew he couldn't be everything at once.

"He can't be everything but he'll try, for us. And for you. Kodiak *will* be there for you."

"What, you're reading my mind now?" A shudder spread across her shoulders.

"You're an open book, Tamaska. Your emotions show up on your face. It's obvious from the…um…discussion, in the car, that you two need some quality time. But everything going on around here keeps getting in the way."

"Does anything stay secret in this pack?" As much as she hated to admit it, maybe Kodiak was right to withhold some information from her. This was already too much to process.

And her earlier understanding, that some things can't be explained, only experiences came back. It went against her nature, but she needed to keep that close.

"Experience is education here. We learn from when we're born. You're trying to do it at once, so stop, let it come, and listen. And privacy? Of course, there's privacy—just not for you. You're human, and Kodiak is about to become the alpha." Roan squeezed her again as they paused beside one of the torches.

At least Roan was turning out to be friendly. Not everyone in the pack stood against her.

"So, be patient and wait."

Gain friends one at a time.

Her chat with Roan alleviated fears she never realized had

been hiding within. She'd been so intent on accusing Kodiak for everything he did wrong—everything she did wrong—that she'd missed a simple way to help him and the pack.

"You've got it."

Maybe rushing into her transformation wasn't such a good idea. She wanted to become a shifter, without a doubt, but she was already in shock. Her mind had been paralyzed since she'd first seen vampires drinking blood, let alone fighting wolves.

She needed to center herself, to ensure she was ready for a step that would change her life forever. Be patient and learn to absorb all the experiences. Good and bad. After the change, there would be no going back.

Roan lowered his voice. "The ceremony is important to him. He's grieving Olcan and still in shock from killing Shota. Until the ceremony is complete, the pack has no official leader. Anyone could step up to claim the position if they wanted. Kodiak's the choice and we know it, but...you saw Shota. Things happen under pressure. And there's the threat of vampires. So go easy on him, *and* yourself."

His words shocked her. "I thought it was a done deal that he was the alpha."

"Not until after the ceremony," he said with a shake of his head.

She closed her eyes a moment. "Which is why he wanted this done tonight."

"Exactly. See, you're learning quick."

Tamaska glanced at the night sky to see the moon peeking behind a cloud. It was almost full. Odd. "Shouldn't the moon be full during the ceremony?"

"Why do you ask?"

Tamaska shrugged. "Seems like it should be, that's all."

She couldn't explain how the thought randomly popped

into her head. Then again, maybe it wasn't so random. Maybe ancient knowledge had awoken within her mind.

Or maybe she was full of shit, clutching away at straws.

"It should be," Roan said, forehead creasing with worry. It was the first time Tamaska had ever seen him look outwardly concerned.

"Is it bad that we're doing it tonight, then?"

"I hope not."

She shivered, hating the helpless feeling rising up. "So, why don't we wait?"

"Because the pack needs a leader to recover and gain strength. There's no time to wait."

Tamaska hoped Kodiak knew what he was doing, missing the full moon by pushing up the ceremony. That wasn't fair. She knew he did. But she worried. She couldn't stop.

Everyone there was exhausted from the fight, the burial, and clean-up. Kodiak had insisted they were safer at the hut than in the clubhouse, but the way Tamaska's belly twisted made her uneasy.

"Don't worry, Channing's been all over the security," Roan said. "We're safe here."

Tamaska clenched her jaw. She trusted Kodiak, but that uneasiness crept over her, like a mist hovering above the ocean.

"I should get you a blanket."

"No, I'll be fine." Whatever happened, she needed to stand in her own strength.

While they talked softly, the pack moved closer to the light, naked and waiting silently.

A thought struck her. "Do I need to take my clothes off?"

"No, only the shifters. We'll transform."

Tamaska didn't like the way her clothes marked her as an outsider. Because of course she didn't. Though if things worked out, if she could hold on to her hot headedness, she wouldn't be an outsider much longer.

"I'll get you a chair," he said, "then I'll go and get myself ready."

"I don't need a chair."

"Right, and risk the wrath of Kodiak? No way." He pointed to her. "You need to rest. I don't want you fainting during the ceremony."

"Sitting will show I'm weak," Tamaska said. The tablets had eased the pain in her head, and she wasn't about to stand out even more by lounging around while everyone else stood.

"Suit yourself. But I'll put one here, anyway. To appease the next alpha." He squeezed her arm and moved away, slipping into the darkness before she could reply.

Tamaska stood at the edge of the circle, behind the pack. No one looked at her.

Roan returned with the chair, then took off once more and she just...stood. Sticking out. A sore thumb with a sore head.

She remained silent, practicing her new approach of waiting patiently instead of rushing in and taking over. More than ever, she wished for Kodiak to be beside her, guiding her, supporting her.

I can do this for Kodiak. For us.

A drum sounded, its beats steady and strong and echoing through the night air. Tamaska found herself drawn into the rhythm, although her body rippled with nerves.

Ash walked into the circle, naked. She held a handmade drum made of animal hide against her chest and beat it with a small, ornate padded mallet.

Kodiak followed her. Tamaska's breath caught in her throat at the sight of his stron, perfect form. His torso muscles, strong and toned, begged for her touch. She pouted her lips, remembering the kisses they'd shared and longing for more.

For a moment, she closed her eyes to cool her thoughts. If things went well tonight, maybe they would have some time together. Until then, she would do what she was worst at —waiting.

Ash stood in the center of the semi-circle, Kodiak by her side. He looked serious, eyes fixed dead ahead, and the only sound in the night was the drum beat.

The two turned around, facing the flames and the pack members waiting in the shadows.

Ash held up the mallet as the echo of the last beat reverberated through the clearing.

"Shadow Pack, come forward." Ash spoke clearly and confidently.

The members moved into the semi-circle marked by torches.

Tamaska's heart ached to be part of the Shadow Pack. To be there for her man. But even if she had wolf shifter genes, she was primarily human.

She stayed at the edge of the light, the boundary between the new life she wished to embrace and the old one she wanted to leave behind.

On the outside looking in, Tamaska sensed the deep, unique relationship between the pack's members. Despite all they had gone through, they stood almost shoulder-to-shoulder with each other, naked, vulnerable, yet radiating strength.

They walked the worlds of both humans and shifters, sworn to secrecy while duty-bound to protect both races. Two worlds stood threatened by the power-hungry vampires and their need for domination and chaos.

She admired them all, especially Kodiak. While the pack

had just been attacked and left weakened, no signs of their defeat remained—only power and strength.

No doubts clouded her mind. That was the life she wanted.

And ff she was going to be hunted by vampires either way, she wanted superhuman strength and the support of the pack. It made sense to become a full shifter.

She also wanted to be with Kodiak. Completely.

Could he turn me tonight?

That was wishful thinking at its best, but it gave her courage. She stood still, waiting for an invitation into the family she wanted to call her own.

CHAPTER 12

 odiak

HE DUG his toes into the dirt. The earth offering him the grounding he needed as his stomach knotted.

Ash, in charge of the night's formalities, stood beside him in the semi-circle, her drum now quiet. They were all ready to start.

Kodiak had imagined his alpha ceremony differently, in a world where Olcan willingly transferred his responsibilities to Kodiak instead of getting killed by vampires.

It hurt. What he'd give to have Olcan watching, being there to help the transition. He knew the pack had needed a leadership change and he suspected Olcan did, too, which is why he'd pushed Kodiak so damned hard.

He should be here.

Not dead.

And Tamaska... He sensed her to his left, in the shadows. The rest of the pack stood in the light.

His chest tightened. She should be there with them. With him.

But his own stubbornness had gotten in the way. They'd never let her be part of it, not even if she'd transformed already. Not even if they were all open to his ideas of a more modern pack, one that could weave progressive thoughts with the ancient ceremonies and ways.

He was so damned aware of her. Had been since they'd first met and butted heads.

She'd proved her strength more than once, but her inability to follow him made him stand back. Grow hard with her. He had to. The pack would never accept her otherwise. They weren't mated. He couldn't have favorites. Especially an outsider. A human.

It would come, but later, when all this was done, the danger passed.

He had thought about taking her aside for a talk before leaving for the ceremony, but Ash had caught him first to talk about the information she'd found. Then, it was time to leave, and once more, his plans to talk with Tamaska were put on ice.

Would any of the others fight him for the alpha position? He didn't glance about, but the thought was there, anyway. And it happened. Often.

Here the danger was the upheavals, the attacks and deaths and the new unknown threats from the vampires they all faced. It was natural to strike out and place blame where none lay.

So if someone was to challenge, now would be the time. The sanctioned time.

He wasn't sure he had it in him to risk another fight to the death with one of his own. Out of all the pack, Moki would be the most likely challenger. Thankfully, he hadn't caused Kodiak any further issues. But there was always the risk that Moki had been quietly garnering support from others.

"We are here to inaugurate the new alpha of the Shadow Pack," said Ash, her voice ringing clearly in the crisp night air. "Kodiak, the Beta, is next in line as the one Olcan chose to succeed him if..." Ash faltered, a fleeting tide of emotion flooding over her before she regained control of herself. "Olcan had chosen Kodiak to be the next alpha. The succession is clear."

Kodiak's stomach fluttered as if housing restless moths that wanted to escape. He inhaled, slow and deep. This was it —the moment when he found out for real if anyone wanted to challenge him over the alpha position.

Kodiak didn't want to fight again, but he would for Olcan. The old wolf shifter had trained him and trusted him to lead the pack after he was gone, and Kodiak would do that to honor Olcan's memory.

Plus, there was Tamaska. He wanted to look at her to see her eyes on him. But he didn't. He forced his stare ahead, to toward the circle of his pack. As alpha, he would be better able to protect Tamaska. It was his position, and he wouldn't let anyone take it from him.

"According to your sacred rights as a member of the Shadow Pack, step forward if you wish to challenge Kodiak for the position." Ash beat the drum once. The vibration washed over him as he held his breath.

He looked his pack's members, lit by orange flames. Channing lowered his eyes respectfully, along with Roan and Fern. Then, he found Moki. The shifter held his gaze.

"You have until the end of ten drumbeats to make your intentions known. Otherwise, you will be expected to pledge your alliance to Kodiak wholeheartedly."

Ash pounded the drum.

Ten...nine...eight...

Kodiak counted automatically. He locked eyes with Moki, and neither backed down.

So be it, then. Kodiak darkened his glare, daring Moki to come forward.

Five...four...three...

Kodiak tensed, readying his muscles for a fight. This was his position, and he would keep it no matter what.

Two...one.

The last beat resonated through the space.

Moki didn't move into the semi-circle where Kodiak and Ash stood.

Kodiak growled softly, but Moki didn't lower his eyes. He knew, right there, he'd always have to watch his back around that one, but at least he didn't need to fight again. The pack had agreed to take him as their leader.

"The Pack has spoken," announced Ash.

Ash turned to Kodiak.

> "By the power of the ancestors,
> shared with me,
> you are given the position of alpha.
> This comes with the responsibility
> to lead with strength and fairness,
> to ensure the pack continues to grow,
> to protect humans, to slay vampires.
> In the way of the alphas who have walked before you
> And the ones who are yet to emerge,
> you continue our line.
> Give this power only to those
> Excelling in control over their forms,
> Both human and wolf.

"Kodiak, do you swear to lead the Shadow Pack?" asked Ash.

"I do," he said.

"Will you continue until you are no longer able, whether due to injury, poor health, old age, or death?"

"I will." His skin prickled at the mention of death. It wasn't his he feared for, but Tamaska's, his pack's.

"Your hand." Ash unclipped a small ceremonial knife from the back of the drum.

Kodiak held out his left hand.

Ash drew the knife over his palm, and blood spurted from the cut. Then, she did the same to her own palm.

"With your blood." Ash turned his palm so his blood dripped onto the dirt beside their feet.

"With my blood." Her blood splattered onto the dirt to mingle with his.

Kodiak recited his pledge.

"I give my blood to the pack
As they give theirs
Blood, ancestry, past, present, and future
Bind us together as one
To fight the evil around us
To protect the weak
With courage, strength, and fairness.
I will bring this pack into a new era of growth, abundance, and peace.
This is my pledge."

"We accept and hold your promise," the pack responded in unison.

"With the pack's blood, the pledges are sealed."

One by one, the pack stepped forward to slice their palm add their blood to Ash and Kodiak's.

"We accept your role as alpha."

"We accept," responded the crowd.

"We support you for the sake of the pack. The pack protects us and preserves the knowledge of our ancestors for future generations. For Shadow Pack!"

"For Shadow Pack!"

Kodiak squared his shoulders and lifted his chin, power rumbling through him. It was done.

Now he looked at her and she struck him hard with her beauty, her soul. It shone so bright right then he could barely breathe.

Tamaska stood just outside the edge of the semi-circle. Tears slid down her cheeks, but her face shone with respect and awe.

Kodiak wanted to include her in the ceremony, but with Moki snapping at his heels, Kodiak couldn't invite her to become a pack member without risking a challenge. And she couldn't participate in the last of the evening's proceedings, either.

She'd still have to wait a bit longer. While that would hurt her in the moment, she'd hopefully understand his actions in time.

"Who will be beta of the Shadow Pack?" asked Ash.

"Onai will be beta," Kodiak answered. The decision was an easy one. Onai was loyal to Kodiak and to the pack. If anything happened to Kodiak, Onai would see the pack into the future and continue looking after Tamaska.

Ash bowed her head in acknowledgement. She lifted the mallet, then beat the drum.

"Come forward, Onai," said Ash.

Onai moved to stand in front of Kodiak and Ash.

"Will you swear to support me as alpha of Shadow Pack?" asked Kodiak.

"I will."

"Do you agree to become the beta of Shadow Pack?"

"I do."

Kodiak took Onai's bloodied hand in his and pressed their palms together. "As our blood mingles, we join together for the pack. We unite to keep us safe, to train our pups, to ensure there are wolves left to fight as long as vampires walk the earth."

"The third in line for alpha will be Channing." It was risky to choose someone so young, but Channing had performed admirably in Kodiak's team and had taken the initiative to organize security back at the clubhouse.

"There's still the right of challenge," called Moki.

"There is," Kodiak said, not liking the underlying tone, "but the vampires must be dealt with. Our secondary and tertiary leaders will prove their worth through their performance. Then, we can reshuffle that line up, if necessary. There's been enough infighting. It's time for us to work together, not indulge in petty, ego-fueled squabbles over position."

"I agree," said Skoll.

"Me too," Jaha said.

"And I," said Fern.

Moki lowered his eyes. Lacking the support of the pack, his request was squashed.

The swearing-in ceremony was nearly complete.

Ash beat her drum, silencing everyone. "The alpha has spoken."

Another drumbeat. "Channing, step forward."

The young shifter moved to stand with Kodiak, Ash, and Onai.

"Do you agree to become the third in line for the alpha position?" asked Kodiak, looking Channing squarely in the eyes. The pup stood confidently, having matured by figurative years in just the last few days.

"I do." He eagerly held out his bloodied hand.

Kodiak smiled. Despite his youth and inexperience,

Channing was a good choice for the pack. Kodiak pressed his palm against Channing's.

"With our blood, the promise is made."

Ash beat the drum.

Kodiak stepped forward, ready to address the pack.

"The last few days have been the darkest our pack has ever faced. We will rebuild and move on. We will make the vampires pay for trying to destroy us."

A few cheers erupted from the pack's members as some excitedly punched the air above their heads. Kodiak paused, allowing them to express their excitement. Even if it was one borne of grief, they'd all earned it. And the excitement honored Olcan.

Now, it was time to celebrate. The ceremony wasn't quite complete. Their wolves were about to be let loose, and they would participate in a hunt to commemorate the change in leadership.

"First…" Kodiak let the cheers quiet down. "We will allow our wolf forms the opportunity to embrace our new structure, to be free, to heal, to rejuvenate, to mate, or to hunt."

Whoops echoed from the pack. Strengthening their bonds through hunting or mating, according to individual preference, would be the best way for Shadow Pack to recover from the vampire attack.

He glanced at Tamaska. A stormy expression crossed her face, and she folded her arms over her chest. He hid a small smile. He wouldn't mate tonight—at least, not in wolf form.

Before handling anything else or indulging himself, Kodiak needed to run with his pack and lead them in a hunt. His wolf gnawed frustratedly inside him. But his wolf would have to wait a little longer for that, just like Tamaska.

"Then tomorrow at first light, we return to the clubhouse and plan our attack on the vampires."

More hoots and whistles erupted from the pack. Their

energy peaked, and he sensed their wolfish desire to roam, to enjoy the freedom they would never have in the city.

"Let's go!" Kodiak punched high in the air as the pack screamed their approval.

Kodiak raised his arms, then released the internal barriers that held back his wolf. Familiar pain burst through his body as bones broke and muscles shortened or lengthened. Then, he crouched on all fours, howling at the sky.

The ceremony would have been more powerful if the moon had been full—but it was close, and the energy rippling through him was nothing like he'd ever experienced. Strangely, his connection to Tamaska and his human form remained, as if connected by the invisible threads of fate. He couldn't let his wolf have full reign yet, so he needed to be careful.

His paws landed on the dirt, touching the edge of the blood spilled to inaugurate him as the alpha. In his wolf form, his strength had increased, and he was much stronger than before.

A warning snarl escaped Kodiak as Moki, also in wolf form, came closer. Kodiak was ready to fight anyone unhappy with his appointment as alpha.

Moki veered away with his tail between his legs, which pleased Kodiak.

Kodiak howled again in a lower pitch, signaling the others to join him. As the pack transformed, they joined their howls to his. Their voices glided up and down, giving beauty to the sound.

He sprang forward, rushing away from Tamaska. He hoped she would be all right for at least half an hour, and then he could return to her without the others noticing. By then they would be hunting, running, mating, or otherwise distracted.

As for him, he would lead the first hunt of the night,

according to his right as the new alpha. He dashed between bushes with great agility, swerving left and right as if pursuing a deer. He luxuriated in every sensation his wolf form afforded him, overjoyed at the chance to loosen his self-control for the special occasion.

Deer scent proved easy to track as the pack, respectfully running behind him, spurred him on. After tracking it for the better part of half an hour, Kodiak found the deer. Its small tail flicked nervously behind it. He calculated strategic changes in direction that would leave zigzagging through the scrub to bring down the deer and send its soul fleeing to the underworld.

Kodiak crouched low behind the bushes, not wanting to be seen, eyes fixed on the alert fallow deer.

He needed to strike quickly, before the deer ran off or another wolf got to it. Kodiak wouldn't put it past Moki to try and steal his moment of glory.

Seizing his moment, he sprang out from under the bush's cover, rushing the deer. He leaped into the air, then clamped his teeth around the tender skin of its neck, claws raking across its flesh.

Blood rushed into his mouth, the glorious taste reminding him of past fights with vampires, where he could taste whatever blood they'd consumed.

The deer put up a fight, but Kodiak was more powerful. The deer was his.

He shredded its body and tore open its hide, ready to feast. His wolf side hungered, not just for a hunt, but for fresh meat.

Kodiak ripped open the deer's chest with only one intention—to find and eat its heart.

The heart, still warm, was torn from the deer and consumed quickly, a fitting reward for the new alpha.

Once he had his fill, he howled with his nose to the sky.

The howl would signal the kill's location to the rest of his pack, so they could fill their stomachs as they pleased. Then, he raced off.

He detected Tamaska's scent easily and found her sitting near one of the torches by the front of the hut. She hadn't wandered off into the scrub, where the wolves hunted. The pack wouldn't hurt her, but she;d been left alone after the wolves scattered for the hunt.

The need to protect beat louder than the drum had.

Crouching in the shadows, he changed back to his human form. He grabbed some leaves and tried to wipe some of the deer's blood off his skin. His wolf resisted, eager to get back into the scrub to hunt, to enjoy its true form.

He stepped towards her, his feet padding softly across the dirt. "Tamaska."

She whipped around to face him with red eyes and tear-streaked cheeks and his heart squeezed painfully.

"I'm sorry, but I had to do it this way. There was no time."

"I know. But that doesn't make it any easier," she responded, getting to her feet. It hurt that she didn't rush to him, wrap her arms around him. Kodiak suspected that the deer blood alone would be enough to keep her away.

She wouldn't like the next event of the evening, either. He couldn't leave her outside alone. It was too dangerous, even here.

"Come this way, to the hut. You'll be more comfortable there." He didn't wait for her to follow as he strode over to the wooden structure where they'd made love the other night, an act that had cemented their fledgling bond.

Kodiak opened the door and motioned for her to step inside. He hated to picture how messy he looked, how he must smell after taking down the deer. That would be enough to put anyone off.

Tamaska didn't seem bothered. She hesitated, then walked through the doorway.

"You'll be safer in here. I'll be back before sunrise." With that, he left the hut, then closed and locked the door.

"Kodiak, come back!" she yelled from the other side of the door. "You bastard!"

"At sunrise. Wait. Please." He sensed the pack calling for him, desperate to know where their new leader had gone. He needed to run with them.

He transformed into his wolf form and ran into the scrub with Tamaska's cries of protest aching in his ears. And he hoped Tamaska would forgive him when he returned.

CHAPTER 13

 *amaska*

Tamaska punched the door of the hut. Pain ricocheted up her arm, but she didn't let that stop her from hitting the wood again. Blood oozed from scratches on her knuckles, and she screamed in frustration.

"Kodiak, you fucking bastard! Come back here and let me out!"

She wasn't some damsel in distress who needed to be locked up. It wasn't like she could hurt anyone, or even get hurt. The pack was obligated to protect her from harm. And no vampires were here.

"Kodiak!" she cried when he didn't return. "Don't leave me, please!

No answer at all and she didn't know if he was still out there. Probably not. He had things to do. Shifter things, and he...he didn't trust her.

Tamaska kicked the door. Her toes slammed against the

end of her boot, adding to the pain thundering through her body.

What did he want to do? Go off and mate in his wolf form? That's what this was really about, right? Just because she wasn't a wolf, would he cast her aside instantly?

She screamed again. "Fuck you!"

With his special wolf hearing, Tamaska was sure he could hear her, making his refusal to return and explain himself worse. She kept returning to the thought that he wanted to mate in his wolf form.

"And why not fuck me in human form, if that's all tonight is for?" she yelled.

Why hadn't he?

She pressed her lips together to stop the tears, and swallowed over the lump in her throat as rejection ripped at her heart with its own set of claws.

This is how she'd been rewarded for waiting patiently at the hut after the entire pack changed into their wolf forms and ran off. They abandoned her without a word, without any explanation. She hated them all.

Still, she couldn't shake off her desire to be one of them. And despite everything, she was drawn to Kodiak. Even though he was a wolf, her irrational feelings for him only spiraled.

I might be a wolf, too.

The thing is, though, she'd never be proper a wolf not to them. Even if she had wolf shifter ancestry or DNA, those genes were dormant in her, leaving her 100% human and unable to change forms.

Even knowing that, she'd listened to Kodiak, waited around, and looked at what happened. She was alone in the hut while he was off roaming the scrub doing fuck-knows-what. Isolated, she ran wild, imagining everything he could be doing.

She was she knew, as she forced herself to calm down, being unfair, a baby. But she couldn't help it. Being abandoned hurt, no matter if there was a ceremonial reason for it.

Tamaska huffed heavily and nursed her sore hand. She needed to clean herself up. She went into the bathroom and washed up. The cold water stung her hand, but the scratches were superficial and would heal quickly.

She splashed some water on her face, and took deep, calming breaths.

This might be part of the whole ceremony, but locking her up instead asking her to stay in wasn't on. And if he even thought about mating with someone, she'd…be very upset.

She made her way back to the living room. Was this how things would be, now that Kodiak was the alpha?

She hoped not. She hoped there'd be some leeway, a little softness, and inclusion for her. She was willing to give up everything for him and he… He didn't bend. She didn't know if he could, as alpha.

Heaviness grew in her heart. That couldn't be right. Even shifters could change. They were thinking beings. They were supernatural and thought and reasoned just like boring old humans. They could change. He could. She knew he wanted to grow the pack in different ways so— There was a time and place for everything. She just was lost and scared and adrift. And if he didn't love her…

She couldn't think that. He did.

Tamaska sighed heavily and flopped onto the bed, looking at the wood-paneled ceiling. Maybe she had to just be the one to give in this time and when things were settled, the vampires vanquished, he could let go of that implacable control. She hoped.

But for now, she'd wait for him. And still she reached for the vacant space beside her, longing for Kodiak to be there.

Memories of the few hours they'd stolen together,

fucking the way two people should when they've just met and were falling for each other, flooded her mind. Her body ached without him, especially since the peace of the hut would be the perfect space to spend time alone, to release some of the emotions that had built up between them, to talk.

Instead, he'd chosen to be in his wolf form and locked her up like a possession.

Tamaska sat up, restless, even though she needed the sleep to recover from her head injury. When she wasn't thinking about Kodiak, fragmented memories of vampire fights came to mind.

If only the hut had a TV or something. She needed a distraction. Lying there alone, too many thoughts haunted her, and she feared losing her mind.

Amdis' words echoed through her. *Your blood... activation... Blood Opal... ancestors.*

She rubbed her temples. Maybe looking it all up, doing some research would help.

But her phone didn't have any signal. She slid off the bed to wander around the room, looking for something to help her focus on anything but being locked in the hut.

Ash's laptop sat on the lounge chair in the corner. Tamaska picked it up and took it back to the bed.

Ordinarily, she wouldn't open someone else's laptop and spy on their browsing history. But she wasn't living in an ordinary world anymore.

She opened the laptop, hoping it might contain some secrets to help her better understand her situation.

No password?

Things were looking up for her. It seemed odd for Ash not to have a password, but maybe she'd gotten distracted by the ceremony.

About a dozen tabs were open onscreen, and Tamaska

flicked between them. Ash had been researching Tamaska's heritage, the Blood Opal, and how to turn humans into shifters.

Horror hit her. Didn't they know how to turn a human? But surely…

Confused, she flicked through all the open files, scanning blocks of text for anything promising. Then, she found Ash's notes.

It's risky to change a human. The moon needs to be full, and they might be unable to rein in their new powers. A new wolf shifter might roam around killing uncontrollably. If the new shifter does survive, they will be weak for weeks after the transformation while they recover.

Tamaska shook her head in disbelief. Surely, turning a human couldn't be so risky. Maybe this was why Kodiak didn't seem keen on making it happen any time soon.

She tried not to be offended as she read on. This time, she found more information about Kodiak's pack.

The Shadow Pack is made of wolf shifters. Their DNA ensures that their skills can be fully developed. No member has ever been human; they are all wolf shifters by birth.

So they only ever chose other pure wolf shifters from whoever was out there? So where and how could she even fit in?

If a single pure shifter had mated with a human, then the shifter genes could have eventually gone dormant after a few generations.

Was that liaison the real reason why her grandparents had come to Australia? If she had shifter blood, of course.

Tamaska flicked back to Ash's ancestry searches. Ash had looked through online immigration records and found many new arrivals to Australia in 1921. She'd even found records of migrants who left Seattle that same year.

But there were no Lanes.

Tamaska frowned. Why weren't there any Lanes?

She'd never been interesting in researching her family history before. Her parents had spoken openly about her grandparents' emigration to Australia, but they'd died when she was a young teen.

No one mentioned a change of name. Her granparents and great granparents on her father's side had been Lanes. If it had been changed then it would have been long before, in the US.

So strange, though. She'd never sensed they'd kept secrets from her, but maybe they had. If her phone had any bars, she would have called her parents immediately and asked them about it.

Then, Tamaska remembered. Of course! Her last name, Lane, was her dad's, and he was Australian. She needed to use her mum's maiden name, Brown. One set had come from the US, the other way back on the convict ships from the UK. So she needed to look up Brown.

Her phone had no bars, but they had wifi in the cabin to her delight.

She resubmitted her information to the ancestry website and clicked to search. She pressed her lips together tightly, hoping this would yield what she needed and shed some light on her family history.

Ornate branches spread across the screen as her family tree was electronically constructed. Elaborate heritage developed slowly in front of her eyes, giving her time to comprehend the information.

Bingo.

She smiled at the screen. There were her grandparents' names, even her great-grandparents' details. Tamaska lost track of time as her family tree was populated with people she'd never even heard of.

How will I know if they were wolf shifters? A human ancestry website probably wouldn't include supernatural information. She snorted at that. What she needed was the supernatural one.

Actually, that probably did exist, but she didn't know how to even begin to find one and she was being invasive enough of Ash's computer as it was.

She flipped through the rest of the open tabs. Ash was an organized and thorough researcher, but Tamaska saw nothing that would help her determine whether her ancestors had been wolf shifters.

Another dead end—

Then, she noticed another open app. She clicked on it, and finally found what she wanted. It showed a site that specifically tracked wolf shifter ancestry. "Ask," she said, "and you will find."

Tamaska filled the screen with the new information she'd found, and clicked to search.

"Fuck!" she exclaimed when she saw a family member whose full name she recognized from the previous site. It lay so many generations back, it was no wonder that her shifter genes were dormant.

Her great-, great-, great-, great-, great-, great-grandparents had been wolf shifters. Their daughter had a red cross through her name, and that branch ended there.

Did she die?

Tamaska typed her name into the human ancestry website and gasped at the information that appeared onscreen. Their daughter had married a human and borne three children.

In front of her lay the moment when her family's shifter genes had been mixed with humans', hundreds of years ago.

Nerves fluttered in her belly. She *did* have wolf shifter genes. That might help her case. Kodiak would have to turn her—he wouldn't be able to ignore this.

Finally, it made some sort of sense that the vampires wanted her. But still, why did they prefer her over a pure wolf shifter?

Tamaska rubbed her eyes. No wonder it took Ash so long to research all of this. Tamaska had only spent the better part of an hour, with all the hard work already done for her, and she was tired. Her eyes hurt. But that wouldn't stop her, not while she was locked inside a hut.

What was so special about her blood or her genes? What made her superior to a purebred shifter?

Or maybe inferior. Maybe the fact it was so dormant and weak meant the vampires could use it.

Tamaska she returned to Ash's notes. She found a list of wolf shifter families with stronger abilities than others. She gasped. Brown was on the list.

Her skin prickled as she processed the new information. Could that be why the vampires wanted her?

Her gut roiled. That was it. It had to be. Now, all she had left to research was the Blood Opal and its potential powers.

But how? The shifters had been doing just that since it went missing. But maybe a fresh pair of eyes...

Ash had noted that the Blood Opal possessed regenerative powers that could be activated by blood. The gem would behave differently depending on the type of blood used to activate it.

A quick scan of Ash's notes revealed that the Blood Opal alone would amplify its user's powers. Weird.

It just didn't make sense that the vampires wanted her blood to activate the opal if it amplified the user's power. That would be her. Or did it mean her blood would strengthen the person who bled her? It wasn't exactly clear and could be read either way.

But either way it was odd. So what if she came from one of the strongest shifter families? Her wolf genes were dormant. And what wolfish powers could the vampires possibly want?

Her gut churned. And if their plan involved her specifically, if they used her blood to activate the gem, it would amplify her powers and turn her into a wolf. Why would they want that?

Because she might go on a killing spree? Her eyes widened as a wave of fear hurtled through her. That sounded like something the vampires would want.

But that was all the more reason to act quickly. The vampires had to be stopped, and the pack needed to turn her as soon as possible. No way could they wait until the full moon. Surely even inactive shifter genes would make it possible for Kodiak to change her as soon as possible.

Eager to find more information, she worked through Ash's search history and added to it. But nothing else Tamaska found seemed remotely helpful.

On a whim, she typed Blood Opal in the human ancestry website to see what would come up. Maybe someone had added supplementary information about their family's property or valuables.

Tamaska brought a hand to her mouth as she gasped.

The Blood Opal had been sold around the same time her great-grandparents arrived in Australia. Someone had uploaded an old hand-written receipt to her family tree's history, and underneath the word *seller*, Tamaska could just make out the name Brown.

Fuck. It would be worth millions. If only they hadn't sold it.

She lay back on the bed, hands on her head. Information

whirled through her mind, trying to connect like puzzle pieces.

They'd probably sold it because they'd needed the money when they arrived in their new country. But more questions began to haunt her.

Had they forgotten the gem's true value within their family, that they needed it to activate their descendants' wolf genes? Or were they trying to keep it away from somebody else?

And was that someone else a vampire?

 odiak

IT WAS hard to walk away from Tamaska's swearing and demands, especially when he had no explanation to offer for his actions other than his duty to the pack. To him it made perfect sense, it was how things were done and even if he wanted to change it now wasn't the time. He couldn't ignore his responsibilities.

Why couldn't he bring himself to explain that to her? Maybe it was because she wasn't yet a wolf and might never be. Or maybe he simply wasn't used to explaining things that were so obvious to him. So ingrained.

But maybe it was something else. Something deeper, harder to put into words.

Because he knew, if he had stayed much longer with her in the hut, he'd never have been able to leave her. If he'd done that instead of spending the night with the pack, he'd miss the opportunity to solidify his position.

That wasn't ego. It was real. An alpha solidified on a solemn and important night like tonight. Especially after everything that had happened. And with one wolf looking to climb the ladder into a command position.

He needed to show his strength.

It was vital.

And something Tamaska didn't get. Couldn't. Not even if he spent hours explaining. And he wouldn't have. He'd have ended up fucking her.

In wolf form, Kodiak roamed for hours with the pack, hunting and even playing in the Australian bushland. The sharp eucalyptus scent refreshed him along with the earthy smells of soil and his packmates. Each smell mingled with the metallic scent of blood from their kills.

That time was necessary for Kodiak so he could exert his new power as alpha in wolf form. The pack needed to shift their pecking order to adjust to their new leader. Once that was done, they would be in a better place to take on the vampires.

Naturally, a few younger wolves wanted to test Kodiak's boundaries with some minor brawls. He surprised himself by easily putting the pups back in their place like a pat on the head or a fatherly bite of reproval, using the years of experience and preparation Olcan had given him.

Like Olcan had done to him and countless others. He looked heavenward and thanked the old Alpha.

Moki kept his distance, which suited Kodiak. Still, it also made him warier. It almost would have been better if Moki had challenged Kodiak openly at the ceremony There were rules with that, and they would've gotten it over with. It seemed like Moki wanted a fight, so it would probably happen at some point.

With him it would be wrong, not so with the others. But it troubled him. Much as the distraction of Tamaska's protest troubled Kodiak, even in wolf form. Her boiling anger and sheer frustration lingered in his mind.

Even from a distance, he sensed her anger. It was as if their bond had gone on steroids after the ceremony and his transformation into wolf form. He had no idea why the bond would be even stronger after that. Tamaska was angrier with him than ever, which should have damaged their bond. Such destructive emotions had the potential to tear apart even the strongest bonds, one thread at a time.

Though now she'd settled, the anger and hurt still lingered beneath the surface.

A young female nuzzled Kodiak, which pushed him out of his head and back to reality. Even though he stood in wolf form, he'd retained a strong connection to his human form. He could only do that because of the pure shifter blood that ran through his veins, through the entire pack.

He planned to break that bloodline by turning Tamaska and bringing her into the pack. More than that, he soon planned to announce her as his mate. But first, he needed to explain what that would mean for her.

The female wolf rubbed her head under his neck. Her intentions were clear—she wanted to mate. Her pheromones hit his nose, a delightful temptation.

He could have mated with her. His wolf form wanted to.

But he didn't. He remained loyal to Tamaska and their promising bond.

Not getting the hint, the female tried again to bury her face in the thick fur of Kodiak's neck. He pushed her away, gently rejecting her, but she came back yet again. She clearly intended to try and to change his mind.

With a gentle swipe to her head and a warning growl, Kodiak expressed his annoyance and sent her away. The longer he remained in wolf form among his packmates, the more advances he'd receive. But he couldn't go back to

Tamaska just yet. He needed to be with his pack, and she needed to cool down deep inside before he could return to her.

It wasn't official, but he already had a mate. He didn't want it public knowledge—not until she was a full wolf. How he wished for that to happen. But he would have to wait. The irony of the situation wasn't lost on him, considering he always told Tamaska to wait patiently for the change.

Needing to run off his mounting sexual frustration, he gave his wolf the freedom it craved and started the run up Mount Solitary.

The climb was easy for him, but exhilarating, especially when he reached the top. For some reason, he could sense Tamaska there with him. His fur stood on end.

For a moment unease trickled through him, like feeling her was a cry for help. But he put it down to his thinking about her, their insanely strong bond.

He stood on the mountain's edge, turned his nose to the sky, and howled a deep song, one that had been passed down from generation to generation. The unifying song had been designed to bind the pack together. His packmates began to join his song, with some following him up the mountain and others remaining where they were. Multiple voices added to the power of their song.

The sky began to lighten as the sun's rays edged over the horizon, announcing its impending presence. It was nearing time for the night's celebration and freedom to end.

Kodiak turned and hurried back to the hut. It was still his for the remainder of the night, and that's where he wanted to be. There with Tamaska.

Will she forgive me for locking her in the hut?

He hoped so.

He figured she'd most likely hold a grudge against him for a few hours. He didn't blame her. What he'd done to her wasn't kind. But it was necessary for her own safety, to protect her from herself more than from the wolves or anything else out there.

He trusted the upgraded security to set off alarms if vampires entered the vicinity. The wolves would respond to an alarm, even if they were hunting or mating. So far, there had been no incidents. And he didn't smell vampires.

But that didn't matter. Kodiak didn't want to leave her alone any longer. He missed her, needed her with a longing that floored him.

Hurrying down Mount Solitary, he moved as fast as he could, allowing his wolf to have its way. He practiced his agility, moving left and right to avoid bushes. His eyes remained sharp and hearing alert, his nose constantly scanning for scents.

Then, something heavy crashed onto his body, slamming him to the ground. He whimpered, more from the shock than the pain. His used a sudden rush of adrenaline to refocus. He breathed in.

Not vampires. His entire body poised to fight.

Wolf.

Kodiak got up. The wolf slammed him again from the side. He landed on his back, scrambling to keep the assailant from hurting him.

Teeth snapped at him, and he growled, pushing against the weight that pinned him down. Their scent announced the attacker's identity long before Kodiak could properly see.

Moki.

Strength thundered through Kodiak, and he pushed through his shock.

His wolf side begged to end the feud once and for all. Kodiak let go of his careful control, allowing his wolf the freedom to fight. It wouldn't be a fair or a good fight, but a fight to the death.

And Kodiak wasn't about to lose.

Moki's claws scraped across Kodiak's back, and he restrained a pained whimper as blood quickly matted the fur on his back.

He growled, baring his teeth and sizing Moki up before returning the attack.

Moki didn't waste any time as he rushed forward, snapping his jaws.

At the last minute, Kodiak sidestepped the attack to get his bearings. Adrenalin coursed through his body, dulling the pain of the wounds on his back. His mind sharpened with the excitement of the fight. Using his years of training, he sized Moki up in seconds.

He faked a stumble, then allowed the wolf to rush in. At the last moment, Kodiak swung. He swiped his claws across Moki's face, blinding him. The attacking wolf whimpered.

That's where Kodiak wanted to stop, but he couldn't. Moki would always come after him unless he put a stop to it. If the wolf couldn't join the pack in supporting Kodiak's leadership, then he would be a liability when they faced the vampires.

Kodiak leapt forward to sink his teeth into the side of Moki's neck. With a shake of his head, Moki's neck cracked. The snap sent a wave of sickness through Kodiak.

But it had to be done.

He held onto Moki, disgusted by the taste of blood in his mouth as the life seeped out of his attacker, his packmate. After laying the body on the ground, Kodiak lifted his head and let out a solemn howl.

Almost instantly, the others joined him. His human side retook control of his mind and communicated to the rest of the pack through their mental connection.

Moki had his chance to challenge my leadership legally. He chose to approach me as a coward and attacked me by surprise and he broke the solemn and binding laws. He doesn't deserve a burial. He doesn't deserve to be mourned. He will rot here, his bones a reminder to those who would challenge me.

He sensed his pack's shock. Normally, they would never deny mourning or a burial to one of their own, but the command would serve as a strong reminder to obey Kodiak.

This death could have been avoided. He made his choice, and this is his consequence to bear.

Ash padded up to Kodiak and nuzzled his neck. He sensed her concern over his wounds.

I'll heal.

The scratches were bad, but not bad enough to hold Kodiak back as they'd heal quickly. They would only pain him for a few hours and remind him of what he had to do.

Shadow Pack, you have a few more hours. Rest before we return to plan our attack against the vampires.

He howled, and the others joined in agreement.

Kodiak left them, pushing through his pain to rush back to the hut. To Tamaska.

On reaching the hut, he returned to human form, unlocked the door, and went inside.

He breathed a sigh of relief. She was there, asleep on the bed.

After closing the door quietly behind him, he locked it again to give him the privacy he needed while wounded. That privacy would also let him deal with Tamaska's wrath over being locked inside.

Kodiak's body ached as he moved. He wanted to reach out and stroke the side of her face, but he didn't want to wake her. She needed to rest, and he wasn't ready to face her anger.

Plus, he surely looked dreadful with blood on his skin and claw marks rapidly scabbing over as he healed.

He went to the shower to clean up. The warm water felt

soothing on his skin. His wounds stung, and the pain kept his mind sharp.

Is this what it was like for you, Olcan, when you began to lead the pack?

Kodiak slowly began to wash Moki's blood off his skin, removing physical evidence of the kill. But the deed remained in his heart.

How many more of his own would he have to fight to unite the pack? Couldn't there be a more peaceful way?

CHAPTER 15

amaska

The knowledge of my ancestors flows though me. In my new form, I know exactly what to do, where to run, and how.

My paws slam into the earth as I run, claws naturally extending into the soil for traction. My muscles adjust quickly, easily powering through the scrubland.

Plant in hues of gray fly past as I run, panting from the exertion. Air rushes through my pelt, tickling my fur, reminding me of what I am.

I am Wolf.

A terrified mouse scampers out of my way. A strength like no other pulses through me as I change direction to snap at the mouse. With its tail in my mouth, I fling my head to the side, tossing it through the air. I send it on its way, giving it another chance at life. I'm not interested in killing right now. That can come later.

My entire being buzzes with something like laughter. My unfamiliar anatomy is amazing, just as I knew it would be.

I turn to glance behind me. I can't see him, my mate. But I know he's chasing me. I know it's him. He wanted me to exist in this form. I am his right as the alpha.

I'm not about to make the pursuit easy for him, even though I want him to catch me. For now, I'm enjoying this form. I want to run, allow myself to savor my shift in eyesight, my amplified hearing, and my sharpened sense of smell.

At this rate, I could run all night. I sprint up the side of the mountain, amazed at the strength and power flowing through my body.

At the top, I'm greeted by the full moon. I lift my head and howl an ancient ode, a tune I know innately.

I hear him burst into the clearing and hurry to the edge of the mountain, where I stand waiting for him. Our noses touch, and my senses explode with his scent, taste, and touch all at once.

I nuzzle into his neck to cuddle, enjoying his fur against mine and his strong form. He pushes back gently. Then we lift our heads to the sky, the moonlight shining down on us, and sing our song together, the notes of our howls haunting the night with delightful harmony. I feel whole, like I've found the part of me I'd always been missing.

Tamaska stirred on the bed, arms still pumping as if she running. A sound had woken her, and she sat up sharply in bed.

What the hell was that? Had someone come in? But she knew. Somehow.

Kodiak.

The dream lingered in her mind, sending her serotonin levels soaring. All she needed now was for the dream to come true, to exist in wolf form for real.

Is that what she'd experienced while asleep? What her wolf form would be like? She wanted to snuggle back between the sheets and will the dream to return.

Her mind tilted toward slumber but, with her senses sharpened from the dream, she heard water running.

Tamaska rose, the pathway to her cherished dream fading.

The sound of the shower running made the hair on the back of her neck rise. Pleasure, fear, that tiny bite of anger still lingering, fueling her blood.

Tamaska wanted to call out, but her mouth dried.

She slipped from the bed and padded to the bathroom door. She tried to open it, but it was locked.

Damn Kodiak, anyway. She threw herself into the door, bursting the lock and the door banged open.

"What the fuck?" Kodiak poked his head out from behind the shower curtain. "*Tamaska?*"

"What, you think I'm not fucking strong enough to survive the change?"

"What?"

She swallowed hard, anger fueling her words. Her breath felt like dragon's fire. She glared at him, wanting...wanting something.

Wanting him.

"I did my own research," she said over the sound of running water.

"So?" Kodiak stepped away from the screen, water still streaming down the sculpted muscles of his chest.

Tamaska's breath caught in her throat. *How can I be so angry and so horny at the same time?*

"I'm strong enough to change into wolf form whether it's a full moon or not."

"Okay..." He frowned.

"What were you thinking, locking me up here while you go out fucking in your wolf form?"

He stared at her, mouth agape. "I did not."

"You did lock the fucking door."

145

"I did that, but what the fuck was the rest of that? You think I was fucking someone? Someone who wasn't you? What's wrong with you? Of course I didn't do that. I locked you in to keep you safe while I went off with the pack."

"*Mating* with the pack." Tamaska put her hands on her hips. "Why else would you leave me?"

"That's not true. And I left because I had to. As Alpha, I needed to run and celebrate with them. It's complicated."

"It's not complicated! You took off and locked me up like…like…a toy! One you didn't want." She blinked hard, hot tears pressing at her eyes.

"Tamaska." He said her name softly, sending shivers down her spine, and the warmth and tenderness in his tone wrapped about her. "I promise you, I wasn't out there mating."

"No?"

He smiled. "I had to go hunting with my pack, but I chose not to mate."

"Chose." She glared. "Why should I believe you?"

"Wrong choice of word, but it was a choice. I didn't want to. Not with them." He lowered his voice. "Because I wanted you. I'm here right now and want you…*right now.*"

The breath left her lungs. Fuck it, she believed him.

Kodiak opened his arms. No words were needed. She wanted him too. Right now.

Tamaska rushed into his arms. Her clothes getting wet as he held her tight. This is all she'd wanted for days, but the last few days had felt like years. She just wanted time with him, to cuddle and…more.

She looked up to meet his eyes. Now, they had time for so much more. She shivered with anticipation.

He pressed his lips to hers, opening her mouth as passion sparked between them. Tongues intertwined to deepen the kiss, unfurling heat and wetness and pleasure and that deep, needing hunger he set off in her, and tension began to leave Tamaska's body.

Not wasting time, Kodiak tugged her T-shirt over her head and threw it aside. She tried to undo her jeans, needing to feel all of him.

"No. My job." His voice was a growl at her ear and it ricocheted through her.

She dropped her hand to his cock, circling it, tugging. "My job," she whispered." He shuddered. He was hard, erect, getting even harder.

He pressed against her as he squeezed her to his chest, crushing her breasts against him. Her nipples hardened as her desires inflamed, out of control.

He was the right fire, the right heat, and he fit her perfectly as her body throbbed with need and pleasure. He kissed a path to her throat, biting his way to her nipple and when he caught one and sucked, her lower abdomen contracted, tight and hard, flooding her with wetness and a deep excitement only he could elicit.

Her pussy throbbed, and she was aware of a space that needed to be filled.

He brushed her back with his hands, sending her senses spinning, spreading flutters of delight over her skin. He clutched her buttocks and pulled up hard, pulled her jeans against her clit as he stretched her pussy to elicit even more desire.

She groaned between kisses, enjoying the sensation of his body against hers and the way he touched her.

He slipped his hands below the waistband of her jeans to rove about her hips. He found her front and freed her button, then lowered her zipper. He brushed against her mound over her panties. Her hips naturally tilted forward, begging his fingers to move deeper, to enter her.

Oh Christ how she wanted this. It was a need that beat

like her heart in her. And she trembled, needing to be naked and have him buried in her.

"Hurry up," she said.

"Impatient," he muttered. "Good things are coming. Fuck I've needed this, needed you."

He pushed the denim down, and she wriggled, letting it fall to her ankles. Then she stepped out of the clothes, lips dancing with his as their hands explored each other's bodies.

He skated fingers up her back, under her ribs, and plucked at her other nipple, and stroked the heaviness of her breasts. Her nipples ached for more almost as much as her pussy.

She ground her hips into him, and his hard cock pushed against her abdomen. He broke their kiss to gently push her shoulder back, then let his hand slip down to cup her breast once more, digging fingers into her softness until she gasped. He teased her nipple again with nimble fingers, rolling it with just the right pressure somewhere between pleasure and pain. Moans escaped from her mouth as she felt herself losing control. She wanted him to thrust into her, take her manic, hard, and fast.

He chuckled. "Steady."

Holding her tight, he trailed kisses down her cheek and over her collarbone, leaving invisible tracks of heat that fueled the flame between them. She held on to his waist, tilting her torso back and pushing her breasts forward. He obediently moved down her chest.

He kissed her hard nipple. Then he took her whole breast in his mouth and moved away slowly, letting his teeth graze gently over her erect nipple, tight with pleasure. A yelp escaped her lips as pleasure shot through her.

He did the same to the other breast, and she ground her hips against him even harder as another wave of delight roared through her.

She leaned forward. Their lips met again with a frantic passion that longed for release. She wanted him inside of her, now. If he wasn't going to do that yet, she'd make her intentions clearer.

She needed him now. It was a savage thing, this need and they were rougher, wilder, more primal with each other and she loved it all. But she needed his cock, now.

Her hand slid over the damp skin of his hips. Gripping his already-hard cock again, she massaged her fingers up and down his shaft, slow and hard. He was more than ready to claim her.

His hands traced the hem of her panties before slipping under the material to clutch her buttocks. This time, when he pulled upwards her wet pussy trembled in a spasmiing, light orgasm. He pushed the material away, sending it sliding down her legs so she could kick them off.

She lifted a leg over his hip, but he quickly pushed it down.

"What?" She moved to protest, to give him another heated lecture. But when his hand moved over her mound and his fingers cut through her moisture, all she could do was groan with pleasure and rock her hips to heighten the sensation. She stayed balanced, her hands on his hips as he made her even wetter.

Then he kneeled to press his mouth into her pussy. Her hands moved to his head to keep her balance. She draped her leg over his shoulder, giving him the access he needed to bring her to full orgasm.

Her noises increased uncontrollably as his mouth moved through her moisture. His tongue circled the top of her slit, playing and teasing her clit until the tension there burst, her muscles contracting wildly as she reached her peak.

She gasped as the last of the orgasm moved through her, and then he stood back up.

"I'm not finished with you yet."

"I should hope not." Her breaths still came quick and shallow.

He chuckled and pulled her into the shower. With water streaming over them, they embraced, kissing. Straight away, her body responded to his touch, her need to feel him inside of her stronger despite the release.

He turned her away from him and pushed her up against the cold tiles to nibble at the base of her neck.

"You ready for more?"

"Yes, fuck yes."

He guided her hips backward while she pressed her hands against the cold tiles and obeyed. His body shook against hers. He explored her belly with one hand, then moved lower before dipping three fingers into her slit and sliding them along her length. He stroked her folds until her muscles ached for him to enter.

He tilted her hips back and angled his cock between her legs, hot and hard and poised at her entrance. She held her breath while he made her wait. Then he thrust into her and she screamed with delight, her muscles contracting tight around his shaft. She never wanted him to move.

No, she did. She wanted him to move in her. Hard and savage and deep.

With one hand on her breast, he worked her nipple. Her breath quickened while her muscles pulsed over him. His other hand circled the tight bundle of nerves above her slit, and tension built quickly within her.

She groaned deeply as he pulled out, then slowly reentered her, matching the rhythm with his hands. He had all of her pleasure points covered. She pushed hard into the tiles, keeping her hips steady so he could rock in and out of her at just the right angle to give her the most pleasure. His cock enlarged inside of her. Her muscles, sensitive to the change, contracted harder, desperate for another release.

With a few more strokes, she tipped over the edge, a third orgasm bursting through her, over and over in waves as she gasped and groaned. He quickened his pace, letting go of her breast to hold her hips as he thrust hard into her until his release came. He shuddered into her.

Out of breath, he leaned over her tenderly, hands over hers on the tiles. His cock pulsed the last of his come inside her, and her muscles tightened. He nuzzled her neck, kissing her gently.

"I've been waiting so long to do this to you. I couldn't hold back anymore," he said.

"Me too," was all she could manage, her breath finally beginning to slow and deepen.

"If only we had longer."

"I know," she answered wistfully. "Though coming twice isn't anything to complain about."

"Only twice?" He nibbled her earlobe playfully.

"Only twice that mattered."

"More next time, then."

"I won't say no to that."

He moved away from her and picked up the shower gel before squirting the fresh, minty liquid into his hands. He began to wash her back, covering her skin with soap bubbles, then migrating to her breasts before moving down her body.

"There might be a third time if you keep that up," she said as his soapy fingers moved over her mound.

He pulled her into him, her back against his chest. "Sounds like a challenge."

Tamaska laughed, wrapping her arms behind his head. "What can I say? You bring out the best in me."

"Then I'd better bring it out."

She sighed as his fingers moved between her folds. Moisture pooled quickly, her body ready and willing. Her breath quickened, and her hips moved to his rhythm. He wound her up until the tension was so tight, she spiraled out of control, her body shuddering with pleasure.

"Three." He smirked when she turned to face him.

Tamaska kissed him gently, sucking on his lower lip. Their lips moved together, begging to stay like that for a moment longer.

Eventually, Kodiak pulled away. "I reckon we're going to run out of water soon."

He turned off the shower, leaned out, and grabbed a towel for her. She took it, drying herself quickly as he found another towel.

Wrapped in dry cloth, they left the bathroom to lay on the bed.

"How long do we have?" she asked, snuggling into Kodiak. She needed to ask so many questions, and she needed to tell him about her research. But here in his arms, she didn't care about those details. All she wanted was to have Kodiak to herself, with no other worries.

"A few hours, maybe less."

Her heart sank a little.

"Hey, at least we put our time to good use." He pulled her into him tightly.

"We did," she answered.

Tamaska felt Kodiak fall asleep and wished she could join him. She was more awake after her nap and the lovemaking. She didn't want to sleep. Even more, she'd dreamt of being a wolf. Memories of that dream urged her to ask Kodiak to turn her now.

But she knew he never would. And that hurt.

CHAPTER 16

 amaska

SHE DIDN'T WANT to move.

Every part of her ached with a delicious rightness. When she stretched it was like a goddess must feel, or a queen. Or, perhaps mate to the alpha.

She sighed, sliding up against the heat and strength of him.

Who knew when she'd get time like this with Kodiak again? This moment was about enjoying the simple pleasures, to be together, in bed, in each other's arms. Kodiak slept, but she couldn't, even though hours had passed. And sleep was the last thing she wanted, anyway.

Her thoughts kept returning to what she had learned, trying to come up with alternative theories. Did the vampires truly want to change her into a weapon of chaos? Nothing else came to mind. She stretched again, his scent surrounding her. Then again how the hell could she think? Her mind was full of serotonin and Kodiak.

Kodiak stirred and kissed her. "You didn't sleep?"

It amazed her, the depth of detail he could sense about her.

"No."

His hand trailed from her breast to her belly. "We've got a big day ahead."

"I know." She paused. "Kodiak, I was thinking… Any ideas on how to make the vampires pay?"

"Damn I need to get up, as much as I want to say here with you." He nuzzled her throat and she arched for him, offering that tender, vulnerable place and he growled softly. "And you, wicked Tamaska, keep making it difficult. Almost like you're disobeying me."

"In you leaving this bed? Fuck yes I am." She held on to him to stop him from getting out of bed. *Just a little longer.*

He groaned. "Would if I could."

She let him go, but he didn't move and a spark of heat raced through her blood.

"Any thoughts or ideas, Kodiak?"

"A few, but we need to call a pack meeting." He held her tight, then groaned with frustration as he pulled away from her and quickly got out of bed.

He dressed, and she indulged herself, studying how his muscles contracted and relaxed as he moved. She couldn't believe how much better she felt after having sex with him.

Bliss vibrating through her body, she lay, still curled in last night's towel. The last thing she wanted was to get up and to return to reality, where the leader of the vampires was hunting her. A reality where the Blood Opal was a dangerous gem, a danger specific to her because of the destruction she could unleash with it.

She took a breath. "I told you how I did research, right?"

"Ash'll know."

He wasn't paying her attention and frustration welled up in her. "Kodiak. I seem to be linked to the blood opal and that's dangerous. I don't want to be a catalyst for terrible destruction if they get hold of me and I'm still mostly human."

"Okay." He picked up a T-shirt, inspected it, tossed it on the bed, and then grabbed a pair of jeans.

His mind was in a thousand other places and he barely listened to her, but she pushed forward. "Kodiak, it's dangerous for me to remain human." She paused. It was true. Not only was it dangerous, but it made her dangerous, unless she could convince him to turn her now. So she went for it.

"I think you should turn me now."

He pulled on his jeans and buttoned them around his waist. "No, it's too risky."

That he paid attention to.

"Because I'll be weak afterward?"

He raised an eyebrow as he reached for his T-shirt. "Who have you been talking to? Roan?"

"No." She forced herself to breathe. I told you I looked stuff up."

"Oh yeah, on Ash's computer. A little knowledge is dangerous."

She looked at him in frustration. If there was ever a right moment to tell him everything, it was now, but she couldn't bring herself to do it.

Christ, she'd tried and he barely listened. He needed to focus on her and the only way she could think of getting that attention was starting a fight. The last thing she wanted.

And she didn't want to ruin their moment or do anything to change their feelings for each other.

This was the happiest she'd been in days, since the attack on the clubhouse. How much damage could it do to enjoy a few more moments of contentment before telling him every-thing? And what would it even do? According to that stuff she'd read, she'd be weak, and maybe she'd be even more dangerous if they strengthened her shifter side?

Shit, she didn't know. What she needed was to dig deeper and she'd do that, definitely.

Kodiak turned his back to her as he pulled on a shirt. And she saw the marks on his back.

Claw marks.

They were healing fast, which was good, but they looked uncomfortable. An unease started to creep into her blood.

"What happened?"

"When?" He turned to her. "Oh, the marks? You should get dressed."

For a terrible moment her imagination indulged in the idea of him with a she-wolf, but as she looked at him, she knew.

He wouldn't.

And trust, it went both ways.

She got up from the bed, the sheet gliding across her skin, still salty from the sweat of sex.

He stared at her naked body as she walked up to him and put her hands on his back, near the marks.

He pressed his forehead to hers and sighed. "It was inevitable."

"What was?"

"A fight with Moki."

"Did you…" She remembered what had happened to Shota. Even though he'd been a dick, it sickened her that he'd been attacked by his own kind.

"Yes."

She embraced Kodiak, and his lips found hers in a slow, drawn-out kiss that gently rekindled her desire.

Kodiak broke away. "We need to get back to the club-house. We've got to plan an attack on the vampires."

Tamaska exhaled, releasing some of the tension that had started rebuild within her. She was worried for him, more than she thought possible considering that it was only days ago when the idea of Kodiak becoming a wolf scared her senseless.

I need to tell him everything I found, all my theories. I have to make him listen.

But how? Especially when he had so much to deal with and what he learned might not get them anywhere except wasting time.

A knock on the door sent her scurrying for yesterday's borrowed clothes, and she quickly put them on.

"We're going soon, get ready," Kodiak called.

"I just need my computer," Ash said from the other side of the door.

Tamaska's hands shook as she picked up the laptop from the floor, where it had fallen during their lovemaking.

Kodiak took it from her, eyeing her, and then passed it through the crack in the door. Tamaska retreated a few steps, so Ash wouldn't see her face..

The other two talks and she busied herself, dressing, and then she made the bed. The smell of their sex lay heavy in the air, delighting her senses and fueling her afterglow.

Kodiak closed the door and turned back to her. His shoulders slumped forward slightly, and a sorrowful shadow etched into his face. "Don't snoop anymore. Once we'll get past, again? We all share but some things are just our alone. Like you for me.

"Like your car."

He shook his head, but the sadness stayed, even as he smiled.

She pursed her lips, stopping herself from asking if everything was all right. After everything that had happened, Tamaska had noticed his change over the last few days. Compared to the first time she'd met him, so much pressure lived in his eyes. The same would happen to anyone who became a new pack leader under such horrific circumstances.

She wanted to ease it, not add to it. She wanted to take it on herself, show him they could share it. But she didn't know how to say it, and she didn't know if those words would help or hurt.

The shifters did things at times so different and to her taking on some of his burden would be a gift for him, but in his eyes it could mean disobedience or worse. What if he took it that she didn't believe in him?

Kodiak went to her, took her hands in his and squeezed. He leaned forward and kissed her. "I'm counting on your help, you know."

His words meant the world to her. "I'm trying." And guilt that came with doubt about whether she was doing the right thing or not in keeping what she'd found to herself after her attempt to share went array a at her.

She wanted to help, not make things worse.

Tamaska didn't know which way she was falling.

"The others are sleeping outside in swags, but they'll be ready soon. We won't have time together again for…I don't know how long," said Kodiak.

"I'm just glad we had this much."

She pasted on a smile. Right now it didn't matter. Did it? He said Ash would know she'd been on her computer and though Tamaska wasn't looking forward that altercation, she hoped it would lead her down the path she was thinking.

Maybe then he'd listen to another shifter, one he trusted. Or…she'd have to make him.

Guilt aside, there wasn't anything she could do. Was there?

"Let's go figure out how to kill some vampires," said Kodiak, taking her the hands.

Excitement rushed down her spine. "Absolutely."

The hut door flung open, slamming into the chair before swinging back. Tamaska jumped, yelping. Kodiak stepped in front of her, the stance so protective she'd have melted had this been any other circumstances.

Ash stood in the doorway, fire in her eyes, anger radiating from her.

"She fucking used my laptop," said Ash, pointing at Tamaska.

"Isn't your laptop password-protected?" asked Kodiak, positioning himself more deliberately between the women.

"Yes, but…" Ash sighed heavily, but her anger didn't dissipate. "She used my laptop. No one uses my laptop."

"I'm sure this is a misunderstanding," said Kodiak, his voice calm and neutral.

"Don't go protecting her because you're fucking her. She has to follow the pack rules like everyone else. And don't go trying to say she doesn't know all the rules, Kodiak. It's common sense not to use my laptop," growled Ash.

"I'm sorry," Tamaska said, twisting her hands, trying to hold back her annoyace. Fine, she knew it was wrong, but she'd needed to do something and they were all more about their positions and doing things right in the pack then actually doing things for the greater good. "The password wasn't set, and I—"

"Wanted to snoop?" Venom dripped from Ash's voice and it took a lot for Tamaska not to step back.

"No." She tried to step around Kodiak. "I was left behind while you all cavorted and I decided to put my time to good use."

"By snooping?"

"No! I told you. Does anyone fucking listen here? Or are you all too self-involved? I—"

"Hey," said Kodiak sharply. "We've had enough infighting, I don't want any more."

"Then tell her not to use my laptop again," said Ash.

Something in Tamaska snapped. "Listen to me, damn you. All of you, that goes for you, too, Kodiak. I get it. You're all upset and stressed and I'm not anywhere near the favorite, but I can help out. I found things about my family, me. About the opal."

"You're a computer expert now? Bringing your great human expertise to the zoo?" Ash glared. "Don't—"

"Enough," said Kodiak.

But she wasn't listening.

"I learned more in an hour than you've managed in days," Tamaska said with a snap. "And you all need to listen."

Fine, maybe she could choose her words better. Maybe she shouldn't have used Ash's laptop without asking, but she hadn't opened emails or looked beyond the areas she needed. It technically wasn't snooping.

There had been a tool and she used it. And learning how to defeat the vampires was more important than Ash's privacy or the pecking order of the shifters. She might not be a wolf yet, but she would still demand her place in the pack.

"Like fucking hell, you did."

A piercing alarm sounded from the hut. Kodiak scrambled to his phone.

"What's that?" asked Tamaska, not wanting to know the answer. Whatever the alarm meant, it wouldn't be good. She wrapped her arms protectively around her body as sudden fear overtook the anger.

"Fuck," said Kodiak, looking at his phone.

Channing rushed in wearing only jeans, terror on his face. "Vampires! Has to be."

"I know," Kodiak said.

"But it's daylight." Channing whipped about, like he didn't know were to look or what to do,

"Thanks, Captain Obvious," said Ash sarcastically.

"Don't lash out at Channing because you're still sour with me," Tamaska said.

"Enough! Girls, you have to let it go, or both of you will end up dead," said Kodiak. "We need to get the fuck out of here."

Tamaska didn't like the edge of panic in Kodiak's voice. Was nowhere safe from the vampires? She still needed to get them to hear what she'd learned—but there wasn't any time with an impending attack.

"Ash, take Tamaska and Channing back to the clubhouse." Kodiak threw her the keys to his car.

Sickness twisted her stomach. Oh God, she needed to do something, anything to help. Running off couldn't be the answer and all she could see, then and there, was the burden she was to him and the pack.

They wouldn't be in danger if it wasn't for her.

Selfish, that's what she was. Completely selfish. She sucked in a breath to try and box in the panic. She might be selfish, but it didn't mean she was wrong. And she couldn't turn time back. This was reality and like it or not, they were all in it.

And she might know something that could help. "I—"

"Tamaska. Please." His gaze caught hers and she shut her mouth.

No one was sitting down for a chat or debate. And insisting would just increase the danger.

"Where are you going?" asked Tamaska, calming her voice as she absorbed some of the stress reverberating around the room. "And what do you need me to do. I might not be strong, but I can help. If you tell me what to do."

"I need to make sure my pack is safe. Just make sure the vamps don't get anywhere near you," answered Kodiak. "So hide or run if necessary and fight with everything you have if you can't. I'll come for you. We all will. But go with Ash and Chandler now."

She stared at the man she loved, working out what he was saying and her heart slammed madly against her ribs. "Kodiak, what are you saying? You have to come with us." No way was she leaving him to those freaks. She couldn't.

"We need a distraction," he answered. "And you get to get the fuck away."

"I can do that for you," said Channing. "You go."

"No way, this is my responsibility," said Kodiak. "I'm Alpha. You all obey me now. Or I'll—"

"You can't go rogue like this," said Ash. "We're a pack. We do this together."

"If I do this alone, there's more chance of us staying a pack. We can't risk losing any more wolves."

"I'll help," Tamaska said.

"No, you won't. Take her the fuck out of here, Ash, *now*."

Ash grabbed her by the arm, the grip bruising her skin.

"No," Tamaska said, but she wasn't strong enough to stop Ash from pulling her outside.

"He'll be fine. You'll see him back at the clubhouse before nightfall," Ash, said but her words weren't reassuring.

"I better fucking see you later, Kodiak," she yelled as Ash dragged her towards Kodiak's parked car.

Pack members in various stages of scrambling out of their swags and dressing exchanged looks of confusion as Kodiak hurried out of the hut.

"The vampires are coming! We need to leave!" Kodiak said. "The morning light should be enough to keep the vampires away, but apparently it doesn't. Not any longer. Daytime no longer offers protection from the enemy. So you must always be on alert. Now go."

Voices rose as panic spread like wildfire.

"Everyone, back to the clubhouse now! Onai, you're in charge until I get there," called Kodiak for all to hear. Then he transformed and ran into the scrubland. His wolf form racing out of sight.

Heart hurting and fear threatening to drown her, Tamaska got into the car, even though she wanted to stay and help Kodiak.

She couldn't shake the thought pounding through her head—what if she never saw him again?

CHAPTER 17

odiak

HE SMELLED THE VAMPIRES. That vile scent that burned its way in to all parts of him. They were closer than he'd like. He moved through the scrub, quietly but quickly. He hoped to ambush them, fight them long enough for the pack to escape, then get the fuck out.

It was a bad plan.

Possibly suicidal.

But it was all he had.

He just hoped it would work.

He would not ask any of his pack to stay behind and help him. That's why he hadn't told them what he planned to do.

His ears pricked as the pack's cars rumbled to life and began to leave. He hoped Tamaska was safely inside the car with Ash, getting far away from the vamps.

He wanted his whole pack to leave, to avoid more deaths. But it was most important for Tamaska to leave. He didn't know exactly what the vampires wanted her for, but whatever their purpose, it would certainly cause problems for everyone. It was his duty as a wolf shifter to prevent that outcome.

And his duty as the man who loved her.

But right now he needed to focus on the duty as pack leader, as a shifter.

It kept things clean, and he could think.

So, once he sorted this—and he would, he had to—he'd head back to the clubhouse and plan an attack on the vampires that they would never forget.

Slowing, he sniffed the air. The vampires lay ahead.

Moving to their left for a side attack, he stayed alert.

The vampires weren't doing much. Kodiak crept closer, paws instinctually padding across the earth without making a sound. That's what he did best—stalk his prey. He hoped his scent was more wolf than shifter, but he couldn't do much about it. Instead, he readied himself, for anything.

He spied the enemy, his greyscale vision sharp and accurate.

Three vampires.

They stood away from each other, looking pale and sickly. Stinking of rancid blood, they moved forward.

Kodiak watched, unable to believe his eyes as the vampires moved into the sunlight. They weren't entirely unaffected. He could see them wincing. The sun still caused them pain, but they could endure it.

His stomach knotted. They really could survive in the light. It was an abomination. What new horrors would they unleash on him with their new power? He shuddered to think.

Kodiak would have to find out later. The trio of vampires moved faster, and the pack's cars were still leaving.

He just hoped there weren't any other vampires lurking where he couldn't sense them.

On his way over, he hadn't detected anything that would suggest more vampires. The problem with their security system was that vampires couldn't be detected on cameras. Their motion could only be detected if the vampires disturbed their surroundings, leaving behind unnatural movement in bushes and branches.

Ordinarily he'd put more value on his sense of smell, but who knew what they had up their sleeves, or how these changes could affect that.

Despite the evidence from his own senses, Kodiak still didn't trust the vampires. Their attacks on the wolves were painstakingly organized, which unnerved Kodiak. They were more organized than ever before. Amdis was too skilled a leader. Kodiak vowed that, when the chance came, he would take out the vampires' leader once and for all.

Yeah, he didn't trust the vampires. He did trust that, no matter the vampires' number, his pack would be able to fight back and win. Kodiak just needed to do the same.

I better fucking see you later Kodiak. Tamaska's last words urged him on as he watched the vampires progress closer to the hut.

He wanted to rip them apart for getting so close to the wolves' inner sanctuary.

As they moved, Kodiak noticed the vampires favored shadows over light.

Attacking the pack as they departed would force the vampires to endure more sunlight. For now, their aversion might still keep his pack safe.

Kodiak considered waiting to attack until the vampires reached the hut, with more sunlight to assist him in the fight.

Then, they slowed, their behavior changing.

He tensed.

They'd detected him.

Still banking on the element of surprise, Kodiak leapt from his position. He slammed his paws into the nearest vampire, pushing him to the ground in one swift movement. He snapped his jaws, sinking his teeth into its putrid flesh.

The screams of the vampire turned muffled as Kodiak gripped its neck with his teeth. Stale blood filled his mouth, and he gagged. He shook his head, breaking its neck before releasing the body and bracing himself to fight the other two.

They weren't there.

Where are they?

He turned around, using all his senses to detect them on his right. He rushed them, unwilling to let the fight drag on. He wanted the vampires destroyed like they'd tried to destroy his pack.

He leapt toward the nearest vampire, growling deep, expecting to connect with the monster.

Then, something hit him.

The projectile was lightweight, but enough to disrupt his trajectory. Kodiak fell to the ground, barely managing to land on his feet inches away from the vampire.

Angry at his mistake, he crouched to leap again. Searing pain exploded through his body.

He howled, trying to push against the sharp tangle around him that restricted his movement. He couldn't fight in this, not fully.

Fuck, what is this?

It wrapped around his sides. The thing wasn't heavy, but it sent pain searing through his muscles, preventing them from working correctly.

He could not take on even one vampire with this around him, let alone three.

He snarled a warning, trying to pretend that he was unaffected.

The vampire he'd planned to attack smirked, standing just out of Kodiak's range. He made no move to fight back.

Why won't he fight?

Kodiak pushed through his confusion and increasing agony. Maybe another vampire was about to attack?

Swinging around, Kodiak tried to ready himself to repel an attack from behind. But he soon stumbled, his muscles betraying him as sudden weakness pulsed through them.

No more vampires appeared behind him. He sniffed the air, trying to find out where the last one had gone. It had moved, now standing next to the vampire he'd leapt toward but barely scratched.

Why are they so confident?

Then he realized with horror what was trapping him. His weakness—a silver net. Yet, the pain was nothing like he'd ever experienced before.

"Amdis was right," said one.

"You doubted, Lazi?" the vampire Kodiak had attacked asked.

"Of course not, Damon. I've just never seen how powerfully the silver binds the wolf shifters. We've haven't fought them in years now, remember?"

"Don't get cocky, Lazi," Damon said.

"I'm not."

"Let's get him into the car and wait this out. This sunlight's going to give me more than a tan."

Lazi snorted. "If you stay out here much longer, you'll to turn to dust and float away. You need Mediterranean heritage, like me."

"Does that protect you from a stake through the heart?" Damon asked

Kodiak whimpered, the pain increasing as he tried to focus on their conversation.

"You've gotta help." The one called Lazi sneered down at

him and kicked him in the ribs. He tried to bite but even that hurt. "The thing looks like he weighs a tonne."

Damon rolled his eyes. "Garrick, get out here and stop being a scaredy-cat. Help us get this wolf into the car before we all blow away like dust in the wind."

"I'm not scared. I thought I heard something in the bushes," Garrick said as he stomped through the bushes to join the others.

He whimpered again, hoping Tamaska was long gone. What a fucking fool he was.

"Well, did you find it?" asked Damon. "The thing in the bushes?"

"It must have been a mouse or something," Garrick said, brushing leaves off his shoulders.

The others snickered as Kodiak lay still as he could. The pain was almost bearable if he didn't move. Did the vampires know who they had caught, or did they think he was another pack member?

"Come on. We all need to lift if we're gonna move him," Damon said.

Kodiak needed to keep his wits about him, try to gather strength and find a way to escape. That was getting harder, though. The silver shot a constant, burning pain into his muscles radiated out to every part of his body. And movement made it so much worse.

"I'm not touching a fucking wolf," Garrick said.

"He's got the silver net on him, he can't hurt you," said Damon. "But I told Amdis you weren't up for the job. And, well, what do you know? You're not."

The longer Kodiak stayed in contact with the silver, the worse he'd get, meaning his people were vulnerable. He couldn't let that happen.

"Not true," said Garrick, stepping closer to the wolf.

"Prove it, then," Lazi said.

Garrick hissed.

Kodiak growled low, and tensed his aching muscles. The silver still worked its painful magic on him but he thought of his shifters, of Tamaska and gathered his will, trying to find the power to break free. Maybe if he could catch the net on something he could get loose. A fight between the three vampires could be his only chance at survival.

"Well, are you going to grab a leg each or something?" Garrick said, standing beside Kodiak's back legs.

"Sure. Then we get him in the car and wait," said Damon.

Wait for what? The night? Until he died? For Amdis and back up? No, he needed an out, and now, no matter the pain.

He tried to move but the fire of the sliver sunk its electric fangs into every part of him. Fuck.

"That's a cramped space for a long wait." Garrick bent down, ready to grab Kodiak's back leg.

"Got a better idea?" Damon asked.

Garrick shook his head. "No."

"Didn't think so."

The vampire's cold hand clamped around one of his back legs, repulsing him to the core. But the ice of the touch somehow soothed the burn from the silver and he seized that reprieve. He thrashed about, and the silver netting slipped off to one side.

"Fuck," Garrick said, jumping back and losing his grip on Kodiak.

"Get the fucking netting," yelled Damon.

Kodiak didn't waste the opportunity. Pain or no pain, this was his chance. He bucked and thrashed, throwing more of the net off him and it gave him some energy.

He swung toward Garrick and clamped his jaws around the vampire's arm.

"Ow! Fuck, get off!" screamed Garrick.

Kodiak sunk his teeth deeper into Garrick's arm, ignoring

the searing pain from the silver still touching him. He shook his head and heard the snapping of bone.

"Fuck!" Garrick howled and struggled, helping Kodiak's teeth cause more damage as they tore through his muscles.

Kodiak let go and threw off the remainder of the silver net. Garrick cradled his arm. Stumbling to get out of the Kodiak's way, he fell to the ground.

Kodiak fixed his eyes on his target and pounced. His jaw wrapped around the vampire's neck. Maybe he couldn't kill all three, or even escape. But it would brighten his day if he could kill even one.

"Get him!" yelled Lazi.

"Grab the net, get it back on him, quick!" screamed Damon.

Kodiak finished the vampire, ripping its throat, before turning to take on the approaching pair. Still weak from the silver and the exertion of escaping, he struggled to stand. But he wasn't about to flee. He had to buy the pack as much time as possible to get away.

"Go around that way," instructed Damon, pointing one way while moving in the opposite direction.

They split up, making it harder for Kodiak to defend himself. But he had a plan. All he needed to do was to endure, to push himself to the limit, and he might just defeat them both.

He ran forward, hoping to confuse them into thinking he wanted to flee. He planned to double back and take them from behind if his body held up. He struggled with every movement, the silver's damage still moving through him, making him weak and sluggish—for him.

But suddenly he yowled and whimpered as every nerve went haywire and a horrendous weight pressed down on him. His footing faltered and collapsed to the ground. The silver net stretched across him, and he'd been captured again.

"Fuck, that was lucky," Lazi said as he rushed up to Kodiak.

"This time, lift him so the silver doesn't fall off," Damon said.

"How? We need to put a muzzle on him," Lazi muttered. "Wrap him up tight."

Damon kicked him "A silver muzzle?"

"Hang on, I've got an idea."

The vampire lifted a thick branch, ready to strike. Kodiak braced himself, too weak to fight back or even move. The silver claimed and bound him.

He'd been captured, well and truly.

Kodiak had failed himself and his pack. His capture could mark the end of Shadow Pack, and he hated to think of what the vampires would do after his wolves were gone.

One thump to the head sent him spiraling into blackness.

CHAPTER 18

 amaska

ASH'S LEAD foot on the gas made good time as they returned to Sydney. The farther she rode from the hut, the more she ached for Kodiak and feared she'd never see him again.

Something was wrong.

She sensed it in her heart, her gut, in every fiber of her being.

"We shouldn't have left him there alone," she said as she shifted in the backseat of Kodiak's car, wishing he was there with her.

"You really struggle with the whole, "Do whatever the alpha says" thing, don't you?" said Ash, looking at her through the rearview mirror.

Tamaska pressed her lips tightly together, biting back a retort. Surely, the pack didn't blindly follow everything the alpha said. That didn't make sense to her, but she didn't want to discuss the technicalities of obedience right now, anyway.

Then again, it really seemed they did. So much of their lifestyle was difficult to wrap her head around and it didn't help she had a pushy nature she tried to quell. She was in their world now, not the other way around.

Ash…she knew the problem and couldn't let it go. Not the fact she'd taken the shifter's computer but no one listened to her. And now…well, now they were in the car on the long drive and the worry for Kodiak at at her and she needed to do something.

Tamaska took a breath. "I'm sorry. I didn't look at anything other than the research on my family and the opal. I was only trying to help. I know It was wrong."

That was a little harder than it should have been, mainly because the tension in the car was pointed at her and apart from that faux pas, she hadn't fucked up—this time.

She'd sat and kept out of things, and okay, Kodiak locked her up, but then…

She blew out her breath.

"I'm sorry."

"I heard." Ash stopped talking. Then right when Channing started to twist about to look or speak to Tamaska she continued. "I'm not going to say it was fine; it wasn't—"

"We're territorial," Channing said.

Ash sighed. "But tensions are high, emotions. And I get it's hard, but you need to just do what you're told. Like we all do. It's how things are done. It might seem stupid to you, but you're not one of us."

Yet, she almost said. Tamaska swallowed it down. For now.

"We all have a tough time with the order and rules here and there, but they exist for a reason."

"What are the rules?" she asked.

"Whatever Kodiak say they are now he is the big boss,"

Channing said, "so we do what he says, and we don't question. He protects, and we—"

"Kodiak's as bad as Tamaska at times." Ash said.

It struck Tamaska right then that Ash wasn't furious, she was scared. Maybe the rules helped. But then again, so did being proactive.

"You're both hotheaded and don't listen."

"Ash!"

Channing sounded scandalized and Tamaska almost smiled.

"He's a good leader, and he's got it in him to be great. I'd follow him anywhere, and I'd punch him, too. But I don't. Pick your fights. This isn't one of them. And you know it, Tamaska."

She rested one foot against the seat, bending a knee to rest her head on. She looked out the window as the rural landscape slowly changed to cityscape. Yeah, she was meant to toe the line, obey and sit back like a good girl, even though she hated it. And his rules...the pack rules...they seemed to be something they all just knew. But it didn't make it easier. It didn't make her worry any less.

"But what if he needs our help?" she asked. "I'm not trying to fight or disobey, but...it doesn't feel right to leave Kodiak, even at his own insistence. Does it to you? Ash? Channing? Roan?"

"He'll be fine, Tamaska," said Roan from the front seat. His face paled from the car's motion.

"Has he contacted you?" asked Tamaska. "Any of you? I know you all communicate through a pack dial up brain service."

Channing snickered.

But she meant it. During the whole ride, she'd studied Ash, Channing, and Roan for any telltale signs that they were using the pack's mental connection. Sitting there with them, Tamaska felt like the outsider she was. It made her sick to think he might be calling out, hurt, in pain or worse, and she couldn't hear him.

But they wouldn't hide that from her, would they?.

"No," said Roan.

"So, you don't know," she said softly, more to herself than to anyone else. "He could be hurt. We should go back."

"No!" Ash pushed down on the accelerator.

"He'll be back, don't you worry," said Channing from his seat beside her, reaching over and touching her shoulder. "You'll see."

Tamaska nodded. She didn't share his confidence. All the information in her head she'd learned bubbled up with nowhere to go. It wasn't about to help right now, just cause more fractures. The last thing they needed.

"He's a great fighter," said Roan, turning around to look at her.

"I just wish he hadn't gone off alone like that." She met his gaze. "I don't know what I'll do if I never see him again."

That was as close to an admission of love she'd give them.

Roan raised his eyebrow as if making a connection—then he shrugged. "I don't hear him, so he's not calling out to us."

"He sent us away, would he?" she asked, "even if he was in trouble? He's not the type to bring others into bad trouble."

No, he was the type to push them away to protect.

If he was here, she'd stangle him. And her eyes burned as she put her fist to her mouth to stop a moan of despair escaping.

"There's no reason to think he can't take on a few vampires." Channing's hand squeezed her arm. "He's not Alpha for nothing."

"I hope he's okay. I hope he's not being stupid and brave." Tamaska pressed her knees together and clasped her hands to comfort herself. She would have done anything to have he arms around her, to hear him reassure her that everything would be all right.

She couldn't explain it to the others, but Tamaska's terrible feeling tore through her faster, right to her gut. Her head pounded, and darkness crept over her vision.

"You should use this time to rest a little more," suggested Roan, his voice soft. "You're still injured, and the shadows under your eyes suggest you could use the sleep."

"She would've slept plenty if she hadn't been messing around with my laptop," Ash said. .

"Oh, you didn't do that, did you, Tamaska?" asked Channing, his voice light.

"Yes and as you heard, I said sorry."

"But are you?" he bumped his shoulder into her, clearly trying to stop her worrying.

"Yeah, she fucking did," Ash snapped. The car started to move faster.

"Slow down, Ash, or I'll throw up," Roan said, turning around to face forward.

"Tamaska, in case you haven't worked this out already, Ash is rather protective of her laptop," said Channing with a wink. He dropped his voice. "And she's worried."

"We all are," Ash said. "I just…I need… Apology accepted. For now."

"Eureka. You're making friends, influencing people," Channing said. Behind his cheer the worry crept through.

But that comment helped ease some of the tension surfacing within her, as did Ash's churlish acceptance of her apology. She smiled back at him a little, grateful for the moral support. Ash still acted like she was simmering over her laptop's lengthy, unauthorized use.

"But you should know, Tamaska, our pack has rules, and they must be followed," said Ash.

"Fuck, Ash, slow down…" Roan's voice went soft.

Ash groaned and rolled her eyes, taking her foot off the gas.

"Never thought you'd have a weak stomach, with all your medical experience," said Ash.

"Motion sickness is different." Roan lay his head back against the headrest.

"Kodiak's not following the rules, going off by himself. It seems to me that your rules only apply to a select few," said Tamaska, taking her leg off the seat in front of her.

"It's different for the alpha," said Ash. "And different for you, because you're not one of the pack."

"Come on, Ash, that's a bit harsh," said Channing. "She's as good as in. You know Kodiak's chosen her."

"Chosen me for what?" asked Tamaska. To change her? But that didn't make sense, that was already on the table. Or wasn't. Or…or maybe it meant he would do it sooner rather than later.

Though, knowing her luck, it probably meant he would sacrifice her.

She couldn't even raise a little humor at her lame personal joke.

"That's for Kodiak to tell you," Ash said. She maintained a steady speed while slipping easily into the parallel lane to overtake a few slower vehicles on the highway back to Sydney.

At least this time there wasn't the prickly belligerence in her tone. But still, she asked, "what is it?"

"This really is Kodiak's news to give," said Channing.

"You can't even give me a hint?" She latched on to this because it was better than worrying. Or, better than focusing in on that worry. "Please."

"I shouldn't have said anything, sorry," Channing said. "Don't worry, I'm sure he'll tell you as soon as he gets back to the clubhouse."

"Secrets, always secrets with you lot," said Tamaska half jokingly. And her gut twisted. It didn't help matter that she had her own secrets now. Even if that was only because no one listened to her when had tried to tell them.

"It's not that bad," said Channing. "Now, there's one less. Don't use Ash's laptop."

"Ash accepted the apology, Channing, so shut the fuck up," said Roan, clutching the door handle as Ash accelerated. "Ash, I'm going to throw up."

"Kodiak will kill you if you puke in his car," Tamaska muttered.

"See? She's learning quick." Channing patted her on the knee.

"Not quick enough. Since we are talking about my computer once more and guilt and blame aisde, you know that you fucked up all my searches?" said Ash.

"I didn't. I made them better," Tamaska said, suddenly sitting forward. "I promise."

"How?"

"You obviously didn't have time to look at them properly. Otherwise you'd know that I'm closer to this pack than you realize."

"What did you find out?" Ash asked tightly.

Tamaska swallowed hard. She had to tell them. Why was it so hard? She knew though. Kodiak wasn't here. She wanted him to hear it from her.

And maybe in regards to becoming a shifter it wasn't much. After all, she wasn't purebred like the rest of the pack. Even though she had shifter genes, she would still need to be turned.

But the rest of it…there was something there. But she needed to get it right in her head, she needed—

"Nothing. You found nothing, just as I expected," snapped Ash. "And fucked up all my searches while you were at it.

You'll have to wait even longer to be turned while I sort it all out."

"I have wolf shifter genes." The words tumbled from Tamaska's mouth before she could think them over.

"Like fucking hell, you do," said Ash.

"My ancestry traces back to the Browns."

"The Browns?" asked Channing with a whistle.

So, it was true. The surname did mean something.

"You said Lane. Not Brown. Lane. Why did...shit." Ash slowed a little.

"My grandparents bought the Blood Opal with them to Australia," continued Tamaska, "and then sold it because they needed the money."

"What?" exclaimed Ash. Her foot came off the gas pedal as she turned to look at Tamaska. "No way!"

"Look out!" yelled Roan as a car approached them from behind a little too quickly.

"Fuck." Ash swerved. The overtaking driver narrowly missed sideswiping Kodiak's mirror, laying on the horn as they passed.

"Yes, and I think the vampires want me in addition to the Blood Opal because it will amplify my wolf side."

"What would that achieve?" asked Channing. "Apart from a lot of dead vamps!"

"An out-of-control wolf," Ash whispered, worry spreading across her face.

Ash's words confirmed Tamaska fears. The vampires' attacks were a calculated effort to capture the Blood Opal and her.

The near-destruction of Shadow Pack was all her fault. Knowing that, there was no way they would ever accept her into the pack.

CHAPTER 19

amaska

HE SHOULD BE BACK *by now.*

She switched off the carpet cleaner, having cleaned the last of the bloodied carpet. Her ears rang with echoes of the machine's loud whirring, nose stinging with the special chemicals she'd been given.

The thoroughly cleaned clubhouse looked even better than before the attack, with clean carpets, fresh paint, and new curtains hung. But evidence of the massacre couldn't be removed so easily from Tamaska's mind.

That would take time.

She might be an outsider, but at least cleaning had given her a purpose for most of the day. Every shifter a job to do, and they went about it in a loaded silence that made her uneasy.

The others left her alone. In fact, they wouldn't even go near her, and that suited her just fine. She had nothing to say to them, nor them to her. Ash was holed up with her laptop. She tried not to take it personally, they'd sorted out the issue, right? So Ash was researching what Tamaska had told her. But still... She wasn't here, and Ash had been one of the few wolves she'd ever felt connected to.

She was here, not in the same room with her, though. And...the worry for Kodiak kept building.

The loneliness didn't help. Apart from the worry and fear, Tamaska longed for him to return. To her. She felt lost without him, unsure of what to do, who to trust—even and she hated to be like this, but even within the pack— and what her future would hold. What if he never returned?

Since discovering her wolf shifter genes, she was spiraling, out of control. Her friend, who she could talk to was dead, and even those in the pack...they didn't understand her humanity on a deep level.

Shit, she didn't even know if Kodiak did, but she knew he'd stand by her, always.

And he wasn't here.

He should be back by now.

As each minute ticked and her fear for him grew, she'd begun to feel less human, as if a change had initiated within her. But the change only felt partial, as if it still needed to progress into something more. She needed to speak to Kodiak about it. To see him. Hold him.

But he wasn't there.

Tamaska pushed the newly hung thick black curtain out of the way to look out the window. There was no sign of him coming down the driveway.

"Kodiak," she whispered. "Please be all right. Please come home to me. To your people."

And to her. She needed him back, alive and unharmed, otherwise she didn't know how she could go on.

Fern crouched outside, changing the plates on the car

she'd used to pick up the carpet cleaners. She planned to return them before the end of the day. Onai, now in charge, had given everyone strict orders to return before sunset and prepare for any potential vampire attacks.

And because of the fact the vampires seemed to be roaming in daylight, a large number of pack members patrolled the grounds.

But under it was a terrible sense of waiting. For Kodiak.

The growing fear made her crazy, angry. And she had nothing to lash out on, and nothing to occupy her time, not since she was done with the damn cleaners.

Fuck. Tamaska hated waiting.

If only he hadn't gone off to be a fucking hero.

She let the curtain fall back and stepped away from the window. It was better not to look outside, as it only reminded her that no one was about to let her go looking, just like no one would disobey their Alpha.

The whole thing clawed at her.

It wouldn't be long before dark. Once night fell, she'd know for sure that something bad had happened, and she wasn't ready to face that.

She needed something to do. Maybe pack up the damn carpet cleaner.

"How many times do I need to tell you to rest?" asked Roan as he entered the foyer. He wore loose track pants and a casual T-shirt. He'd recently showered, and the clean scent of soap lingered in the air.

"I rested in the car," she said, wrapping the carpet cleaner's electrical cord around its body.

"That was barely an hour. That's not long enough," Roan said, helping her move the machine to the front stoop, where the other cleaners already sat.

"That's long enough for me. I can't sleep until he's back."

"I get it, but you need to have all your strength if you want to be turned."

Roan was looking out for Tamaska, and that gave her hope. Maybe it was possible that she would soon become part of the pack. Nothing would please her more because it would please Kodiak. Well, nothing, apart from his safe return.

"I'm not leaving you alone until you rest. Kodiak would have my head if you collapsed."

"Fine, I'll go and rest." She had no chance of sleeping, not until she knew Kodiak had safely returned to the clubhouse, but she agreed to get Roan off her back, and to appease him.

"Good. I'll bring these to Fern so she can return them. Great idea with the carpet cleaners, by the way. I've never seen the clubhouse look so good. And the smell of blood's gone." Roan gently pushed her back inside the house, giving her little choice but to turn around.

Tamaska sighed as she walked down the hallway. When she passed a meeting room towards the back of the house, she couldn't help but glance inside. Ash sat on a secondhand lounge chair, which someone had collected to refurnish the room after they'd tossed the old, bloody furniture. Her laptop rested on a small desk, her fingers moving quickly over the keypad.

Maybe it was time to make proper overtures. And, hopefully, learn something about the research. If Ash decided to share, that was.

"Knock, knock," said Tamaska, entering the meeting room. "New decorations look good."

Ash didn't glance up. "I'm busy."

Shit. She pasted on a smile.

"Can I help?" asked Tamaska, flopping down on a scavenged beanbag nearby. All the furniture in the meeting room was now secondhand, which suited the space. At least, there was no more blood in sight. So...there was that.

"No." Ash tightly pressed her lips together, as if actively stopping herself from saying any more.

"I'm...I am really sorry I took your laptop, but aren't you sort of glad I did? At least I learned more about the Blood Opal and my family line. That's got to be helpful."

Oops, that slipped out, but now it was out there, she waited.

Ash kept typing.

"C'mon. At least we know more now, and that's gotta help the pack." She breathed out. "I'm trying. I just...I just thought if there's a link somehow with me then maybe you can use me. For the pack. F-for Kodiak."

Ash ignored her.

"Fine, I get. You're mad, worried and all the rest. But you're not always going to be able to ignore me." Tamaska moved to leave.

Ash sighed heavily and snapped her laptop shut.

"It's not that."

She turned back to face the shifter. "What, then?"

"You're changing the hierarchy, the pack, our future, and you're risking Kodiak's life."

She stared at Ash. "That's crazy. H-he wanted me to stay. It's his choice. I'm not making him do anything." She bit her lip. "I'd do anything for him and the last thing I want is an upset in the hierarchy. Please. Help me understand."

Ash blew out a breath then shook her head. "We need him back here. I can't be the one to tell you."

"I-is this about what was said in the car? I don't know what it is if you don't tell me." She spread her hands. "Is it about changing me? Is something wrong there? Right? Help me, Ash. Please."

"You don't get it." Ash rubbed her eyes. "Kodiak needs to be the one to tell you."

"And what if he doesn't come back?" The words were out before she could stop them and she wished she could take them back, as if saying them would somehow make those terrible syllables true. She gulped back a sob.

Ash half reached for her but dropped her hand. "We're all worried, Tamaska, but it's Kodiak. He's tough and smart. He'll be back."

Tamaska forced the giant what if back to the bottom of her being and turned on her bravado, all the way up to eleven. "He'd better. I need to whup his ass for making me worry like this."

Ash smiled. "You're a good match for him."

"Except for the times when I don't follow his orders." She rubbed her arms even though it wasn't cold. Inside, she was frozen. And she didn't think she could ever be warm again, at least not until Kodiak came back to her.

Ash shrugged. "You'll get used to it."

Tamaska felt a change between them, like some invisible tension had eased.

"I'm sorry for using your laptop, truly." she said. "I just had to do something. I couldn't sit alone and twiddle my thumbs all night."

"I'm pretty fucking sure that's what Channing does." Ash grinned, and she smiled back. "And I know you're sorry, you've told me a million times and, well...just don't do it again." Ash inhaled slowly. "It's not straightforward with you."

She waited, like she stood on a mountain of shifting, broken glass, for Ash to continue. One wrong move and the pile would give way and that would be that. So she just waited, holding her breath, not moving.

"I've been researching, actually." Ash met her gaze. "I

don't know about transforming you, or if we should because I don't know how your wolf genes will affect the transformation."

"Surely for the better?"

"Maybe. To be safe, we should proceed as if you're fully human and change you during the full moon."

"That's, what…five days away?" She stopped. How the fuck did she know that? She'd never bothered to look at the moon before. Somehow, she just knew the day.

"Yes, and we might not have five days to wait. The vampires want to use the Blood Opal to turn you." Ash picked up her computer and read over something. "At least that's what I make out. I stumbled on a sub-reddit and it's coded but it's shifters, talking about browns and the cursed stone. I'm sure that's the opal. They say the one who has it can control the one who bleeds. It's all jokes and assholery, but there's some nuggets in there. It's gonna take me a long time to go through it and follow what links people put in, or…you know…"

"You mean when they go on tangets about something else that ends up being related? Been there done that kind of rabbit hole," Tamaska said. Of course for her it was about a book she's read. But she got it.

"So I don't know what to do." Ash sighed. "Not without Kodiak.

"Then take the risk and change me now," Tamaska said. "I'm fully aware of the risks. I'm willing."

"I can't." Ash looked away. "This isn't my choice. It's Kodiak's right as our alpha."

"Or Onai's, until Kodiak gets back."

"Onai won't agree to change you."

"Wouldn't sooner be better? Then the vampires can't use me as a weapon." It made sense, and she saw that Ash agreed, so what the hell was the problem? What weren't they saying?

"Yes, okay? Yes it would." Ash looked at her and set the computer back down. "But we need to wait until Kodiak gets back, which will be before dark. It's not much longer, now."

"Fine," Tamaska said, knowing she couldn't force it. But it sucked.

"This is all part of existing within the pack's structure. You'd better get used to it. Stop fighting it, and things will go a whole lot more smoothly for you."

She sighed. "I'll try."

"It's not as bad as you think. You'll see."

"Thanks." Tamaska exhaled heavily. Ash was trying to help, and Tamaska had adapted to so many changes in such a short time. Maybe it was better not to rush into her transformation.

"I've been told to go and rest," Tamaska said. "So...I guess I better obey."

"Good, you should." Ash rolled her eyes. "Rest I mean. Roan is a great healer, you should listen to him. I'll come get you if anything changes."

"See you." Tamaska left the room, satisfied the rift that had come between them over the laptop incident had been bridged.

She stepped through the back door and glanced toward the graves beyond the fence. She sent her silent gratitude out to the fallen pack members. Then, she headed around the left of the main house and followed the rocky path to the long, rectangular dormitory.

Each pack member had their own room—some even had private bathrooms. No one owned anything beyond their necessities. After having had her place ripped to shreds by Amdis, sge knew she would adapt easily to the shifters' minimalist lifestyle. Other things would be much harder: like following the rules, being submissive, and figuring out what the fuck it would feel like to become a wolf.

Her mind turned to her ancestors. What had life been like for the first generation of shifter-human hybrids? Did the fusion even change anything for them? When had the wolf genes fallen dormant? So many questions, no one to ask.

She had half a mind to ring her parents, but they probably wouldn't even know what she was talking about. Even her grandparents probably hadn't known. Surely they wouldn't have sold it if they'd known the value of the Blood Opal?

With way too many questions swirling through her head, she let herself into the dormitory building. Kodiak's room lay at the end of the hall, and she used his hidden key to let herself inside.

His musky scent immediately wrapped about her and reminded her of his absence. Her mind buzzed as memories of their stolen time together at the hut boarded her infinite train of thought. Being in Kodiak's room wouldn't help her rest, but at least she'd feel close to him again.

In a few more hours, she'd know for sure whether he was okay. She just hoped against the brewing heaviness in her gut that her instincts were wrong, that he would be all right.

Lying on his bed, she covered her eyes as if pushing back tears. She couldn't stay stuck in this limbo, being neither human nor wolf shifter. She had to change.

How the fuck was she going to survive in the pack if Kodiak didn't come back?

CHAPTER 20

 amaska

THE DESIRE TO taste it overwhelmed her. She smelled the iron hidden inside red blood like never before. It sent her body shivering with hunger, a hunger laced with so many unfamiliar emotions.

She tracked her prey with heightened senses, enjoying how hard it tried to lure her in. She ran her tongue over her teeth, savoring the feel of her elongated incisors, sharp and ready to sink into living flesh.

She turned to see a male human standing chained, restrained, terrified.

She froze.

This wasn't right.

Didn't wolves track deer, rabbits, mice? Not humans. They protected humans.

She stepped back, her desire to kill evaporated while her blood craving remained.

I have to feed.

The look of terror in the human's eyes stopped her.

He knows I'm going to kill him. But I'm not a killer.

A being appeared next to her.

Expecting to see Kodiak, she turned, ready to fall into his embrace. She couldn't wait to hear his confident explanation. What was happening to her?

She gasped as her eyes locked on the man.

No. Not man.

Vampire.

Amdis

What are you doing here? *She asked without speaking.*

Do you want me to show you how? *He grinned around protruding fangs, ready to feast.*

No! I'm not a vampire. *She reeled backwards, falling away from him.*

He laughed. Take a closer look.

She looked down at the ground, expecting to see paws. Instead, she saw her feet. She lifted her hands to see pale skin.

You need to feed. *Amdis moved closer to her.*

But I've been turned.

Yes, but it wasn't the change you'd planned. You're a vampire now, one of us forever, *he said.* Now, feed!

Tamaska screamed. The image broke away as she bolted upright in bed, tearing herself out of her nightmare. She curled up tight against the headboard.

Her pulse raced, urging her to sprint to safety. Instead, she stayed in bed, trying to calm herself.

What the hell was that? It seemed so real. And the images, the smells, all of it were so fresh she could see it all when she closed her eyes.

She never wanted to sleep again.

Ever.

She lifted a shaking hand to her neck, searching for puncture wounds. She found nothing of the sort. Frantically, she looked around the room, ensuring nothing was out of place. All she'd done was fall asleep in Kodiak's bed.

What the fuck was that dream about?

Had Amdis gotten to her that badly? One one level yes, but there was more to it. Her dreams had been so vivid, so maybe the concussion had messed her up worse than she'd thought.

Or maybe she was an utter mess because Kodiak wasn't there.

She missed with a physical ache that bordered on pain.

But missing him didn't explain the dream. Shit, it was probably a mix of all the craziness and recent crap about the opal and turning her and vampires all over the place.

Grey light hung heavy in the room as a thousand tiny shivers slid down her back. It was nearly nighttime. The vampires would be out now without any risk.

What the hell was she thinking? They'd been out and about in daylight. Early light, and Amdis couldn't cross the light in her place so maybe only some had that new power. Still…last thing she wanted was to sit here, alone.

She slid out of the bed, hoping Kodiak had returned. She let herself out of the room and locked it behind her. Like she was his girlfriend, she thought, and paused, holding the key. Relationship. They'd whispered love talk, and she loved him, she knew it. It might be fast but the word relationship meant something. It meant a future, commitment. Compromise. It meant she belonged to him and he to her.

Were they in a relationship? She liked the sound of that, but her mind skittered from it, throwing early says and needing to get to know each other at her. And then she giggled. Actually giggled.

It wasn't funny, not really, but damn, she was standing here, worrying about that normal stuff on one hand, while on the other she wanted to change and fit into his world and that meant them, together, not Tamaska prancing out into the world to date other shifters or men.

She could come up with all kinds of excuses and reasons why she wanted to change, but the bottom line wasn't just whatever her heritage was, it was him. They both wanted it so they were together in a way that his pack would have to accept.

So yeah, they were in a fucking relationship. Did she know him as she wanted to? Not yet, but in theory that's what a future was, time where you went beyond scratching the surface and finding out all about the person.

And for her, she wanted that with Kodiak. He might frustrate her, but he fascinated her. He drew her in and turned her on more than anyone. He was strong and good and smart and if he was a little bossy, so was she.

Again, something they could work out.

If he came back. If he hadn't managed to get himself killed with his bravery. And—

This wasn't the time. She needed him back, his pack needed him and she couldn't do a damn thing until he did or didn't show. If he did, she'd yell at him and then hold him tight. If he didn't she... She would do something. She knew that.

Beyond that, though, she realized they were all focused on changing her, on the opal and her ancentry.

What about the vampires?

She didn't mean in general the pack knew vampires, but Amdis and his lot. And whatever connection she might have to them—whether she wanted one or not.

The hairs on the back of her neck prickled.

Both species had an intense need for blood, just in very different ways. If she was going to be a wolf, then she'd need to get used to eating her meat raw, dripping with blood.

Maybe she could start by getting some animal blood. Or raw, fresh kill. She could—

Tamaska swallowed hard as horror spread through her. She must've gotten hit on the head really hard. The concussion had messed up her thoughts, confusing her, tricking her into associating a wolf's natural desire for prey with a vampire's demented cravings.

She stepped out into the cooling twilight air. She missed the scent of the bush. Here, a hint of the city's pollution tinged the air, something she'd never noticed, not with Sydney. But now...yeah, she could pick it up.

It still amazed Tamaska how heightened her senses were. Maybe her shifter genes weren't as dormant as she'd thought.

Feeling drowsy and in need of fresh air, she headed for the gate between the dormitory and the main house. She didn't think about where she was going, and only wished for Kodiak to be beside her.

A figure appeared down the driveway up ahead, dark and amorphous in the dusk light.

Kodiak!

Without another thought, she ran toward the figure, willing it to be Kodiak willing him back, safe and sound and hers..

Even as her instincts warned her away, she continued sprinting toward the figure. "Kodiak!"

Suddenly, the figure moved with uncanny speed. It stopped directly in front of her, and only then did she realize her enormous, deadly mistake. Panic flooded through her.

It was a vampire, pale, dressed in dark clothing. Most definitely not Kodiak.

She contemplated the possibility of an imminent, gruesome death at its hands.

"I have a message for you," said the vampire.

"If you've done anything to Kodiak, I'll kill you," she said, finding her inner strength. No way would she let a vampire leave her turf alive.

"We've got Kodiak."

"I'm going to rip you apart." She'd kill it with her bare hands and bathe in its blood.

What the hell was she even thinking.

"Then you'll miss the message," said the vampire, stepping closer.

A whiff of rot wafted her way. Repulsed, Tamaska struggled not to run away from the creature. "Hurry up and spit it out so I can kill you."

"As if you could."

"Just you wait," she said, her head swimming weirdly. She wanted blood. She needed to run. She stood there, not moving. "Talk, or I'll consider the message useless and kill you now."

"We want an exchange. Kodiak for you."

Her pulse slowed, and her heart drowned in dread.

"Where is he?"

"You've got until midnight tonight to come to the Blood Moon nightclub. Otherwise, we kill him. Come alone, or we kill him. You try anything funny, we kill him. Honestly, we're so looking forward to killing him that we're not sure how much longer we can wait. Got it?"

"Sure." Inside, she started to shake and her head swam more but still she didn't move. She wanted to kill the thing and get to the club and save her man. She wanted to go right now.

Horror moved through her at the thought of him hurt. Bleeding. In pain.

"If you hurt him—"

"Come with me now, then. Save him. You for him. Go on you know you want to."

It held out its hand and she found herself reaching for it

as her head swam more and more, almost like her brain was a spinning top. She took half a step and then stopped.

"What am I doing?" What the fuck was this bloodsucker doing to her?

Putting her hand in his was utter madness. She needed to save Kodiak, yes, and it was a trap. Obviously.

But she couldn't go with it.

The thing wanted her to. It was in her head, pushing her thoughts into death and blood and destruction, making her want to take its hand.

But now she'd found the weird link, went both ways. It tried to force her but she could also see its fear.

And Kodiak.

In pain, fur matted, whimpering.

Her heart broke and seeing him gave her strength to step back.

"Vampires!" She screamed it as loud as she could. "Vampires! Hurry! They have Kodiak!"

It stared at her, not moving.

She wanted to grab it, fight it down but it would take her, it wanted her to put hands in it. So she took a big step back.

"Come now."

"With you? You'll never let him go. Negotiate? That's what we'll do."

But inside she was a mass of panic. The vampires had Kodiak. They wanted to trade him for her. It would mean... What, that she would end up as an out-of-control wolf on a killing spree? She'd rather end up as a vampire.

Her breath caught. Had her dream been some sort of warning? And why wasn't it moving.

To her horror it stepped close and she found out why. It brought its hand up to its neck and drew a line and she found herself bending her neck for it.

"Now, just let me sample your fine blood, and I'll be on my way."

"Like fucking hell, you will." Tamaska stepped back again.

The vampire was quick, and she was still groggy from her dream. He rushed her before she had time to react.

Then a shadow appeared from nowhere, pushing the vampire to the ground with a growl. As the wolf ripped the vampire apart, Tamaska put her hand over her mouth to stifle a scream.

When it was over, the wolf changed back into human form. Channing hurried over to her.

"Are you all right? I saw you on the security monitor, but it took me a moment to realize you were talking to a vampire."

"I screamed. No one came."

He shook his head. I heard you talking but not scream.

Tamaska started to shake. It stole her voice, did something…but it didn't matter. Only Kodiak did.

"Channing! They've got Kodiak. They want me, and that's the only way they'll release him." Tamaska suppressed a sob.?

"I heard. Come on, we need to go and tell Onai." Channing held her shoulder and guided her back toward the clubhouse.

Before they ever set foot inside the building, Tamaska knew what she had do. No matter what they decided, she'd exchange her life for Kodiak's.

It was the only way.

CHAPTER 21

odiak

AT LEAST I kept Tamaska safe.

The thought soothed Kodiak despite the pain of the silver chain around his wrists. He was again in human form, naked, vulnerable, unable to defend himself.

At least they removed the fucking net. At least there was that.

It was a small, almost non-existant comfort.

His captors had hidden from the sun until nightfall. It seemed they could only tolerate a little sun.

Then, finally able to move freely, the vampires had forced him into a car and driven him back to Sydney. They'd parked at the Blood Moon nightclub, where Amdis had waited to greet him.

Bile seeped into Kodiak's mouth, bitter, hot and burning at the thought of another encounter with the vampires' leader. They'd confined him to a room with a silver chain around his wrists, anchored him to a ring in the brick wall, and left him alone in the dark.

Tamaska would have surely fled the hut with the rest of the pack. Though Kodiak had recently encouraged them to formulate an attack plan that would exterminate the vampires once and for all, now he hoped against all odds that they'd neglected their duty.

He hoped that, instead of planning an assault, they were seeking refuge thousands of miles away from the city so they could be safe. Then, they could rebuild in peace. A fight could come later.

His thoughts weren't right, his brain a little cold, the silver was taking its toll. If the vampires got whatever they were doing working, nowhere would be safe.

But… His pack… they had Tamaska. They needed to keep her safe.

Onai, I hope you don't fight.

Kodiak was too weak and encased in silver to telepathically connect with the pack. Still, he tried many times, just in case through some strange chance, they could hear.

They'd be listening, trying to reach him. That is, if they hadn't figured he'd been taken, or thought him dead. His stomach churned and nausea rode through him at his failure as a leader.

He'd gone off, on his own, and left them.

Worse, left Tamaska.

He only knew one thing now: The Blood Opal wasn't worth it.

Whatever powers it had, in truth or in legends, the gem wasn't worth losing his pack over. The pack needed to forget about it, to look out for themselves and each other. Otherwise, their pack could go extinct.

No, no that wasn't right. Not the thoughts, not the coldness in his head that numbed his brain. The pack would die if they did nothing. A smart, prepared fight was the only thing to do. They had to find a way to stop the vampires and if the opal had something to do with it, destroy that.

His pack, humanity, depended on that.

Kodiak closed his eyes, trying to squeeze the dreadful thoughts from his mind.

Shadow Pack had to survive, do their sacred job, no matter the odds. If they didn't, the vampires would continue to grow unchecked, and if the opal somehow gave them the powers he'd witnessed like being in the sun, then the human race would end up enslaved for their blood.

A thump forced Kodiak's eyes open. He turned toward the sound as the heavy wooden door creaked open.

Kodiak smelled the vampire and stiffened. He instinctively pulled against his chain, then immediately regretted it as fresh pain burned through already aching muscles. If the chain had been steel instead of silver, the vampire standing in the doorway would have seen the fight of his life.

"Steady, now," said the vampire.

Goosebumps rose on Kodiak's skin. He recognized the voice straight away.

And he felt it, the cold poking at his mind. He was a shifter so the vampire couldn't get in and manipulate him. But he was in silver, had been for the day and he was weak and in pain and the thoughts that weren't right...

Amdis, using his power.

He'd bet his life on it.

Now he figured that out, he could work out the things being put there and what he was thinking.

Never in his life had a vampire been able to do that. But these were strange days.

"Let me loose, you coward, and we can have a proper fight," growled Kodiak. "Tell me what you want and I'll rip out your throat without making you suffer. Don't, and you'll wish you'd died properly the first time."

"When I became so much better than human? Maybe I was born this way."

Kodiak spat at him.

"Not nice." Amdis chuckled. "Not enjoying your stay? Gonna give me a bad review on SnareBnb?"

Kodiak snarled, his wolf side rising to the surface, wanting out. It had been hurt. Badly. It wanted revenge. It wanted Amdis. But the vampires' silver binding was secure. Even if Kodiak transformed, he'd still be trapped. And his wolf would rip itself apart trying to get free, at first in anger and then after going mad with the pain of the silver as it fought. He was not giving in. His wolf needed to calm and wait because Kodiak needed to stay in his human form, think logically, keep a clear head.

His wolf growled, twisting and whining with pain and the need to fight.

Maybe he should let it, maybe—

Oh that coldness in his head. If Amdis wanted his wolf to surface it had to stay down.

If he allowed his wolf to surface, best case would have him enraged and spiraling out of control. The worst case he told his wolf, was death.

But as long as he could speak to Amdis man-to-man, he had a chance of getting out alive—or, at least, a chance to learn more about Amdis' plans.

"You'd better be on your best behaviour, wolf."

"Why the fuck would I do that?" Kodiak shielded his eyes as Amdis turned on the lights. Light burst and made him squint after being left in the dark for hours.

"I'm expecting visitors," Amdis said with a smirk. He stepped closer, then paused a few feet in front of Kodiak.

"Coward," spat Kodiak. Amdis stood just out of reach.

There would be no point in braving the agony of the chain in an attempt to kill the vampire.

But it was interesting the vamp didn't trust Kodiak. Good. It meant fear and fear always meant mistakes.

He growled low and long, giving his wolf that.

Amdis clicked his tongue disapprovingly. But he moved back a little more.

"I thought you'd want to help me welcome our guests," said Amdis. His hands rested casually in the pockets of the long tailored jacket he wore over a shiny black shirt, leather pants, and boots shined to perfection.

The dapper must be to hide the rot.

"Why would I want to do that?"

"Because one of them will be Tamaska."

The first thing that hit him was terror. The next...

Red. Hot. Fury.

It seared through Kodiak. He lurched in Amdis' direction, wanting nothing more than to tear him apart. But the silver chain pulled him back, and he stumbled to regain his footing even as the pain raced through him.

"What the fuck did you do?" Kodiak's gut knotted sickeningly.

The vampire smiled. "I sent her an invitation."

"Leave her out of this!"

"I can't," he said. "She's vital to my plan."

Fuck. What the hell had she been trying to tell him back at the hut? He'd had so much going on he hadn't heard and then Ash got upset... He took a breath and met the vampire's eyes, trying to see past the cold, white face.

But the only thing he saw was smug evil.

"Which is?" Kodiak asked.

He waved a hand. "Rule the world, you know, the usual shit."

"Tell me!" Kodiak said.

"Better yet, I'll show you. It will be quite the show, when she arrives. I'm really doing you a favor in all of this, you know."

"Like fucking hell, you are," said Kodiak.

"No need to be angry, wolf. I'll take good care of her." From the distance he put between them he made a show of leaning in, still staying far away from Kodiak. "Really good care. If you know what I mean. Have some fun."

Torture? He was going to torture his woman? Not while he breathed."Taking care of her doesn't mean killing her."

"Oh, no." Amdis paused for dramatic effect. "I don't want to kill her, I just want her blood."

Kodiak stared, horror shooting through him of different levels because fun might mean—oh God. If this fuck laid one finger on her sweet body he'd— He struggled to get his rage under control and stoke calmly. "Her blood? When have you ever stopped at that?"

"I will. I promise." Amdis put his hand on his chest, a solemn look spreading over his pale face before he broke into a fit of laughter.

Kodiak yanked impatiently on his chain, then grimaced against the fresh pain that sliced into his skin and reverberated deep in his muscles.

"She won't come." Well, Kodiak hoped she wouldn't. "She's forgotten all about the Blood Opal."

"Oh, it's not the Blood Opal I've promised her."

Kodiak's chest tightened as he watched Amdis walk the invisible perimeter of the chain. He didn't want to know what Tamaska had been promised.

But he had to know. "And what's that?"

"I've promised her your freedom." The vampire took a a couple of steps in as he said this.

Kodiak growled. Ignoring the chain, he leapt forward with hands outstretched and lashed out at Amdis. He clawed the vampire's face with human fingernails, leaving three bleeding scratches.

Amdis leapt back, right up against the opposite wall,

But that one taste of violence against the fucker wasn't enough. Kodiak wanted more.

Too bad the coward had moved way out of his reach.

Amdis hissed in response, fangs bared as he touched his face. Sticky blood oozed from the scratches.

"I'm surprised at you, wolf. I thought you'd be more grateful than this. I've given you the chance to get out of here, to return to your pack." Amdis spun away from Kodiak, sending his coattails flying before he strode to the door. Then, he paused and turned back.

"Congratulations, by the way, on becoming alpha. Though you may well be the shortest reigning alpha in Shadow Pack history."

Amdis slipped through the door before slamming it shut behind him. The echo bounced around Kodiak's small prison.

He growled, thrashing against the chain with all his strength to go after Amdis. But he wasn't strong enough. He collapsed on the floor, and not even the cold stone could ease the burning pain in his muscles or where the chains touched him.

He knew in his heart that Tamaska would come and free him. It was the stupidest thing she could do, but she still didn't understand the world of vampires and shifters. Given her penchant for disobeying instructions, it was inevitable that she would find a way to convince the others to join her or slip away alone to find him.

He loved the little fool for her ridiculous ways. But not this. In this he hoped to the heavens that she'd be smart, get furious and wash her hands on him. He fucking prayed his pack would tie her up and lock her the fuck away until they'd dealt with all this.

But Tamaska was Tamaska. Resourceful, tenacious, the most stubborn and irritating thing he'd ever met. And she got to him like no one else.

She'd come.

He knew it.

Tamaska wouldn't see the trap coming, and Kodiak had no way to warn her.

She wasn't part of the pack, so he couldn't use the pack connection to communicate with her, not even after she got close.

Maybe others would go with her? He could try and communicate with them. However, he lay underground, surrounded by earth, stone, and brick, insulated from the rest of the world and wrapped in silver. It would be difficult to establish a connection with even a dear packmate under those circumstances.

Tamaska wouldn't be careless enough to go alone, would she?

But even as the thought formed in Kodiak's mind, he knew that she was.

Chained and unable to help her, weakened by silver, he couldn't be the protector she needed. And that cut him more deeply than a silver chain ever could.

CHAPTER 22

amaska

THE IMAGE of the vampire's dark, sunken eyes, pale skin, fangs, and black clothes burned into Tamaska's brain, and Channing's worried face both reminded her that her encounter hadn't been a dream. It was real, and Kodiak was in trouble.

It didn't matter it had taken on a dream-like state, what happened was real and it scared her half to death. Whipped her into a cold, dark fury, too.

The fucking vampires had Kodiak.

They were hurting him.

She knew it.

Tamaska tapped her feet, unable to stand behind Ash's lounge chair. Ash's laptop lay open as usual while her fingers flew over the keyboard.

When she'd stared into the eyes of a vampire as he told her that his comrades had captured Kodiak she'd wanted nothing more than to morph, there and then, into a vicious wolf who lived to tear apart bloodsuckers.

She didn't even care it was insane to want that. They had him and they had to pay. All of them.

"Calm down, Tamaska," Onai said, "your energy is dark."

"They have him."

"Yeah and they want you," someone said. "What's the problem?"

Onai turned and growled then put his hand on her shoulder. He came in close. "It got into your mind?"

"Like it was fogging it and manipulating thoughts. It wanted me to give it blood, and it wanted me to take its hand and go with it willingly." She drew a breath. "I don't think it could take me and I don't know why."

"I know they can glamor, but it doesn't sound exactly like that."

She shook her head, aware of the dark looks from the pack as they came in. Something had changed. Perhaps they blamed her for Kodiak's capture. Or maybe they were sick of the interloper.

She didn't know and right then, she was finding it hard to care. Everything was focused on Kodiak.

"I don't know what they did, but I resisted it and then Channing came." She looked at Onai. "I have to go and get him back. I have to."

He pressed his lips together.

Fern pushed past Tamaska and bumped her abruptly without bothering to apologize. The shifter's vibes felt more than prickly as she moved to the other side of the room.

He squeezed her shoulder. "Everyone's on edge, but Tamaska you don't think they'll just give him up for you? Why? If you turn up, they'll just take you and kill him, or keep him to ensure you do what they ask."

Because they promised! The words reverberated through

her, but she didn't say them out loud. It sounded crazy. Worse it sounded like she was a vampire lover.

And below all that she could almost feel him thinking, almost hear him saying, *kill him or worse.*

Or worse.

She shuddered.

"We'll deal with this," he said, and moved to the front.

The pack had now mostly gathered in the meeting room and they had to cram into the space around the newly sourced secondhand furniture. They were a little diminished in numbers but they were strong it was as palpable as her fear, that strength.

The air hung thick and stuffy with hints of fresh paint. And she kept skittering back to the image of an injured Kodiak in wolf form, bleeding, matted fur. Her heart wept.

Onai stood near the door with his arms folded across his chest, welcoming the others with a clipped nod as they entered.

No one spoke. The silence weighed in the air.

Tamaska wanted to scream, she wanted to lead a charge, go Van Helsing and find a pitchfork. She wanted to demand they go now.

She didn't want to put anyone else in danger, either. What she should do is slip out and get him. And she'd do that, but she was nowhere near the door and since the vampire incident, they hadn't, she realized, left her alone. Someone had always been with her.

Making sure she didn't run off like she needed to. Run off and... What? Fight the vampires on her own?

Thing was, if she had to, she would.

This was Kodiak. She'd do anything to save him.

"You've probably heard," Onai said, his deep voice strangely out of place.

It should be Kodiak standing here.

A lump of emotion welled inside Tamaska's throat, hard and painful. This was all her fault. The man she was falling for, had been taken and she was responsible. She needed to go, rip out throats, sink her teeth into horrible vampire flesh she—

Had to stop that line of thought.

And she had to do something.

Onai sought her out and met her eye. "Amdis has Kodiak."

No gasps echoed through in the room. A few shifters shuffled, shifting their weight as they waited for Onai to continue.

"He left me in charge until he gets back, and I promise you all that he will come back."

The hairs on the back of Tamaska's neck prickled as a shiver slid down her spine.

He will, she promised herself.

"We only have until midnight, which doesn't give us much time to plan a rescue," continued Onai. "We'll—"

"No. There's nothing to plan," Tamaska said. "They want me for him, so I'll accept the exchange. Kodiak needs to be here with his pack to put the vampires back in their place."

"He would never allow that, so neither will I," said Onai.

"I don't care," she said. "They want me. In return, they'll release Kodiak, so I'll do it."

"I'm not asking you to do that." He paused. "In fact I'm ordering you not to do that."

She sucked in a breath. "But it's the only way to ensure Kodiak's release."

"He won't like it if the vampires capture you," Onai said. "And that stands."

No, Kodiak wouldn't like that at all. But that wasn't what Tamaska had in mind. And she wasn't a member of the pack. Couldn't be if he never returned. Because there was no way she'd be able to stay, constantly reminded of him.

But it wouldn't come to that. She wouldn't let it. She was smart. And she could think outside boxes. It had come with her job. And she'd been great at her job.

"I know, Onai, but please…listen. I have a plan. Will you listen? I know I'm an outsider, but you all opened your doors so I beg you'll listen." Christ, she sounded pathetic, but she needed to find a way to get them…get Onai…to listen, and pleading worked better than demanding. She hoped.

"Will you?" She asked.

Onai sighed. "Go ahead. I'll listen."

"Thanks. Assume I go. Once they think they have me, the vampires will be distracted. Then, you can launch an attack on them." Tamaska hadn't had much time to plan. But her desperate need to free Kodiak before the vampires killed him made her willing to propose the half-baked suggestion.

"Like a Trojan horse of a kind, I guess. I'm bait and then we take them." She wiped her sweaty hands down her jeans. "And if it doesn't work, you get him out. No way am I going to be the cause of his death. All I have to offer is my life for his, and I'll do that willingly."

"It's way too risky," said Onai.

"I don't care." She looked at him. "It's my life, so—"

"It's not just risky for you, but for everyone in this room. Plus, the vampires will be expecting us to retaliate."

Tamaska coiled her hands in frustration. "There has to be something I can do. I'm not totally useless. I can fight."

"You can't." He shook his head. "You're not a wolf shifter."

"I have shifter genes."

"So what? You're not pack." He growled softly at her.

Tamaska closed her mouth, but she wasn't about to give up. She would put her life on the line if it helped get Kodiak back.

"Then make me part of the pack. Turn me now." She

didn't even know what possessed her to say that. She wouldn't even be able to shift.

Onai raised his eyebrows. "No way."

"Why not?" The words flew from her, like they had a life of their own. "The vampires won't be expecting it."

"You'll be too unpredictable!" Ash stood. "Or the change could make you so weak, you'd be unable to fight."

"I'm sure I'll be fine. Turn me." She couldn't stop them. They were right, turning her wouldn't be the way to do it.

"Kodiak will have my hide if I listen to you."

"No, he won't, because it will save his life and mine. It will save the pack." A weird confidence coated Tamaska's words,. This was the way forward.

"What's wrong with you, Tamaska?" Ash pushed her way to her side. "You know how it works with the shift, if it works. The risks. The only ones it would help would be the vampires."

That thing that made her speak all that left her and she knew Ash and Onai were right. She put a hand to her head and almost swayed. Fuck, she hoped the vampires weren't reaching her here. She didn't feel weird like she did outside, but... Maybe the pressure had gotten to her.

Or maybe she was losing her damned mind.

"I..."

"Okay, here's another problem." Onai pointed at her. "When you arrive—even if you're human form, and that's assuming you instantly gain perfect control over your shifts after you're turned—the vampires will smell you. They'll know you're a wolf."

"I don't know what's wrong with me." Her heart sank, and her gaze dropped to the floor. "I'm just trying to help. I want —I need to do something."

"Don't we have a way to mask our scents?" asked Channing, rubbing his chin as he stepped forward.

"We do, but her scent isn't the only problem," answered Ash. She finally stopped typing and looked up from her screen.

Tamaska's breath caught in her throat.

"I didn't mean for her," Channing muttered, but no one was listening. And Tamaska couldn't find it to ask what he meant.

"Tell me," Onai said, tight-lipped. "What's this latest problem?"

"The vampires want Tamaska's blood because she's a Brown. You know, the ones who brought the gem to Australia?"

For a moment, Onai didn't speak, then he whipped his head to face Tamaska, then to Ash. "What? You found all this out...when?"

"Well, Tamaska found some of it," said Ash. "But I've done extra digging since then."

"And you found what, exactly?" he said. Fill me in, and don't hold anything back."

"As we suspected, the Blood Opal has powers. Under the right circumstances, like a full moon, the gem will enhance the properties of whatever blood it touches," said Ash. "When it comes into contact with human blood, it grants humanlike properties, such as the ability to tolerate sunlight. The vampires most likely got that added bonus after consuming human blood that had touched the Blood Opal."

"So, why Tamaska's blood?" Onai rubbed his hand over his forehead and closed his eyes. "What could they possibly do with her?"

Ash looked at her and then Onai. "Create a wolf shifter."

A murmur ran through the assembled shifters.

"But vampires surely don't want to become wolf shifters," Onai said. "Why are they doing this shit?"

"No, they don't, which is why they have to do things a

little differently. That's why they took Kodiak." Again, Ash looked at her. "They won't consume Tamaska's blood; they'll filter it back into her body, forcing her take on the change. Her dormant shifter genes will wake up."

"Which means she'll become a wolf shifter? That would be helpful for us, wouldn't it?" Channing asked.

Ash shook her head. "No, because she's going to be an out-of-control wolf shifter."

"Oh…" Channing looked down.

Onai glanced at her. "Fuck."

Tamaska didn't fully understand the flash of concern in Onai's eyes as he glanced at her.

"Are you sure?" asked Onai.

"Sure enough." Ash nodded. "My conclusion is based on the properties of blood and opals, as well as everything they represent. I found instructions for old rituals on the database, the same rituals they used on shifter-human hybrids. When a daughter of the Browns refused to continue our pure bloodline and married a human, their children were fine. They were both wolf and human. But with the next generation, it was harder. They had to use the Blood Opal to activate their children's wolf shifter genes, if the children wanted to become shifters. So, the point is, if her blood comes in contact with the gem, it won't be good."

"What, it would activate her wolf genes just like that?" Channing looked at her like she was part interesting bug. That sounds crazy, you know."

"I believe it will happen. It makes sense." Ash stared him down then looked at Tamaska and then Onai. "Her family brought the Blood Opal to Australia to prevent it falling into the wrong hands. I've gathered they had to keep it hidden, and they accomplished that by selling it."

That was a stupid decision. Tamaska didn't agree with what her grandparents had done.

"So, you're saying that if she was turned using the Blood Opal, her shifts wouldn't be regulated by the moon's phases like ours? And then her animal instincts would take control of her, dominating her human mind," Onai asked.

Ash nodded. "Which means she'd be out of control."

"Why would that be so bad? I could kill some vampires for you," Tamaska said, hoping...she didn't know what she was hoping. That they'd just shove her out the door to bring back Kodiak?

"It's not that straightforward. You could kill us, or a human, and then we would be forced to kill you," said Ash.

"I'd never do that."

Ash took her arm. "Not on purpose, but the point is you don't know, wXe don't know! And we have to be sure."

She took a shaking breath. "So, change me, then. I'll be a wolf shifter, but I'll stay in human form, right? I'll be weak and without powers. But that will mean the vampires can't touch me. It's the safest way. I'll go and make the exchange." She licked her lips. "It's the only way. If I don't go, they'll kill Kodiak.

Onai folded his arms. "What do you think the vampires will do if they smell wolf on you?"

"We'll mask the scent, like Channing said," Tamaska said. "I get it's risky doing it now, but surely not as risky as me going in human and the vampires using the opal. Or them killing Kodiak."

Another murmur rippled through the room.

"What if that doesn't work?" he asked. "What if we don't get to you in time, or you change forms accidentally? They'll tear you apart once they realize you're useless to them. They want to use you for destruction and chaos, and we can't let that happen. Not even to save Kodiak."

"No. He can't die. H-he can't."

"We do't let it happen." Onai said.

"You can't guarantee that. I'm the best bet." A terrible one, perhaps but the best they had. She knew in her heart that everything Ash and Onai said was true. The vampires weren't going to be so easily fooled. But she couldn't give up now. This was her chance to help the pack and to get what she wanted —to save Kodiak.

"We've masked our scents before, when we went to the nightclub," said Channing, earning a glare from Ash.

"See, it can be done." Tamaska said.

"But Amdis will be expecting us to play tricks, to try and rescue Kodiak without making a true exchange." Onai sighed "We'll have to be smarter than them."

"So, what's the plan, then?" Tamaska massaged her temples in tight circles.

Onai inhaled slowly. "We'll use you as bait, then leave with you and Kodiak in tow. And kill some vampires."

Tamaska's stomach tightened. "Let's do it, then."

"All in favor?"

The pack lifted their heads and howled softly, music vibrating through the room as each wolf contributed a unique pitch.

Tamaska swallowed hard as the howls raised goosebumps on her skin.

Kodiak wouldn't like Tamaska's plan. But the tables had turned and, for once, she would have to rescue him.

CHAPTER 23

THE PLAN TO use her as bait was risky.

She knew that. But what else could they do?

Silently, she went over the details one more time as Channing drove the van to the nightclub—go in, make the exchange, wait until Kodiak was safe. Then, all hell would break lose.

Her nerves were stretched tight. And worry nibbled at her. So much could go wrong.

Everything hinged on the plan's perfect execution. But they'd only had time for a single discussion and a few questions, before hitting the road and hightailing it to the Blood Moon Nightclub—the last place Tamaska had ever wanted to return.

But that was the least of it. The fact they hadn't had much time, the fact the clock ticked down, and the fact she hated the club with a passion…it didn't matter to her, not really.

What did, what gnawed at her deep where she tried to hide it even from herself, was the her part of it.

Even if the vamps didn't cotton on to the plan, didn't know of the shifters who'd be waiting to attack, what if they got in her head again?

She didn't worry about them reading her mind. She didn't think they could do that, but they could manipulate her. Poke inside and stir things up.

But she knew the feeling, the strange dreamy, swimmy feeling of it, the way thoughts that weren't right would insinuate themselves into her.

Tamaska had to be on high alert for that.

And do everything like they planned.

"Easy, right?" she muttered.

"No, it's not." Channing glanced at her as he picked out a good parking space. Close enough yet far enough away.

She sighed. "I was being sarcastic."

"Sometimes it's hard to tell." Channing finally parked a ways down the street. "The perfect distance, as Onai instructed."

"I'm right here, Channing. And yes, it's as good a place as any." Onai tapped a finger on his thigh.

Channing snorted. "Trying to do it right, that's all."

"You are."

Everyone was on edge and tensions mounted by the second. For her, it was almost unbearable.

They were cutting it close. Her gaze kept darting to the digital clock on the dashboard.

She swallowed hard as she noted the time. Ten minutes before midnight.

Like a close shave it was. And no safety blade in sight.

She shivered.

"Cold?"

"I just want this done with and Kodiak back," she said, looking at Channing.

"Are you in yet, Ash?" Onai asked, impatience biting into his words from the passenger seat.

"Hang on a minute…" The shifter muttered a little under her breath then made a triumph sound. "There! Yes, I'm in. Their security is shit."

"I bet it is. We're lucky I upgraded ours," said Channing.

"Don't get too excited, pup," Onai said. "That vampire messenger got way too close to the clubhouse for my liking. You'll need to get back to work on our system and make those sensors extra sensitive."

"Do you know how hard it is to calibrate the security cameras to detect vampires, which can't be recorded? Fucking impossible. So, cut me some slack." Channing slumped, and even in her anxiousness, Tamaska's heart went out to him.

She liked the kid. Young man. Young shifter? Blowing out a breath she counted to ten, and tried to get herself back on track.

"No way." Onai ruffled his hair. "You'll get it fixed. Every pack member's life depends on it. What would've happened if the vampire had made it past the gate and all the way to the front door? More lives could've been lost today. It was lucky that Tamaska happened to see it." Then he lowered his voice. "And you saw her. So you're getting there. Kodiak has faith in you. Me..? Meh."

"I got to her in time to help," Channing said, outraged at the last part. "No one got hurt, not even Tamaska."

"You did."

"And," he adds not looking at Onai, "I saw her, and raced to help. So there's that."

"I know," said Onai. "And I'm gonna tell you what Kodiak would, we need to improve. All of it. We'll have round the clock patrols, but I want you to review the system when we get back and make sure it can see farther down the driveway, maybe some kind of movement detector? Like…"

Tamaska shifted. "What about super fast movement, car or more, as well as just the fine tuning? He did get there and stop whatever that vampire was trying to get me to do."

And she knew how that sounded. She didn't want them to stop her at the last minute. They couldn't. Not when they were out of time. Not when Kodiak relied on her. "I was able to resist, but he saved me."

"He doesn't need defending, do you, Channing?" The shifter growled in answer to Onai. "We can all work to improve things, attitudes, training, security. Can't be too careful, you know."

"You sound like Kodiak." Channing clamped his jaw shut. "Consider it done."

Tamaska's stomach tightened painfully. He sounded like Kodiak? A reasonable, non-spiky version she didn't know? Then again, maybe she brought it out in him. That and the stress of everything.

And with them, things had moved so fast and now… now… He could die.

She closed her eyes and forced herself to try and calm. That's what they were there to prevent, Kodiak's demise. Tamaska rubbed a hand on her stomach as if that could help ease the pain inside. She opened her eyes. Even though she hadn't been to the gym lately, everything that had happened, all the fighting that had unfolded proved to be the best work out.

If she survived and even if she got to fulfill her legacy, she'd devote time for combat training and learn some krav maga, anything that could enhance her strength and skill.

Of course thinking about it didn't do anything but distract. But that was good. Because too many memories flooded her mind as she looked down the street and caught a glimpse of the nightclub.

Inside that place she'd seen her first vampires drinking blood from humans. Outside the club had been her first time seeing a wolf, and she'd been scared out of her mind. Although she'd hung onto it for all those years, her fear of dogs had lessened the more time she spent with Kodiak.

It still flared up sometimes, especially when she saw the old scars on her arms. Yet, there she was with a pack of dogs. She couldn't deny that her fear still existed, as it simmered under the surface, but she had it under control.

And she'd come so far in such a short time.

She inhaled slowly, eyes fixed on the front door. Oh, she might feel the lick of dehabilitating fear. Of what she'd find, of what the vampires might do to her. But nothing on the planet could stop her going in. Nothing.

He would do the same for me.

And if he did, she would be furious, just as he would be with her.

She knew it, felt it, accepted it. That unwavering knowledge.

It wasn't that she couldn't live without Kodiak, but she couldn't live with herself if she didn't try to free him. And she'd much rather a world with him. She'd rather that than anything, even if he banished her, she could move on knowing somewhere her Kodiak still lived and breathed.

She needed to get him out. She—

"We've got your back, remember," Onai said, interrupting the thoughts swamping her.

"They'll know you're here. Maybe you should park another block away?" said Tamaska. She leaned forward in her seat to look through the windscreen.

Channing said this was the perfect spot, but now she

wasn't sure. She was minutes away from going in, minutes from midnight and nothing could go wrong. Nothing.

"The vampires surely know we wouldn't let you come here alone," said Ash. "They risked coming to our place. They need you to walk in on your own. For whatever reason, but they'll expect us to be around."

"And that's going to be a problem," said Tamaska. "Right?"

"They won't know how we'll come in, though," said Channing. "It's going to be fine."

Tamaska wasn't convinced, but it wasn't like they had any better options. They couldn't just leave Kodiak to his fate among the vampires.

"They won't know where we are, Tamaska. We've all masked our scent and dropped off pack members around the nightclub. They'll stand ready to launch the attack. I figure they'll decide there's only one or two of us here. They're arrogant, they don't think we can plan. Besides, those bloodsuckers will be so distracted by you, they won't realize we're all here until it's too late," said Onai.

That was the best plan they could come up with in so short a time. Still, that knowledge didn't calm Tamaska's nerves as she sat in the van, waiting for the clock to tick closer to midnight.

"I should go in now. They said I have until midnight, not turn up on the dot."

Onai sighed. "Ash thinks they need you at midnight, right?"

"It's what makes sense. They could have said eight or ten or even one a.m. but midnight's always significant in paranormal worlds. They need you at midnight. So we wait until as close as we can. It'll push them to further distraction," Ash said.

"We hope." Tamaska twisted her hands together.

"We're here with you. Stick to the plan. Tell them you'll

do nothing until they'll free Kodiak. If they couldn't touch you but tried to lure you into touching them it might mean something, so don't touch them until Kodiak's out the door. Then, we'll take care of the rest," said Onai.

Tamaska nodded, her stomach rippling with nerves. Shit, she hoped with everything she was they were right.

"I've disconnected their security," said Ash. "We're good to go."

"Perfect timing," said Onai.

The clock on the dashboard ticked. It was one minute to midnight.

Time to go.

"See you on the other side," said Ash as Tamaska opened the van door.

"Likewise."

Tamaska got out of the van, and headed fast towards the Blood Moon Nightclub.

A parallel memory flooded her mind, the memory of walking toward the nightclub with Tahla beside her. Tamaska had been so innocent back then, so blissfully ignorant of the darker life she was almost a part of. Then there was the time she snuck into the nightclub to get the Blood Opal back. She'd known so little then. She didn't know much more now, yet she felt entirely different. It felt as if part of her had awakened, and was never, ever going back to sleep.

What would this visit to the Blood Moon bring? No she had to stop that line of thought. She had to be strong. Had to trust. Freeing Kodiak was all Tamaska cared about. It was the only goal that mattered.

The front door of the nightclub opened, and Amdis stepped out.

"I knew you'd come." He gestured for her to step inside. "Leaving it to the last minute, but on time."

He held out her hand and she fought the compelling need to take it. She squeezed her fists, hard.

"Not so fast. I want to see him," Tamaska said.

She needed to stick to the plan. Have them get him, bring him out.

"Come in and see him."

Tamaska shook her head. "That wasn't the deal. You bring him out and then I'm yours."

"I don't think you're in a position to negotiate little girl." He laughed. "Are you?"

"A deal's a deal and I'm not moving until he's here. And free."

The vampire breathed out in a low hiss. "But you want to come inside, don't you? You want to know what our magnificent plans are…"

She did. She swayed towards him half lifting her hand before she snapped herself back into reality. Her hand came down hard against her side. "No. But I'm here. And I'll go with you. If you send him out."

"He's inside," said Amdis. "Waiting for you."

"Then let him out. He's not who you want." Tamaska narrowed her eyes at him.

"You're sure about that?"

"Yes."

"Or maybe," he said, we'll keep him to keep you in line."

She started to tremble. "N-no deal."

"You sure? Or is it you think you have some feral bargaining chips?"

"What—"

Amdis snapped his fingers. A chill went down Tamaska's spine. A loud noise erupted from behind her, then yells. She spun around. And she shook her head in disbelief and grief. "No!"

"Yes," he said as vampires started attacking the van with a ferocity that frightened her.

"No…" she moaned wanting to rush back and help her friends, but Kodiak's imprisonment rooted her to the spot.

"You were told to come alone."

"And you promised you'd release him. I don't do what I'm told," Tamaska said. The knot in her stomach tightened, folding in on itself.

"You should, or more lives will be lost. Including your own." Amdis gestured for her to enter.

She had to. Because if she didn't…

Kodiak would be lost. She couldn't—wouldn't let that happen.

Admis held out his hand but she gave it a wide berth and she didn't miss the flash of irritation.

But she did it. She stepped inside.

It was foolish.

A death wish.

It was the only thing she could do.

Because with the screams and cries that rose up around the nightclub she knew the vampires were attacking the pack full force.

There was no more plan, and she had no idea what to do.

And no one would be coming to help her.

CHAPTER 24

odiak

THE CLOMP OF footsteps approaching his prison dragged him into full alert from his pain-filled twilight. Not sleep, not wakefulness, just…surviving.

Someone was coming.

And it woke up all his senses into a howling fire.

Kodiak sniffed the air and gathered his strength. He needed to be ready…to fight, to kill…to try and escape.

Somehow, someway, he needed to fight off the pain.

The silver chain jangled as he stood up from the cold stone floor.

It was hard to guess the time, down there in the dark. The silver blocked his innate sense of the time of day or night, or when the moon approached fullness. Without the chains he'd have known if it was midnight or midday, even if he was locked in a windowless space. With the fucking chains it was just endless dark that never ended.

Like a timeless void that sucked at his soul and will.

He had no idea how long he'd been trapped. He did know that, left alone, he'd had way too much time to think. And judging by the maudlin turn of thought, it had definitely been a while.

He sniffed again, and an odor he hated crept closer with the footsteps.

The metal lock creaked, and the bolt slid aside. Kodiak smelled two vampires on the opposite side of the door, stuffed full of blood that wasn't their own.

The door burst open and he was hit, full blast with the stench. And he tried not to gag.

Two male vampires walked in, dressed in black, hair slicked back. They looked at him, their ugly, pale faces twisted into contempt. And they opened their mouths and revealed their fangs with a hiss.

Theatrics, sure, but theatrics with teeth—literal and figurative. And the hiss was a warning, a provocation. A signal they could turn on him in an instant.

Drain him dry if they wanted.

Those things were plain as day, loud as if they'd spoken the threats.

Kodiak tensed, ready to defend himself. Had they finally come to drink him dry? It wasn't something vampires did or even liked to do. Something about shifter blood repulsed them normally, maybe even affected them detrimentally. It was only ever done to kill. But right now, the way they looked at him, the evil intent and silent message in their eyes, it seemed like they definitely wanted his blood.

Or wanted him to think that.

But who the fuck knew? These weren't ordinary times, So with walking in light maybe they'd developed a taste for shifter blood. Like it was end of days or some such shit.

He stared them down and they stared back, their glassy eyes exuded hunger as they approached him.

He flexed his hands, opened and closed them, testing how much he could endure. Quite a lot, even with the burn of the silver that buzzed like an electrical current. He then settled on tight fists.

It was a fallacy, he knew, his supposedly getting used to the silver. He wasn't. No shifter did. The silver worked its insidious magic and destroyed. And Kodiak, Alpha or not, wasn't any different from any other shifter. The longer the silver touched him, the weaker and less likely to defend himself he became.

And the fists he made were like a baby's, pathetic and useless compared to their usual power.

Did they know? Of course they did. They understood the evils of silver on his kind.

Still they looked at him like a tasty treat.

And he couldn't fucking stand it.

Kodiak wasn't about to let them drink from him, no matter if they'd developed a taste for shifter blood or they just wanted to torture him and kill him the way he never wanted to go; been drained by a vampire.

The drinking of blood had a vile, intimate feel to it. Invasive. Wrong. No way he'd them take his life without putting up the best fight he could manage.

Which wasn't much, he knew, but he'd fight. To his last breath.

He waited for the attack, for them to leap on him and rip into him with their disgusting fangs.

But they made no move to do such a thing. They just leered at him.

"What? You think we want your blood? Your repulsive, stinking, tainted blood? Not fucking likely. Not when we have a tasty treat waiting for us," said one of the vampires. "Come on, doggie, you're going for a walk."

"Like hell, I am." Kodiak aimed an uppercut at the vampire's face, unable to stop himself.

Before he could connect with its face, the vampire moved sonic fast and something heavy wrapped tight about his wrist, sending sparks of pain shooting up as it pulled his hand down. Excruciating fire shot up his arm, and he groaned, almost falling to his knees.

"Your new leash. You're lucky we're not putting it around your neck. Make this hard for us, and that's exactly where we'll put it," said the other vampire, hissing close to Kodiak's ear. "Maybe tight enough to cut off your air supply."

There was something in the hiss from the other one which made the vampire with the threat step back.

Did they need him for something?

I'm not beaten yet, then.

But fuck, whatever they had on him tightened when he moved, and the more tried to get it off, the more it gripped.

The vampires laughs. "Fucking dogs," one said. "Brainless, all of them. Look at it shake. Maybe we should get him a cone from a vet, stop him gnawing."

"Nah, its weak."

Anger surged.

Kodiak glanced down at his hand. Silver netting wrapped around it, but he couldn't shake it off. Ignoring them, he tried again, testing it. The more he tried, the tighter it got. And then a shot of pain froze his entire arm.

He clamped his teeth together to stop screaming out.

But, he'd found the limit of this type of netting. The more he moved the worse it got and then it sent out a blinding shot of pain at its limit.

The vampires laughed at his moan as they untethered

him. They wrapped a length of sliver chain around his wrists before removing the horrible netting.

Maybe, he thought, maybe he needed to work with that kind of bind. He tried to think back to how he got out of the larger net, but he'd been a wolf then and everything was hazy with pain and cold.

"Come along, dog." With a single tug, the chain bit into Kodiak's wrists, burning into his skin. He yelped as they forced him to follow them out of the room.

He hated the fucking chain but it was more bearable than the fucking net. That...that was something else.

"Hurry up," one grumbled as they tugged him up the stairs.

His muscles struggled to obey him, but Kodiak kept slipping, the confinement and silver having already weakened him more than he'd thought possible.

Gritting his teeth, Kodiak tried to keep up. His skin glistened with exertion as he followed the vampires up the stairs.

Didn't they say something about a tasty treat? The altar lay this way, to the right. But they didn't turn that way, instead, they turned left.

At least they were leading him away from the altar where he'd watched them drain Tamaska's friend of blood.

He wanted to say it was a good sign, but his instincts suggested otherwise. Obviously they weren't going to drain him, but at least they didn't want him to watch them murder someone else.

At least...

His mind started to swim and a coldness touched it, sending him spinning into numbness, but he managed to drag himself back into the now. It didn't matter if he wanted to be somewhere else, if the numbness of the vampires trying to probe his head made him lightheaded and feel less pain, that wasn't a place to be. That way led to unconsciousness, subservience, bending to their stinking will.

So he silently gathered himself, made himself sharp, and dove into the pain.

He hated it, but there was something there they didn't like either, and if he had to be nearly driven mad with silver's bite, then he'd take it. Especially if it kept part of him from them, kept him in the moment.

And he suspected they wanted him half out of it all.

Kodiak endured.

The vampires pulled him through the door toward a big open space. The dance floor—or at least it was a dance floor at night, when the Blood Moon nightclub was open to the public.

Kodiak noted the private room to his left where he'd taken Tamaska for the first time, right there in the nightclub. Hot, lustful thoughts burst into his mind, adding to the inner well of strength he needed. Even memories of sex had power.

He deliberately dragged his feet and stumbled to soak in the memories as he went by that space completely.

And they loosened their hold a little as they slowed down, snickering at his weakened state. The urge to try and fight swept him but he clamped it down.

He needed to know where they were going, what they were doing, and he had to let them think he was weak. That part wasn't hard; he was, but he wanted them to think the weakness had him beat.

The only thing to beat him would be death, and he didn't want to tempt that until he had to.

He walked a tiny bit faster, stumbling and the vampires slowed some more.

They snickered even more and started to go at a snail's pace, clearly thinking they were hurting his ego. And he stored up the pathetic amount of energy that pace gave him.

"What, is this your idea of a walk? Pathetic," Kodiak said with a growl, hoping they'd go even slower.

They looked at each other, then at him.

"Poor doggie feeling sad?"

They slackened his chain. He cupped himself, trying to look like he needed to feel less vulnerable.

He didn't enjoy them looking at him, but that stood for when he was clothed, in wolf form or naked. And it struck him. Suddenly, horribly. His wolf. The silver had weakened him so much that his wolf no longer pushed to the surface, demanding freedom.

He could feel it, the pain and the fight that it only weakly held. Like an injured creature it curled on itself a mirror of what his mind wanted him to do.

Maybe his wolf part was taking all that on to give him a chance at survival.

But they tugged him again, to get him moving, and he had no option but to do so.

A few orange lights glowed between boarded-up windows on the paneled wall, equally spaced to push away the shadows. Aboveground once more, Kodiak could tell it was nighttime.

"Should I tell you to take me outside? I need to piss." He could do with the feel of the moon on his skin, to combat the permanent ache of the metal. That and maybe a chance to escape.

It was a long shot, but you never knew.

"Shut it," hissed one of the vampires.

The last thing Kodiak wanted to do was invoke their wrath, but he needed to. He opened his mouth, ready for another snarky comment. "I'm not going to just stand around, chained up like a pet."

One made to speak when he stopped and turned.

A movement in his peripheral vision caught Kodiak's attention. He turned his head, too.

Then he caught her scent, sweet and fresh and his, and his worst fear came true.

Tamaska had come.

CHAPTER 25

Tamaska

Pain flooded her heart as she caught sight of Kodiak standing there naked, clearly weakened.

He struggled to stand and there were marks all over him, bruises blooming on his ribs and cuts, too.

A wild anger whipped through her and she wanted to destroy these creatures who'd dared hurt him. She wanted to go to him and wrap herself around him, holding him, as if her touch could somehow heal him.

Or she could protect him.

Tamaska forced herself to stand there, keep her face as neutral as possible, but one of the vampires started to laugh as he caught her eye.

"Sweet on the doggie, are you? Pathetic."

"Watch it," Amdis said to the vamp from behind her.

She didn't turn. If she did, she'd be laying hands on him and even if it was in anger, she feared that would be enough to give them what they wanted.

Because so far they hadn't touched her. Not yet. And

maybe for what they were to do, they needed her to initiate it.

She squeezed her hands into tight balls and whispered, "Kodiak."

One of his eyes was bruised, his cheek grazed, and he was still the most handsome man she'd ever seen. Even weak, he was strong.

Because roles reversed she didn't think she'd be standing, when they—

Tamaska frowned. Her man barely stood on his own, yet his wrists were bound by a thin chain by the vampires. And... he wasn't fighting.

What the hell had they done? "Kodiak..."

He lifted his head and through it all the faint glitter of his eyes, the anger she was there, the heat and desire for her; the defiance at these monsters for keeping him like an animal. Less than an animal. It was all there and it almost undid her. Because even she could see how close he was to being broken, how his sheer stubborn will and resilient strength of character kept him in one piece.

Tamaska pushed down her rising emotions. She had to keep her wits about her. Because one wrong move and all would be lost.

She was just human, no matter what genes lay latent in her blood, but even she could sense that.

She turned so she was face-to-face with Amdis. And she lifted her chin. "We had a deal."

"And you're here," he said.

"You promised you'd release him if I turned up." She fought the urge to glance at Kodiak, scared another look would send her self-preservation and common sense tumbling and crumbling to dust. "So let him go. He's no use to you."

The vampire smiled, looked past her to Kodiak. "Hear that pathetic shifter? She thinks you're useless."

Kodiak growled and the pain hidden there cut into her deep.

"No," she said. "I said he's no use to you."

"Maybe I changed my mind. Maybe my vampires want to use him as a chew toy, or something for the newest additions to cut their teeth on. And I do mean cut."

"Let him go."

"Make me," Amdis said, holding a hand out to her. "You know you want to try. Here, take my hand."

Kodiak made another sound like pure pain and misery and she wanted to cry.

"You promised." It's all she had and she clung to it. "Or I'll make sure you don't survive this."

Amdis threw back his head and laughed. "You hear that? She's threatening me. A girl. Human girl who fucks animals like the one here, she's threatening your king." He considered her. "And how are you going to do that? With the back up you're counting on? They're too busy involved in their own fight. Or they're dead."

"Fucker." Kodiak spat the word and one of the vampire's tugged hard on the wire making him howl.

"Are you going to rescue him, all alone?"

Amdis motioned to her with his fingers and stared hard, and inside she went dreamy, floaty and she wanted to rip his throat out. It would be so easy to do. All she had to do was grab him, bite—

Something shot through her, like a cry. A command and she scrambled back, Amdis' hold breaking. He glared past her to Kodiak. "Keep out of it. No one wants you here."

"Then let him go."

But the vampire had felt it too, like she'd been hauled

back to herself, out of his psychic clutches. And she could almost feel the soothing heated touch of Kodiak, his fingers at her nape, his voice whispering to her to hold on.

And his pain blasted into her and she opened to it, wanting to take it.

Just as suddenly it stopped and she staggered, breathing hard.

What the hell was that? Kodiak. It was Kodiak. It didn't matter it made no sense, it was. She knew it. It felt as if Tamaska and Kodiak were bound by their own chain, something invisible.

Is this the bond he keeps referring to?

Warmth flowed through the bond, cooling the rage to lay hands on the vampire, giving her hope. She could feel him. And unlike the vampires, it seemed right when Kodiak touched her in a psychic way. He wasn't in her head, trying to manipulate her thoughts, but it was like he felt what she did, and she felt his pain.

And his strength. It gave her hope.

Despite Kodiak's weakened state, he was alive. He was there. Tamaska was infused with new strength, and that new strength, he stood only a few feet away.

"Look who I have," said Amdis, smirking as he shifted focus to Kodiak.

Tamaska gathered her strength and stood, waiting to see how this played out, waiting to see if she could find a weakness, a way to break Kodiak free.

"I see why you want her; she's pretty, and tasty." The smirk broadened into an evil grin. "Such a delicious little snack for me. And you brought her here, just by being stupid enough to get caught. The alpha and the snack."

Kodiak growled. "Let her go. You have me, so do what you want to me. Just let her go."

"But I really, *really* want her." Amdis stepped toward Kodiak, shoes clicking on the polished dance floor. "Rather surprising, isn't it?"

The rhetorical question hung in the air between what she could see as three powerful forces—Amdis, radiating confidence; Kodiak, bound; and herself—only important because of the opal, but important. And she fought the paralyzing fear that built inside her.

She was more than destiny and unlike anyone else in here, she was human...closer than any of them, anyway. Even Kodiak who grew up in the pack. And she got the feeling after her colleague who'd been turned, that vampires forgot their humanity.

Or maybe they lost it when they died and returned as soulless creatures. It didn't matter. She was human and had the best and the worst of all that. Fickle, sneaky, tricky, stubborn, smart, wily and full of the kind of bad decisions that just might save them.

Because all she had to do was grab the opal, grab Kodiak, and run. Anything pointy would serve as a weapon. Broom, broken chair. Fuck, she'd somehow make a Molotov cocktail and burn the place with herself in it if it meant killing them.

She's do anything and everything she could think of.

Including biding her time.

The two vampires stood ready behind Kodiak. One held the chain, and appeared to suffer no discomfort from the contact. That same chain, wrapped around Kodiak's wrists, left burns across his skin. The sight made her stomach churn nauseatingly.

What was it? Not metal, as in steel. Because this was hurting him and he touched all kinds of metal. Silver? Or something else? Something rare? Wasn't there something in lore about silver bullets?

Tamaska eyed the surroundings, looking for hiding places, ways to fight. Exits.

Problem was they could move super fast, and sniff out a human or a shifter, so they could find her and Kodiak even if she managed to get him free and hide. And Amdis was here. How many other vampires lurked in the shadows?

Come on, you can get yourself out of this fucking mess.

All she needed was a brilliant idea. But until that happened she'd wing it and right now it meant stretching out the time. It had to be after midnight, so she hoped that helped in her favor. And the more she learned the more she had time to find a way out.

"I bet you thought you would always keep her safe." Amdis walked up to Kodiak, staying just out of his reach.

Even with him chained and weak they seemed scared of getting too close. She looked at Kodiak but he was focused on Amdis, even though she couldn't shake the feeling he knew her every movement.

"That I would never get my hands on her—or, should I say, sink my teeth into her?" He leaned close to Kodiak, deliberately baring his fangs while maintaining a healthy distance.

"But that's exactly what I'll get to do right now," said Amdis, straightening and squaring his shoulders.

"Like hell, you will," growled Kodiak, straining against the chain. Only for a moment, though, as the pain seemed too much, and he had to relent.

"She's mine," taunted Amdis, "and I will finally put a stop to this game of cat and mouse. Now, I can test my theories about the Blood Opal and her blood."

"I don't think he can touch me," she suddenly blurted, needed to give Kodiak something to hang on to. "They tried to get me to touch them when they came to me earlier, and when I got here, Admis did the same." She looked at the vampire. "You can't, can you?"

"Maybe I'm waiting."

"Or maybe," Kodiak said, "you know if you do you'll what…? Not die. But… I'm betting whatever you lured her here for works better if she intigated touching. Isn't that right?"

"Shut your fucking mouth, dog," Amdis said with a snarl.

This time Kodiak cut a glance at her. "Don't touch him. Don't touch any of them. Even in anger. If you only listen to one thing from me, Tamaska, listen to this."

Amdis threw his head back and laughed. "But you don't tell her to run, do you?"

Kodiak was right, because the resentment and goading in the vamp's voice was thick like cake.

So she joined the verbal attack. They wouldn't let her go, and Kodiak was right, she couldn't let them try and manipulate her into touching Amdis.

"You promised to release him," said Tamaska, holding her chin high. "That's why I'm here. Let him go. Demand they let you go, Kodiak."

"He's got no power, tasty girl." He glared at the shifter. "Do you?"

Kodiak shook his head but said nothing. His subtle, helpless actions wounded Tamaska. She'd never seen Kodiak submit to anyone, and had never thought she would.

"He's stronger than you think!"

"I think your boyfriend here would have something to say about that," said Amdis. "Considering his…unfortunate state."

"I don't know how many times I have to say it, but we had a deal so—"

"Don't ever make a deal with a vampire," interrupted Kodiak.

Tamaska's heart sank at the coldness around her and the censure in his voice. He pulled back, angry, even in his weakened state. Maybe she'd gone about rescuing Kodiak all wrong. Maybe if she hadn't involved the pack—

No, the vampires want this. But she pushed the agenda that the two of them were fracturing rather than bonding. This is what Kodiak wanted…right?

"I haven't made any agreements with you," snapped Tamsaka. "I've been very careful since I got here. I haven't let Amdis trick me and I'm not the one standing chained up and naked."

"And you never fucking listen." Kodiak's words were so soft she almost missed them, but they were razor sharp and Amdis looked like he was being fed a meal.

Oh Christ, she hoped she was right and Kodiak was also trying to create a feeling of dissent. And it hurt to say the things she'd said to him, just like it hurt to hear his words.

She swallowed, taking in a gulp of air, her misery somehow real and Amdis bared his fangs in a grin and rubbed his hands together.

"Don't tell me, Tamaska, you're not listening to your alpha. My, my, you will get yourself in an awful lot of trouble by breaking the rules. Lucky you're with me now. We're on the winning side of this little war."

"I haven't made a single deal with you, Amdis," Tamaska said.

He laughed. "I hope you don't think the dog's joking here, he means it. They always do. Then again, they're a subspecies. Not worth my time." He looked her over. "And then there's you."

"Say what you want to me. I'm not touching you and I'm not listening. Not until you let him go." She folded her arms as if she had confidence. "Then we can talk. You and me."

"You need to educate her about her new supernatural lifestyle. Her ignorance has made this all too easy for me," said Amdis, glaring at Kodiak.

"Wait, what?" Tamaska whirled around and looked at Kodiak. "What does he mean?"

"She hasn't touched you. And there isn't an agreement. You forced her."

Admis nodded at his vampires, who pulled the wire tight and Kodiak tumbled to his knees, he breathed hard and heavy before he shakily pushed up.

"These aren't normal rules, I suppose," Admis said. But my place, the opal and the ancestor of the opal's owners and I can do what the fuck I want."

"Listen to me Tamaska. Run. I—I didn't know this." A cry broke free as the vampires pulled the wire again and he landed hard, this time he only made it to his knees. "If he's saying this and needs your touch, then...then this must be right. Fucking run."

She looked about and made half a move before stopping as Amdis came right up to her and she narrowly missed touching him.

Oh, God. It was a trap. She didn't even understand most of it, and even Kodiak was surprised, but she stood still. She could keep trying to run, yes, maybe even make it. But she wasn't leaving Kodiak and Admis could move so fast that she'd end up touching him. She stared the Vampire down. "I'm not going anywhere. Not without him. And I turn down this so-called agreement. Deal's off."

Amdis curled his lip. "Just walking in here was agreement enough. You're now bound to me."

"Fuck, no," said Tamaska. Her attitude riled Kodiak, she might as well turn it on Amdis. "I say no. Ever hear of women's lib?"

"What the...?" Amdis narrowed his eyes. "Do I look like I fucking care about human rules. Come here. Now."

The need to go to him was almost overwhelming, but she fought it.

"Or maybe I just wanted Kodiak…" Amdis clucked his tongue. "Maybe I was counting on you being too predictable, Kodiak. Rushing after the vampires and leaving your pack made it so much easier for us to capture you."

"Fuck you, Amdis! Let him go," she said. "I don't believe you."

"She says that but look." Amdis raised his hands. "I'm not holding her, she can leave and yet she stays."

It made no sense he only wanted Kodiak. No, he was trying to confuse them and make her touch him, but something came to her.

"Do you have the Blood Opal?" she asked.

He sighed. "I do, right here inside my jacket pocket. I keep it close to my undead heart as a reminder of my ultimate plan to improve the life of every vampire. If you want it, come and get it."

"Tempting," she said, "but no."

"What if I said I'd let him go and let you touch the opal?"

"I'd say get your damn story straight," she said.

"Tamaska…go…"

She ignored Kodiak, even though it hurt him. But Amdis was throwing everything out to see what stuck, what would bring her close. He'd gone from taunting Kodiak, to taunting her, to arguing and then flipping the script and claiming Kodiak was the one he wanted.

Maybe time was running out or he was getting impatient. But they were at a weird stand off so she pushed her questions.

"How do you plan to do that?" she asked. "I thought you'd already improved their lives after using it to help them tolerate sunlight."

He jerked a little at that. It had only been a guess, but if she'd hit on a truth, maybe that meant her other theory was also correct, that he wanted to use the Blood Opal to turn her into an out-of-control wolf shifter and hunt down the Shadow Pack.

Maybe that's why he needed her to touch him. It would make their bond strong and her psychosis worse...

"If only you'd seen what we did to your friend, and all the others who have come here searching for something beyond their reach. Instead, they've found us. They've discovered a new way of life. And, what can I say? We're hungry for them and their blood.'

"So, what? You bleed out a human, and infuse the blood with the Blood Opal's energy, then have one of your vampires drink it?

Is that going to happen to me? She shivered involuntarily.

"Ahhh, Kodiak, I see why you like this one. She's a clever one. She's worked it all out," said Amdis.

"Stay away from her," Kodiak said.

Amdis chuckled, a nasty sound. "It's late for that."

"Can I see it?" Tamaska asked, her heart pounding loud and clear. A dangerous, half-baked plan started to form.

"I hear that a lot, so you must be more specific. But it's good to know you've got eyes for me, as we will be the winning side. As you know."

"The Blood Opal." She looked at him. "Please?"

Amdis couldn't help himself. He reached inside his jacket pocket, drew out the Blood Opal, and held it up for her to see.

Even the room's dim light was enough to catch the polished surface of the gem, reflecting its beauty. Tamaska's breath caught in her throat. Such a stunning gem was worth well beyond seven figures.

If she touched him, then it would be bad, it seemed, but if she got him to do it, then...then maybe...

"Give it to me," she said.

He shook his head. "Come and get it."

It was time for it to return to her family. Better yet, to return to her—for good.

She held out her hand.

CHAPTER 26

amaska

SHE BROUGHT HER HAND UP, right up, opened palm.

"Tamaska, no."

She ignored Kodiak and put on a dreamy little smile, like she'd given in to the manipulations Amdis was trying to do to her.

He brought the opal down. Not quite touching.

And Kodiak's gaze burned hot. "It's so pretty," she whispered.

"Stop, Tamaska, please! Fight him!"

She ignored the pained cry of Kodiak and Admis grinned at her like he had her, like they were the only ones in the room.

And she couldn't look at Kodiak, because if she did, her resolve might crumble and the terrible manipulations she was attempting wouldn't work at all.

"It's all yours," Amdis said. "Yours and mine, the things we could do."

"Yes, yes." She shifted closer to Kodiak who struggled, even though the wire's burn must be agonizing.

Amdis followed.

And she brought her hand up a little higher. "I want it…" The words came out almost as a moan.

Kodiak snarled and one of the vampires cried out as suddenly the shifter hurled himself up to get Amdis.

Everything seemed to happen at once.

Kodiak howled as the other vampire hit him with a net and he went down so hard she felt it. Amdis was knocked forward and to right himself, his hand came down and touched hers.

She snatched at the opal.

Amdis snarled.

The heavens failed to open and lightning failed to strike, but the vampire had touched her.

It was going to happen, she knew that, but this way, now it had, she had freedom.

Tamaska moved fast. She executed a spinning round-house kick, knocking Amdis hard and sending the Blood Opal flying out of his hand.

"Bitch!" he said, and he dove then, to try and catch the gem. He missed it completely.

It skittered and she used her momentum and shoved him hard, running for it. She had it in her sights. She reached down and—

Something slammed into her back, right between her shoulders. Hard. Air rushed from her lungs and she couldn't keep her footing. She slipped and crashed face-down on the floor with a scream.

Desperate not to lose the gem, she pushed herself up.

Adrenalin pumped through her body, giving her the boost she needed to keep going. She reached for the gem, but the Blood Opal was too far away. Stretching as much as she could, she pushed herself into the air, skidding forward. One of the vampires near the writhing Kodiak—she couldn't let herself think of that—kicked it as she reached for it, sending it into the air.

Cursing she twisted and lunged, her outstretched hand openingnto catch the priceless stone.

She missed and the vampire kicked it again. She leapt for it.

It wasn't enough.

The gem fell just out of her reach and hit the floor hard. A shard chipped away as the gem bounced, then slid to a stop.

Fuck. Did it break?

Did opals break? And if so was this good or bad for her, for the shifters? The vampires? Christ, she didn't know but she still needed to get it.

Tamaska shimmied along the floor, desperate to reach the gem. A commotion erupted behind her, but she focused on the Blood Opal. Its two parts lay side-by-side on the floor. She almost had it, one more shimmy and—

Something grabbed her around the ankles.

"No, you don't."

Automatically, she flipped and kicked Amdis hard. Now he'd touched her she didn't care. She kicked him again for good measure, that one for Kodiak. He cried out and one of his hands lost its grip, giving her the chance to kick some more and try to fend him off.

Tears burned her eyes as she grappled with him. All she wanted was him dead and Kodiak safe. This time, she aimed at his groin, not knowing if that would affect the bloodsucker, but she did it anyway.

The Opal had been so close to becoming hers once again. "You can't have it, stupid bitch. And now we're bonded!"

Bonded? She felt nothing but hate for him, certainly not a bond. Unless...unless it had to do with who had the damned opal.

"Give up or they'll kill him."

"No, you won't." She kicked him again, hard and tried to turn to get the opal.

He grabbed a kicking leg, his cold fingers digging deep. "Do you know me?"

"No," she said, "and I don't want to. And you won't hurt him because you know I won't help."

"I. Don't. Need. Your. Help." He grabbed higher.

She put all her strength into her next kick and sent him stumbling back.

Kodiak moaned but she couldn't do a thing until she got the opal, and she wasn't about to give up, not when the opal was literally within reach.

The vampire grabbed her again. Something snapped inside her, releasing fierce energy. Strength flooded her as she kicked at Amdis.

No way would she let him use her blood or turn her. She'd rather die. And she couldn't let him hurt Kodiak any further. She'd kill this bastard and drink his blood if she had to to save Kodiak.

"You can't win this," hissed Amdis as his fangs elongated, prepared to bite.

"No, you can't." She freed herself from his grip and skittered backwards, before jumping to her feet.

But a glance at Kodiak cost her dearly. Amdis rushed her, and his hands wrapped around her neck before she could defend herself.

"We already touched remember? You're mine. It's a weaker link than I'd have liked but it'll do. You should have listened to your dog and stayed away." He didn't look at Kodiak as he directed his next words to him. "I'm doing you a favor by taking her."

Tamaska turned to face Amdis. "Asshole."

His dark eyes sent sharp, cold chills coursing through her like icicles.

She forced herself to relax, even though it went against her instincts. Tamaska had to escape with the gem and Kodiak, no matter what.

"You're not going anywhere," said Amdis. His hands relaxed around her neck, enough to give her the chance she needed. She threw her arms up, flicking his hands away while diving into a squat.

Then she swung a leg out and swept it around Amdis. It connected with the back of his knees, forcing a reflex that sent him crashing to the floor. His head landed hard with a sickening crack.

Scrambling to her feet, Tamaska moved toward the Blood Opal. Then, the sight of Kodiak changed her mind. He was up, barely, and he had managed to get the net off and tried to fight the vampires.

Tamaska rushed to Kodiak instead of the opal. He was already bruised and battered with new scrapes and bruises and he swayed, his two vampire attackers clearly taking sick pleasure in hurting him. They circled him, striking him harder and harder in turns, tormenting him. Even as he tried to fight.

The silver reflection around his wrists caught her attention. The chain tethered him to one of the vampires.

Tamaska grabbed the chain. Small and delicate, it didn't seem nearly enough to bind Kodiak. But it had still rendered him weak, unable to properly defend himself.

It had no effect on her. Surprised, she tugged at the astonishingly strong chain. The vampire holding it stumbled towards her, the unexpected force unbalancing him.

A well-executed kick to the vampire's guts sent him doubling over, and he dropped the chain. Moving faster than she thought possible, Tamaska unwrapped the chain from Kodiak's wrists and pulled it off him.

His demeanor changed immediately. He stood up, no longer vulnerable, and flexed his arms. He was still weak but he seemed to get stronger by the second.

He growled as another change occurred within him, and Tamaska stepped back fascinated she'd never seen him change and she couldn't move for those moments, chain in her hands.

Within seconds, a wolf stood before her, eyes ablaze with anger, his majestic ochre pelt bristling. Kodiak spun, leapt gracefully into the air, landed on one of the vampires, and tore it apart through its unsettling screams.

Now that Kodiak could fight, Tamaska turned toward the Blood Opal. Amdis was on all fours, patting the ground as he searched for it.

"Oh, no, you don't." She rushed forward and kicked him hard in the guts, pushing him over.

He turned and hissed at her. Then rushed at her.

Fear chilled her blood, and her whole body ached as if icicles circulated in her veins. She froze, shocked at his speed.

She shouldn't be. She'd seen it before, but so close...it scared her. How had she ever thought they could run away?

Then Amdis sprawled on the ground with Kodiak snapping at his face.

Tamaska exhaled, she thought she spied Blood Opal She sprinted around Kodiak and Amdis as they fought. She had to get the gem. She couldn't let it remain in the vampires' hands.

It wasn't there, just a shard of glass reflecting low light.

"Oh no!"

She searched frantically but didn't see it. Dropping to her knees, Tamaska slowly picked her way across the floor with trembling hands. It had to be there somewhere.

A whimper from Kodiak made her jump. They both fought fiercely, giving their opponent a run for their money.

Hang in there, Kodiak.

The need to feel the Blood Opal in her hands jolted Tamaska into action. She searched for the gem's cold, solid form as she moved across the floor, hoping her hands would feel anything her eyes missed in the dim lighting.

Tamaska widened her search, moving in larger circles.

"Come on, come on," she said, glancing over her shoulder to see Kodiak and Amdis still fighting.

Did Amdis take it already? She shuddered at the thought, refusing to believe it.

Her fingers touched something hard and cold, and Tamaska picked it up. The largest piece of the Blood Opal. Stunning even under subpar conditions, it caught enough dim light to show off the amazing shades of red embedded in its pearly reflections. A new lightning-shaped crack carved its way down the middle of the gem and extended into countless branches, some of which led to where a chip had broken away.

She returned to her search, determined to find the other piece she'd seen break off from the gem. Had that shard been the only one?

Tamaska continued, pushing away the sounds of snarling. She couldn't leave the last piece of opal in the nightclub. If she did, the vampires might be able to use it against her.

She slipped the opal fragment into her pocket, then scanned every millimeter of the floor around the gem's point of impact.

Behind her, the fight intensified. She had to dive out of the way as the two rolled over each other.

Then, she saw the small piece that had chipped away from the Blood Opal.

Before she could snatch it up, Amdis rushed over to her and pushed her to the ground.

"I can't let you live, not when you're destined to do so much more," said Amdis.

Where was Kodiak? A cry broke as she turned.

Kodiak lay on the ground, unmoving.

"Nooo…" A keening broke from her like her heart shattered.

A slamming door made them both jump.

As Amdis turned Tamaska swallowed her grief and hauled ass up from the ground and kicked the shard from Amdis' hand.

She picked it up, then turned as the wolves poured into the nightclub. For the first time in her life, her childhood fear didn't surface, didn't cripple her. Her time spent with the pack had healed her.

"You haven't seen the last of me," said Amdis. He was outnumbered as the pack members hurried into the night-club, and he knew it. Instead of fighting alone, he chose to flee.

In a shadowy blur, Amdis was gone. He fled the nightclub, but Tamaska didn't care. She held both pieces of the Blood Opal in her hand, and they fit together perfectly.

The gem was finally hers, right there in her hand. It might have broken, but it still held breathtaking beauty. She slipped it into the pocket of her loose trousers, hands trembling.

Had they really done it? Could she dare to hope it was all over? They had the Blood Opal, and Amdis couldn't turn her.

Even though they'd touched…

The pack rushed to Kodiak's side and nuzzled him. He barely responded.

Tamaska fell to the floor beside him to put her hand on his bloodied fur.

Please, please be all right.

He didn't move.

CHAPTER 27

amaska

SHAKING, she gently stroked Kodiak's fur. His breath came fast and shallow as pain raked through him.

"We did it. We have the Blood Opal," she said, unsure if he could hear her. "And I'm so sorry I said those things. You know I was just trying to throw him, right? You were magnificent. My hero. Oh, Kodiak, please…please don't die…"

He made a tiny moan but the panting, shallow breaths worried her.

Everything in her twisted and guilt came crashing down. She'd said those horrible things to him. What if he believed her? After all their fighting and her stupid, pushy ways…he might.

She wanted to say she loved him that he was everything, a true leader and so brave, that how he'd fought the horrible chains was… She didn't have words.

She wanted to tell him that the fights, her anger and resentment of being locked out...her disobedience...that was just her trying to find her way, to adjust, to fit into a world she was only beginning to understand.

But she couldn't.

All that was selfish.

And not one word of it would make things better.

She'd thought she could walk in there and just save him.

Deep down though, she knew she'd had to. Even now. It might have been wrong, she might have put everyone in danger, but she had to. What else was she meant to have done?

Let him die?

"It's going to be all right," she whispered, kissing his furry head, breathing in the scent of him so clean and pure that lingered beneath the blood and gunk. "You're going to be all right. I know it."

Then his breathing got shallower and panic scrabbled at her and she looked up.

"Roan?" she called.

Oh, God. She hadn't...where was he? Had he survived the fight outside? And what about the others?

Roan approached, changed back into human form, and knelt beside Kodiak.

"Will he..." The words stuck in her throat.

He touched her shoulder as he knelt close to Kodiak and put his nose to his, closing his eyes. He seemed to listen, then he nodded and looked up at her, face grave.

"I think so," Roan said. "But we need to get him out of here. There are still vampires around."

"Kodiak, can you walk?" asked Roan.

Kodiak trembled, and Roan dragged Tamaska backward. She fought until she realized her shifter was changing back into human form. But to her eyes, it didn't seem right. The transformation was slow and painful. Not quick and easy like Roan's had been and she pushed a hand against her mouth to stop a cry escaping.

Kodiak fell, but with a groan, pushed himself into a sitting position.

And all she wanted to do was grab him, hold him. But she couldn't move. Roan kept his hand on her shoulder like a warning to stay put.

"I think so," said Kodiak breathlessly.

He stumbled as he tried to get to his feet. But he fell and the freeze inTamaska broke. She shook off Roan and hurried to Kodiak's side, helping him to stand with Roan's support.

"I'll be all right in a moment," said Kodiak with a gasp, and he leaned on Roan.

She bit her lip, tears slipping free. "I was so worried…"

He didn't speak to her as the rest of the pack suddenly burst into the room, like they knew he was up and about.

Tamaska had never been so happy to see the rest of the before. Right now they represented a kind of home, familiarity and every face she saw meant someone else had survived.

Channing approached, then changed back to his human form. His skin held onto the remnants of a fight, spotted with bits of fur, his own blood, and someone else's.

She felt about for the opal. It was there, and she found that wire was there, too. She must have stuffed it in there without thinking. She pulled it out to ask someone, but Channing went to pass her and she reached for him to hug him. So happy he'd survived. She'd grown fond of him.

But he didn't seem pleased. In fact he backed away, arms raised.

Bile rose in her mouth. They all hated her. She looked about and the rest backed away, including Kodiak. She looked around, scared and took one step towards Channing. "Please, what—"

"Keep that away from me." Channing scrambled farther away from Tamaska, fear in his wide eyes as the wire swung out.

"This? But—"

"What are you doing with a silver chain?" asked Ash after she morphed into human form. She backed away, too, eyes accusing.

Tamaska looked down at the silver chain in her hands, which was so delicate yet so strong. "It was around Kodiak."

"Silver is our one weakness. Keep it away from us," said Ash. "Now. Never, ever bring silver in here. Ever."

"Noted." She rolled up the chain and shoved it into her pocket.

"We should get out of here," said Onai, nursing an oozing cut on his shoulder.

"Let's go. Stay alert, they won't let us go easily," said Kodiak, pushing Roan away so he could walk. He only took a step before stumbling, which prompted Roan and Onai to catch him.

Tamaska hurried to assist them, but Kodiak veered away, bumping into Onai, who cursed as the wound on Onai's shoulder widened, and more blood spilled out.

"Get the silver away from me," growled Kodiak. "Now!"

Ash pulled Tamaska aside. "He's too weak, after so much exposure. Now he's more sensitive to it."

"I didn't know," said Tamaska, moving away from Kodiak while all she wanted was to be as close to him as possible. "Th-they threw a net on him, too. I think it was silver."

"Bastards."

She almost threw the chain up behind the bar, but stopped. Because what if the vampires did come back and they found it? And then used it...? She couldn't be responsible for that. Instead she bundled it right at the bottom of her pocket and put the opal over it.

No, she couldn't risk leaving it. She'd nearly lost him. And he was still weak, he'd used his strength to fight and save her and it tore her apart with guilt.

She looked at his male beauty. To her it shone, even when he was so beaten up.

She…she could've lost him. Just the sight of him filled a hollow within her she hadn't realized existed.

Is this part of the bond between us?

As they moved towards the exit, Tamaska stretched her senses into that bond. It was strong. And now she knew Kodiak was all right, it was a warm, unbreakable glow. Did that sensation mean that a growing, all-consuming emptiness would threaten to consume her if something bad ever happened to him?

She swallowed hard.

"I reckon you're getting it," said Ash, walking alongside Tamaska.

"What?"

"The bond thing," said Ash.

"How did you know?"

Ash shrugged. "I just did. Maybe you've become part of the pack already."

A small smile wanted to break free. From Ash, that sounded like high praise. And she hoped the shifter was right. Being part of the pack would be being part of a family.

And it would mean she'd be able to be with Kodiak.

If he still wanted her.

But she hoped he did. From the bond, it seemed like they were all right, or would be.

She wanted, she realized, it all.

This new life felt like hers, despite being so different from her human life. Although it had rocked her to the core and totally torn apart all she'd ever known, she ached to be part of that new, parallel life, the one bursting with wolf shifters and vampires.

Okay, maybe not the vampires.

"Hang in there," said Ash, stepping away. "And lose the silver, yeah? It's giving me a headache."

'I don't know what to do with it," said Tamaska. She pulled it out of her pocket, and every nearby shifter immediately moved away from her. "If I throw it, what if the vampires get it?

Ash threw her hands up. "Argh!"

Tamaska couldn't believe something so mundane and flimsy could be such a powerful weapon against the wolf shifters. She made a mental note to toss her silver earrings later. As a matter of practicality, her love for silver was now over.

Get rid of it," Ash said. "Now."

Startled, she threw the chain down, then let it slide across the floor.

"I don't think you should've done that," said Channing.

Tamaska didn't even get to ask why before a vampire dropped down from the upstairs balcony and snatched the chain.

"Fuck," said Tamaska. Right after she'd said that about the stupid chain. She'd thought the fight was over—she'd been banking on it.

"The fight's never over," Ash said before changing into wolf form. "Sorry about making you chuck the chain."

Tamaska watched in horror as two more vampires closed in, baring their teeth and hissing.

"If I can't have you, Tamaska, then I'll kill you and your friends," announced Amdis from the safety of the balcony.

"Coward," Tamaska yelled back at him. She moved out of

Roan and Onai's way as they hurried over to help Kodiak walk. "It's because I've got the opal, isn't it?"

His eyes lit up and she bit her lip.

"Tamaska!" That was Channing. "Don't tell him!"

"Get Kodiak to the van, and get out of here," Tamaska said.

"You're not their alpha," said Kodiak. "I am."

"I'll stay," said Onai. "You go."

"You will not. You're both too wounded. Get the fuck out of the way so you don't get killed, or kill me instead," said Tamaska firmly. She was the only one there that could tolerate silver, so it was up to her to retrieve the chain. Shadow Pack's hierarchy could fuck off—a strict sense of order wouldn't save them now. They needed more.

"Take the opal," she said, loudly as she could.

She didn't say who. She wasn't giving it up on the off chance Amdis could sense it. But she figured if he didn't know who had it after her unfortunate slip it might help.

"Go," she hissed.

"No—" Kodiak said.

Tamaska missed the rest of his protest as she rushed toward the vampire who'd grabbed the silver chain.

Ash, in wolf form, snapped at his heels, distracting him. Tamaska took the opening to rush in and grabbed the dangling length of silver. She began to dart away, but the chain pulled taut, stopping her in her tracks.

She turned to see the vampire laughing at her, pulling the chain to reel her back to him.

That hadn't played out quite the way she'd imagined. She redoubled her efforts, straining against his pull. But he was too strong.

Time to mix things up. She released her grip on the chain, and the vampire was taken unaware. He stumbled back-wards, the momentum overpowering him—but he wasn't the only one affected. Tamaska couldn't keep her balance, either, and she tumbled forward landing on the vampire.

She screamed and pushed it away as its fangs approached her skin.

Ash leapt to her aid, snarling before pushing Tamaska out of the way. A sharp pain tore through her upper arm as she rolled away.

Ash fought the vampire, but her movements were slow, fatigued. The vampire easily gained the upper hand.

Tamaska gripped her left bicep, trying to quell the blood spurting from her wound. She winced as she got to her feet. There was no time to worry about an injury, especially a bloody one. After all that fighting, the vampires would be hungry, and she didn't want to become their next target.

The chain slipped to the ground.

Tamaska snatched it up. Immediately, Ash's fighting improved. Soon, she was tearing the vampire to pieces.

She pushed the silver back into her pocket. She couldn't let it fall into the vampires' hands again.

The rest of the wolves were still fighting the vampires, wounded and struggling but slowly gaining the advantage.

Tamaska rushed toward the door to keep the silver safe, hoping that would be enough to help the wolves finish off the few remaining vampires.

"This isn't over!" yelled Amdis. "Mark my words.

"No one says that," she said. "And it's over!"

"Your blood will be mine." Amdis smacked the railing, then turned and strode away.

After the pack finished off the last vampires, some switched back into human forms. They protectively closed ranks around Tamaska.

"Channing, go help them bring the van up. We need to get the fuck out of here," Tamaska said, out of breath. She was touched that they were finally treating her like one of their own. Had she finally proven herself to them, or was it a result of her bond with Kodiak?

Right then she didn't know or care; her wound still bled and everything hurt, and she missed Kodiak with a physical ache.

"Okay," said Channing before leaving through the exit.

"If silver is your weakness, then what's the vampires'?" Tamaska asked. "Garlic? Holy water?" She tried to recall the fantasy movies she'd watched over the years.

"No, don't bother with that. The only thing that can stop them is light," said Ash, limping up to her.

And yet, they now could somehow move about in the sunlight.

Because of the opal. Because of her family. Because of her.

"Come on, we need to get out of here. We got what we wanted," said Tamaska, pushing those thoughts down as she touched the pocket where the Blood Opal lay.

They made their way outside into the night. No one was around, which felt suspicious. Surely something must be lurking in the shadows—more vampires? Or something even worse.

The pack must have looked like a walking advertisement for the world's darkest kinks, pouring naked out of the nightclub, smeared with blood and cuts.

The sound of the van chugging through the cold of the night drew Tamaska's attention down the road, the vehicle their only hope of getting out of there. How many of the pack had been wounded? Tamaska would have to include herself in that tally, her wounds finally throbbing as her body broke down the surge of adrenalin.

Channing eased the van up the road, then stopped with a jolt to let in the passengers.

"Hurry up," he said. "There's more of them out here, in the shadows."

"What? We can't just drive around until the sun comes up," said Tamaska. "And how exactly does one lose a vampire, anyway?"

"Always with the questions." His tone was mild and light. "Don't worry. I've had the outside of the van reinforced. We're safer in here," said Channing. "Those of us who can't fight so well anymore are, that is. The rest can fight!" He glanced at her arm. "What happened?"

"I…don't know." Tamaska slid into the backseat next to Kodiak, who had a blanket around him. His eyes flickered open, and he smiled at her. She took his hand and squeezed.

"I'll meet you at the clubhouse," said Ash.

Her heart lurched. Kodiak had said those same words to her, and that hadn't turned out so well.

"Get in," said Tamaska.

"No, I can still fight. We're a pack. Besides, Roan must stay with you to look after the wounded."

"Make sure no one else gets wounded," said Roan firmly. "I've got my hands full."

"And you make damn well sure you find your way back to the clubhouse," she said.

"I will. We all will." Ash flashed a grin. "There are hardly any vamps left out here. Once you leave, they'll give up. They need to regroup. This round goes to us."

"Kill a few more, just to be sure," said Tamaska.

"I will." Ash closed the door.

Tamaska eased closer to Kodiak, but he winced. She quickly pulled away, afraid he didn't want her, afraid he was in pain.

Just plain afraid.

Channing sped away from the Blood Moon nightclub, the speed gluing Tamaska to the hard backseat.

"Take it easy," Roan called out. "I get sick, remember?"

"They have pills for that," said Channing, refusing to slow down even as something solid struck the front of the van.

"Fucking vampires," said Channing. "Get him, Ash, get him."

Tamaska shifted to look out the windscreen. Outside, a vampire limped away with a wolf hot on its heels.

Channing pumped the brakes and spun the steering wheel in a sharp turn, sending everyone sliding to the right.

"Do you need help?" asked Tamaska.

"I'd say get the gun out of the glovebox and start shooting, but that's probably not a good idea in the city after dark," said Channing.

"Probably not." She slammed into Kodiak during another sharp turn, then righted herself. She remembered the silver in her pocket. The chain was probably causing residual damage even as they rode in the van. She took out the chain.

"Hey, get that covered or something," Roan, said wincing in pain as he turned to check on the injured in the way back.

"Sorry." Tamaska opened a metal toolbox by her feet and tossed the silver chain inside before closing the lid.

"That's better." Roan handed her a wad of bandages. "For your arm. Press on them hard to stop the bleeding."

She took the cloth and pressed it into her wound. She hated feeling so helpless.

Then Kodiak squeezed her hand. The world turned bright for her.

Maybe all she needed to do now was sit beside him and hope for the best—that every wolf would make it back alive.

CHAPTER 28

 *amaska*

PACING KODIAK'S ROOM, she completed another lap, hand still pressing the now-bloodied cloth into her left bicep.

Roan inspected the cuts and abrasions on Kodiak's body. Some of the smaller scratches had already healed. It amazed Tamaska how quickly the wolves could heal, especially since her wound had only just now stopped bleeding.

They'd made it back to the clubhouse without any more incidents. Now, they waited for the others to return. Tamaska couldn't stand it. She wanted to have them all back, to know they were safe. Channing had taken his post at security, along with the others Roan had finished patching up.

"I should be out there helping," she said. She wanted to be here, too, watching over Kodiak, but the guilt of getting them into all this trouble ate at her and if Kodiak was going to be fine then that's where she should be, helping.

But Roan shook his head. "You need to be in here."

Panic flared up and she grabbed Roan.

"Will he be all right?" asked Tamaska. He was weak, and it hurt to see him like that, but if something horrible was wrong, then—

"I just need rest," said Kodiak as he waved a hand in the air, looking pale and ashen. The remainder of his wounds, though fading worried her.

"Are you sure? He—"

"A lot of rest, Tamaska" said Roan, standing. "And some tablets to help."

Roan rummaged around in his bag, then handed some white pills to Kodiak.

"Do I have to?" asked Kodiak. He glared at the pills like they were the cause of all his problems.

"You're lucky, Kodiak. No one else in the pack could withstood the pain of silver, and you did. But you're going to pay for it."

"How much?" He accepted the tablets, then swallowed them. He grimaced.

"Not money. I'm putting you on bedrest indefinitely, for a start," said Roan. "So rest."

"I can't do that." Kodiak shifted on the bed, aiming to get up, but his body protested. He groaned in pain before flopping back onto the mattress. "You can't do that."

"I can and you don't have a choice. If you don't take it easy, you'll make things worse in the long run. You'll stay weak, and you know that'll threaten your position as alpha."

"But he'll get better if he rests?" asked Tamaska suddenly anxious.

Roan looked at her. "As long as he doesn't overdo it."

Of course Kodiak would overdo it. He wouldn't be Kodiak otherwise.

And it wasn't over. They all knew that. Especially Kodiak. He didn't have to tell her, he wanted his revenge, to end this horror show so badly the room almost vibrated with it. Although Tamaska had reclaimed the Blood Opal, the vampires were most definitely still a threat.

Who knew what they would do, now that their precious gem had been lost?

Tamaska took the Blood Opal out from her pocket and looked at it. The stone reflected the room's light, showing off its brilliance despite a crack down the center and a missing shard.

"We got it back?" asked Kodiak. He held out his hand, and Tamaska gave him the gem.

"I think it's broken," said Tamaska.

"No way to know for sure, I suppose." Kodiak turned it over in his hands.

She rubbed her arms. "Amdis didn't go after it, not once it cracked."

"Hmmm, you could be right. We can always test it."

"How? We don't want my blood coming in contact with it."

"That ship's already sailed," said Kodiak, his voice light.

A chill ran through Tamaska. "What?"

Kodiak held up the gem. "You've got blood on your hands."

"Oh...I thought I was being careful." Horror spread through her.

"It's not doing anything," Kodiak said as he handed it back to Tamaska.

"Maybe it needs more blood?" But somehow, she knew.

Turning it over in her hands, adding more of her blood to its surface, didn't provoke a change in its appearance. Even as her blood soaked into the gem, no power was released, no abilities enhanced. It was no longer a threat to her or a boon to the vampires.

"No, it's broken. I know it." It was a relief to say the

words, knowing the security that had been granted to her after the gem's destruction. But the stone had also made her feel connected to her ancestors—part of her lineage that, until recently, had been hidden and forgotten.

"It's yours now," Kodiak said, interrupting her thoughts.

"I don't know what to do with it." Her whole plan in retrieving the Blood Opal had been to return it to its owners so she could get on with her work as an event planner. But there was no going back to that life. She no longer belonged to that world, and her urge to give the Blood Opal back had disappeared. It was part of her heritage. "All this…for nothing."

"Not nothing. If it isn't working then you fixed the vampiric problem. They should go back to their normal light hating selves," he said. "I'm not saying they'll give up coming for us; Amdis has an ax to grind. And we're not going to let them rest and wreak their regular havoc, either."

"I hope that's true," she said. "I just…I guess I hoped the opal could bring us something, but now it's not even worth money."

She placed its two pieces on top of the bedside table.

"You don't have to decide anything right now. But at least you've learned about an entirely new world," said Kodiak.

"A world I want to be part of, fully," said Tamaska, looking deeply into his eyes.

He nodded. "I'll turn you at the full moon, in a few days," said Kodiak.

Tamaska smiled, joy surging. "You will?"

"I will. On one condition."

"What?"

He took her hand and linked their fingers. "That you become my mate, in both human and wolf forms."

"Is that because of the bond thing you keep mentioning?"

"Yes." He studied her face. "You feel it?"

"I do." Tamaska's heart swelled and she couldn't keep the smile from her face.

"Then you'll be my mate?"

"I will." She leaned over, and kissed him softly. His salty taste burst on her lips, along with his promise.

Their kiss deepened, rolling slowly, full of passion, heat, and sweetness. She wrapped her arms around him, falling into the world of the kiss, of all it held and he pulled her closer, growling softly so that her body came alive with that sweet ache of need.

"Sorry to interrupt you two lovebirds, but I haven't finished," said Roan, clearing his throat.

"Oh, I'm fine," said Kodiak. "More than fine. And would be even better if you went the fuck away."

"Yes, I see you are, but Tamaska isn't," said Roan, holding up a needle and thread.

Tamaska swallowed hard, and stood. "Is that for me?"

"Yep. Now, sit back down so I can stitch you up. That's a nasty gash."

Tamaska sat next to Kodiak.

"I need to clean it up first," said Roan, putting down the needle and thread. "This is going to sting."

Tamaska braced herself and he got himself ready.

"Fuck." Agonizing stings flooded her senses as he started to clean the wound, and she closed her eyes and held her breath.

"Fuck. Are you done yet?" she said, her voice tight with pain.

No one spoke for a long moment.

"Just getting started." Roan patted the wound as he cleaned the outside with gauze. She moaned at the pain. "How did you get this gash?"

Tamaska didn't like his tone. Something was wrong.

"I don't remember. Everything happened so fast." She opened her eyes and frowned.

"It doesn't look like a fang mark," said Roan. He turned her arm to one side, then the other, inspecting the wound.

"What else could have made it?" asked Tamaska. "A knife?"

"It's not a clean cut, so it can't be from a knife." He looked at her with concern in his eyes, then glanced at Kodiak.

"What, then?" growled Kodiak. "Out with it."

"It was a claw."

"What does that mean?" Tamaska glanced from one of the men to the other. "K-Kodiak?

"Are you fucking sure about that, Roan?" asked Kodiak.

"Yes."

"Think, Tamaska," he said. "Were you fighting near any wolves?"

Tamaska paused to think. "Only Ash. Come to think of it, she pushed me off of a vampire. That's when I hurt my arm."

"Fuck," said Kodiak. "Oh, fuck."

"I need a little more than that to understand what's going on here." She snapped the words, as fear and confusion pecked at her.

More silence. Finally Kodiak muttered something then looked at the other shifter. "Would that have worked, Roan?"

"No way of knowing." The shifter cleared his throat. "It's not the full moon."

The panic was in full swing now. Was one of the vampires a different sort of monster? Had it done something terrible to her? Or...Or... "What the fuck are you two talking about?"

"Ash has already turned you," said Kodiak. "Potentially, anyway."

Now she couldn't speak. Tamaska just stared. Thoughts ran like crazy in her brain. But she took deep breaths and made herself speak. "How?"

"She scratched you," said Kodiak.

"But that was an accident. She can't turn me, not like that. You're going to turn me." Tamaska stood, panic in her voice, in her veins. She stared at Kodiak. Then at Roan, finally at Kodiak once more. "I mean, I can't be."

"Nothing like this has ever happened before, I'm not sure if you've been fully turned or not."

More panic rushed her and her throat started to close over. "But isn't that dangerous?"

Kodiak nodded. "Very dangerous."

"So, what do I do? Am I going to turn into a wolf at the next full moon?" asked Tamaska. It was a wonder she wasn't screaming or fainting. She just stood there. Not knowing what the hell she should do.

"Is she, Roan?" asked Kodiak.

"Maybe." He started to stitch the wound, and she flinched.

"And what happens if I don't?"

"You could die," said Roan softly.

"So, what do I do to stop that from happening?" asked Tamaska. She couldn't stop the panic now, it shook in her voice. A couple of minutes ago she'd been so happy, and now...now...now she might lose him. Fuck, she might lose her life. "Is there?"

"I could bite you on the full moon," said Kodiak.

"Good. Do that, then." That didn't sound so hard. She breathed a small sigh of relief . "Just bite me, and I'll know that you're the one who turned me."

Kodiak remained silent.

"There's more?"

"If Ash is the one who turned you, then you'll be linked to her."

"Like our bond?" Suddenly her eyes widened. "Will that go? Will it?"

"No, nothing can take that away from us," said Kodiak.

"This is different. She's the one who'll show you how to be a wolf."

"So, she needs to bite me?" But…she wanted that to be him, her soon-to-be mate. Or would it just put a stop to that too? Tears burned her eyes and she made a small sound. "I… why can't it be you?"

"She has to do it, Tamaska. To make sure you transform properly," said Kodiak.

"No. You're the one who's supposed to bite me," said Tamaska. "You. So I can be your mate. So I can be truly bonded to you. It has to be like that. I might have latent shifter genes, but I'm still on a level human and…if you don't then what happens to us?"

Kodiak and Roan exchanged a look.

"Well, there's no point in both of us biting you." Kodiak tried to take her hand. "It might confuse you when you're in wolf form."

"Like hell, it will." She snatched her hand away.

"You don't understand the risks. I don't want to lose you." He stared at her. "What if you change, but can't control yourself and get trapped in wolf form?"

She shook her head. "I won't."

"You are so fucking stubborn," he muttered. "You also don't know that, none of us do. That's the fucking point."

"What about my genes?" She pointed at the broken opal. "I've got genes that will help me transform properly. It'll be fine."

He grabbed a pillow, punched it, and put it behind his back as he sat up. "You just said you wanted it to be me because you're still human, even though you have those fucking genes. You can't have it both ways, Tamaska." Kodiak took a breath. "And I can't be sure."

"I can."

"You can wish, but you can't be sure." He crossed his

arms. "No one can. And I'm not risking it. I'm the fucking Alpha. I'll be your Alpha, so start obeying me, starting with this or—"

"What? You'll banish me?"

"No, I'll put you over my knee and fucking spank you." He looked at her. "Tamaska, I'm saying not to protect you, now, come the fuck here."

Kodiak held his arms out toward her. She paused, wanting to argue some more because he was wrong, but also she really wanted to go to him and have him hold her and wrap her in the comfort and love she could see.

Tamaska sighed and got on the bed, snuggling down into his embrace. He didn't feel like his usual strong self, but it didn't matter. It was Kodiak, holding her and that was everything right then. Everything.

"We will work out it, Tamaska." He brushed his lips over her temple. "Our bond is more important."

"I don't like not knowing. Everything is so…complicated." She buried her head against his chest.

"It won't be like this forever, I promise."

Tamaska hoped that was true.

"I'll leave you two alone. Remember, you're meant to be resting," said Roan.

"Yeah, yeah. Go get some rest yourself," said Kodiak.

Roan closed the door softly behind him.

"Oh, that reminds me," said Kodiak. He moved to brush her hair with his hand.

Her body responded to his touch, and she held him tighter.

"What?" asked Tamaska, enjoying a moment of peace with him.

"You were doing that whole bossy thing again, you know," he said.

"I couldn't help it."

"I know. Don't tell anyone, but I'm glad you did."

"You're kidding me, right?" She sat upright to look directly at him. Was she hearing things? "You also just berated me and threatened to spank me."

"Spanking you might not have been strictly disciplinary." Kodiak chuckled, his eyes fluttering between open and closed as he struggled against the sleeping pills Roan had given him.

"Are you kidding?" she asked coming back to settle against him. "About being glad?"

"Nope. Not kidding. But don't do it again."

Tamaska smiled. Maybe a grey area existed for her within the pack after all, a role where she could belong without having to be so submissive.

"I did save your ass," teased Tamaska.

"Yes, lucky for me, you did. I think I've still got you beat, though."

"What do you mean?"

"I've saved your ass more." He reached around her waist and pinched her hard on the ass.

"Ouch." She laughed, slapping away his hand.

"Damn Roan for giving me those pills." Kodiak drew his hand back, letting it droop to his side. "Otherwise, I'd give you a thorough checkup."

"When you wake up, then." She squeezed him tight. She was grateful they were together and they'd survived another vampire attack.

But it wasn't over. Would they survive the next one?

CHAPTER 29

amaska

SHE AWOKE, terrible pain throbbing in her arm, a reminder of her unwelcome, improper change. She snuggled closer to Kodiak and tried to ignore it and find comfort in her dreams.

But those seemed to be light in supply for her.

Light streamed into the room, and Kodiak remained asleep, thanks to the medication.

She took a slow breath as she let herself dive into the moment. Of what it was and what it meant.

She was here. With Kodiak.

He's asked her to be his mate, his parter, one of his pack. She'd nearly lost him. On so many levels, she'd nearly lost him. But now…

He slept. Alive. Hers. Safe.

Tamaska sighed softly and ran her fingers over the side of his face, her skin tingling at his warmth. Reveling in the stubble there.

Yes. She had come too close to losing him. Way too close.

It wouldn't happen again. She would chain herself to him if she had to. She smiled to herself. She wouldn't have to do that to stay connected with him, not since she'd learned the true nature of their bond.

Her head still spun a little at that, how the bond was more than love or duty or something like marriage, it was belonging, love and blood and bone and minds and hearts. They were mates.

And it was all such a beautiful thing.

Like him.

He could make her want to spit broken glass when he got her mad and she'd crawl over fire to save him. He could also make her melt with a look or a touch or a word, and they made love…

"Kodiak," she whispered, wanting to say his name, like it cemented everything.

The bond was strength and warmth flowing between them, reassuring her of their connection, was like nothing she'd ever felt before. Is this what it meant to be a wolf, to be part of a pack? If it did, she rather liked it.

Hunger drove her away from the comfort of the bed. Who knew when he would wake up? She felt the pills were strong because the man was like an ox, and to get him asleep would take a lot. The fact he'd fought the silver so hard for so long…

He needed the sleep.

Of course, having thought that, he'd most likely wake soon.

If she was quick, she might get back before he stirred. Then, maybe, they could have some intimate time together, to help keep their bond strong. Obviously.

The excuse for sex made her smile. She'd use it on him in the future as a joke, a tease, maybe a way to smooth future fights because she knew there'd be some. They were both too strong willed to not clash from time to time.

Tamaska slipped off the bed. Already dressed, she left the room, heading for the clubhouse kitchen.

The house was quiet in the midmorning as its residents slept off their injuries from the fight last night. Most had chosen to sleep in. But the pain that had stopped Tamaska from sleeping any longer, was still there, the stitches pulling tight whenever she moved.

Tamaska opened the fridge. To her disappointment, there was a lot of meat, like the pack was ready to throw a big barbeque. Not what she wanted to eat right now. She picked up some cheese, broke off a chunk, then nibbled on that while searching the cupboards.

Some biscuits were about all she could find, so she snacked on them while making a cup of instant coffee.

"What are you doing up?" asked Ash as she entered the kitchen. She looked like she'd been out for a run or working out in the gym.

"I could ask you the same thing."

"I'm not injured, nor do I have a boyfriend." Ash winked, pulling some juice from the fridge and pouring it into a glass.

"Coffee?" asked Tamaska, ignoring Ash's insinuation even as her skin heated.

"Sure, thanks." Ash sat on a stool behind the high counter as Tamaska made the coffee. "What's on your mind?"

She paused, looking down at the coffee. "What makes you think there's something on my mind?"

"It's a pack thing. I'm right, so spill."

Oh, shit. Roan hadn't said a word. Did she even know? It didn't sound like it and Ash was pretty much what you see is what you get kind of woman, which she respected, so she hazarded a guess Ash was still in the dark. She flicked the shifter a glance.

"They think you changed me," said Tamaska, handing Ash a cup of coffee. "Is that even possible?"

"I'm sorry, but yes." Ash wrapped her hands around the cup as steam snaked out from its top.

She nodded. "So, that means you have to show me how to act in wolf form, or something like that?"

"I do." Ash put her hand on Tamaska's arm. "And I'm pretty sure if you know all this—which I didn't, not the scratch part—you'd know I'm the one to show you. I have to be."

Exactly what Kodiak had said.

She took a sip of her coffee. Then looked at Ash.

"I wanted Kodiak to show me," Tamaska said with a small sigh.

"I know." Ash took a deep breath. "You know what, though?"

Tamaska frowned at Ash. It was amazing that she'd already healed from her injuries. "What?"

"It's better if I show you," said Ash. "How to do all this."

"But he was meant to turn me and he would have shown me so how is this better?"

"Do you really want your mate showing you?" Ash shuddered. "You don't want to hate him. Anyway, you need someone with time, not that I'm idle, but we're talking Kodiak, the Alpha. He's going to be too busy running the pack. With me showing you how to be a wolf, you'll get to spend as much time as you want on learning and training. And when you spend time with him it'll be good time, not training." She raised her brows up and down.

Tamaska rolled her eyes. "Stop that."

"You know I'm right. More training time means you'll be a better wolf. Knock his wolf socks off, and win over his inner wolf, get it panting!"

She laughed even as her head spun. "Ash."

"I'm right and we both know it."

Tamaska saw Ash's point. "Does that mean answering all my questions, too?"

"Yes." Ash smiled.

"Even the dumb ones?"

"Even those," she said to Tamaska with a dry note of humor.

"And you'd have to answer them? You don't have to get permission from Kodiak?"

"I don't." Ash took a mouthful of coffee.

Tamaska sighed. Her now-impossible vision of the future was a lot to let go of, but one thing was for sure—Ash did have more time to teach Tamaska how to be a wolf, to function within the pack. With a surprise connection forming between them, Tamaska could learn so much, so quickly, rather than always waiting for Kodiak.

And, Ash was also right about how it meant her time with Kodiak wouldn't be training or resentment from her or from him over that aspect. It would be just them. And she wanted that, she really did.

"I look forward to having you teach me," said Tamaska. "Thank you."

"I want to say my pleasure but we'll probably hate each other for...oh...a week. Even when us shifter go through training you hate the trainer for a period of time. People ride your ass so damn hard." Then she grinned. "And I'm going to be no different."

Tamaska gave a small laugh. "Thanks."

"It's a compliment. I think this will be good. And, uh, sorry."

She looked at Ash. "How about we call it even. I used your computer and you accidentally turned me."

"We-ell..."

She stared, oh, God. Ash was going to hold the computer thing over her whenever the whim struck.

"It's a deal." But she touched Tamaska's hand a moment. "Seriously, I told you I forgave you. I hope you can forgive me for this."

Apart from Channing and Roan and maybe Onai, she got the feeling that she could now count Ash as her friend. Hopefully she'd end up proving herself more and others would accept her. And Kodiak…maybe she could make him proud.

"I can't wait get started," Tamaska said.

"First things first. On the full moon, I'll turn you properly. Then, we can start your training."

"I guess it's only a few days away, so I guess I can wait." Tamaska raised her cup of coffee. "Cheers. Seriously. Thank you for helping."

Ash clicked her cup against Tamaska's. "I should warn you, I'm a taskmaster. You might not like my methods."

"Now, you tell me," said Tamaska, laughing.

"I've got to go check on Channing and the others. I'll see you later," Ash said with a sigh.

"Bye." Tamaska finished her cup of coffee. She shivered, knowing she was already a wolf but hadn't yet been turned. All too quickly and yet not quickly enough, that was going to change.

Now that lunchtime had passed, Tamaska figured it was time to check in on Kodiak, maybe wake up. Maybe they could get naked…if he was up to it. With a smile, she returned to his room and opened the door quietly, expecting to see him asleep on the bed.

Instead, the room lay empty.

Where the hell was he?

CHAPTER 30

*amaska*

It was hard to breathe. Panic fluttered fast and wild in her veins and she rushed from the room.

Where could he be?

Had the vampires come? Taken him? It was daytime, but she couldn't help herself from expecting the worst. After all, they'd come and taken him during daylight hours last time. Maybe the residual power from the Opal infused blood still lingered in them?

Or what if it wasn't that but something else? It hurt to breathe as she turned and made herself run.

She rushed out of the room and repeatedly yelled Kodiak's name, hoping he would answer her.

But he didn't.

"Hey, what's going on?" asked Channing. rushing up from the basement.

"He's gone," she stammered. "He's not there! He's gone!"

He looked at her like she'd gone mad. "Who?"

"Kodiak. Who do you fucking think? He's not in his room where I left him." Tamaska clutched at him. Like that would somehow right whatever was wrong. Like it would bring him back.

"I'm sure he's taking a piss or something," said Channing.

"I don't know—I don't feel…" The bond between them felt distant, as if he was no longer close. Emptiness yawned inside of her.

Had the vampires gotten to him again?

She couldn't stop coming back to that. Over and over again it spun in her head

They had gotten in once before. It could happen again.

Worse she'd left him. Let it happen.

She had to say it. She needed to say it. She opened her mouth as she clutched at him, but no words came.

Kodiak had become her world so fast she hadn't noticed, and yet she somehow always knew it from when they first met. So how could she have let him be snatched.

"Do you think…"

Channing shook his head. "No. No way. I'd have seen them. Or not seen them but detected them, and you'd have noticed. So would have everyone else who's around. We can fucking smell them and…" He took a giant deep breath and released it. "See? Vampire-free air."

Her throat was hot, closed up and her eyes burned and blurred. "What if they have a spray, too?

"That's dumb."

"It isn't." She shook her head, teetering on some kind of edge. "This is all my fault. I should have been there, in that room, watching him, defending him. He's hurt, he's—"

"A shifter," he said softly. "The strongest I know. He's healed up."

"You don't know that." She let him go and started to frantically move about the room. She needed a weapon, something. "I have to find him. You have a gun, right? Give it to me."

His eyes went wide.

"I'm going to kill whoever took him. I'm—"

"Ash!" Channing called into the basement. "I need your help!" He stared at her. "You can't have a gun. We don't know who has him or if anyone does or—"

"What is it?" Ash came running up the stairs looking about. Her gaze fell on Tamaska and turned completey serious and the shadows of anxiety from the last day turned darker under her eyes. "What's going on?"

"Kodiak's gone." The words tumbled out. "It's the vampires, I know it. And Channing won't let me have a gun. I need car keys."

"Tamaska!"

"No," she said. "I'm going after him. They probably have him at that horrible club. Oh, God they had those silver nets. They'll kill him."

"You need to calm the fuck down." The savage tone of Ash's voice slapped Tamaska across the face and her panic shifted from planetary meltdown to something manageable.

And she put her icy fingers to her hot cheeks as Channing backed away towards the basement door like they'd both lost their minds.

Ash let out a breath and took her hand and squeezed. "Panicking won't help. We've been through a lot and you got thrown right in. But you know what? You proved yourself a worthy mate to Kodiak—"

"Mate?" Channing grinned. "That's great!" Then he frowned. "I mean buck up, Tamaska, no way vamps took him. We'll get to the bottom of this. I promise."

"Just don't," Ash said, "fall apart now. I'm sure he's here somewhere. Maybe he went for a walk?

But she shook her head. "He wouldn't just leave. He'd let me know." Tamaska looked at Ash. "He'd let kme know. After everything he wouldn't just go."

"Not unles he had a good reason," Channing said.

"Like what?" she snapped. "Last time we wasted so much time and he nearly died. He can't go through that again. He can't."

A muscle worked in Ash's jaw. "I'm sure he's around here somewhere," she said. "He's got nowhere else to go."

"Take her downstairs and review all the security footage. I'll run around the compound and see if I can find him," said Channing. "Because she's got a point. Last time we did just assume he was okay. I'm sure he is, but we should check. I'll go, you both look at the footage."

He took off and the worry grew on Ash's features, even though she tried to hide it. "Come on Tamaska, down this way. Let's see if we can spy on him. Because yeah, it's weird, but he's here somewhere."

"Can you call out to him with your pack link?"

"Hang on." Ash tilted her head as she stared past Tamaska a look of concentration on her face, one that grew the longer she stayed silent. Finally, she shook her head. "Fucking hell, the asshole's blocked me."

"Or maybe something happened—"

"Tamaska, he's definitely blocking. It's…it's hard to explain, you'll have to experience it and practice it, which we will, but I know he's somewhere, and he doesn't seem to be in distress, but he's just not there, you know. Blocking me, that's what he's doing."

But Tamaska wasn't so sure. They hadn't picked up on stress when he was taken by the vampires, so maybe if they had him again, they'd done something.

Or maybe he'd taken off.

But the moment that thought came she dismissed it. He'd

never shirk his responsibilities. This pack and his role as alpha mean too much for him to do that, and he wasn't that kind of person, anyway.

With a sigh, Tamaska followed Ash down the steep stairs into the basement, which was full of security devices and monitors.

"Wow," she said, momentarily stunned out of her now low-key panic mode.

"This is our most recent upgrade, where all of our money went," said Ash. "The best of the best."

Ash sat on a swivel chair, motioning for Tamaska to sit beside her.

"It's impressive." But her anxiousness made her unable to sit still. Yeah, it was impressive, but it was hard to care when the man she loved had gone missing.

Her heart kept coming apart and smashing back together.

Ash typed away at the keyboard, and computer screens flashed between scenes. "Let's start here."

The screen showed the hallway outside Kodiak's room. Tamaska shifted uncomfortably in her chair. At least there wasn't a camera inside their room. Nothing seemed private around the pack.

What was she thinking? He was gone and her brain worried about modesty?

All she wanted was Kodiak back. If she got him back she'd pitch a tent in the living room and reside in that with him. Because he was all that mattered.

"We'll find him, don't worry."

Tamaska's throat constricted. The growing emptiness inside of her argued otherwise.

She studied the screens through occasional flickers, but there was no movement around the room. Then, she watched an image of herself exit the room.

Tamaska sat up straight, hands clutching the swivel chair's arms. Her breath caught and froze in her lungs.

This was it. The moment of truth.

Not long after, Kodiak left the room dressed in jeans, a shirt, and sneakers. His hair was messy, eyes dark and tired. But he looked determined like he had a mission to complete.

What is he up to?

If he was off to kill vampires she'd… She'd rush after him, that's what.

"To be expected, right?" said Ash.

From somewhere she found a smile and put it in place. It felt sickly fake and greasy.

Ash frowned as she clicked on the keyboard, getting the cameras to track Kodiak's movements.

They followed him outside, and Ash flickered between different cameras positioned around the compound.

Then he did something that astounded her.

He got into his car and drove away.

Without a weapon. Without a back up.

Just him and his stupid fucking car.

Driving away.

"He's not, is he?" asked Ash.

Tamaska knew the answer to that. He was.

They watched him drive away from the compound.

"Where the fuck is he going?" asked Ash.

"I don't know, but I'm going to fucking kill him when he returns for leaving without telling me." And Tamaska meant it.

Love or no love, she was fucking killing him.

Dead.

CHAPTER 31

amaska

SHE RUBBED the tops of her shoes into the clean carpet, wondering what on earth could make Kodiak leave her like that.

What the actual fuck was his problem?

And it wasn't just her he'd left. No, he'd left everyone.

Maybe the vampire's had addled his brain or his long contact with the silver had made him insane.

Or maybe he just wanted a good ass whipping and this is the only way he could think of.

Her fingers curled tight. And just maybe he'd decided to go after the vampires and get himself killed.

She swallowed that one down, deep.

Ash and Onai discussed the situation, trying to figure out what was going on, while Channing reviewed the footage again for anything that could give them a clue about Kodiak's intentions.

The same two safe questions played in her mind on repeat. What had happened to him, and what would she do if he didn't come back?

"Do you think he's left us for good?"

"Do you, Tamaska?" asked Onai.

"No." Could she be sure? But she raised her chin. She didn't think any of them thought he would, her included. It was nice they asked her but... They asked her. Like she counted.

But she'd trade that acceptance for him coming in through the doors at this moment.

"But..." She licked her dry lips. "I just don't know why he'd do this, or where he'd go."

Unless he went after the vampires.

Tamaska had said it before and if she kept saying it...what if it made it true?

"This isn't like him. Something's up," said Onai, pushing a hand through his hair. "Maybe he got bitten by one of the vampires, or they infected him with something."

"Roan checked him out last night, though," said Ash. "No marks or bites. He was weak, but...that was to be expected. There was nothing that even remotely suggest they did something to him other than get violent."

Her stomach lurched at that.

"Or maybe," Tamaska said, "he just left because he could. And he's a rat bastard."

"I'll go find him. You two stay here and watch in case he comes back." Onai hurried away.

Ash looked at her. "Men."

"I'm definitely going to kill him," said Tamaska. "I don't care if he went for a drive or went vampire hunting, I'm killing him." She paused. "Kodiak. Not Onai."

"Figured." Ash sighed. "You might have to get in line.

Onai's pretty worked up. He's not showing it like a normal person, but I know him and he's worked up."

"Me too," she muttered.

"He is, but so am I. On the inside." Ash grimaced. "And he is being a rat bastard. Kodiak. Not Onai."

"I know who you meant." Tamaska flexed her fingers, then tightened them into fists. "And he better not kill him before I do."

Onai had barely made it halfway down the driveway in his vehicle when another car came into sight.

Not just any car...

"It's Kodiak's," said Tamaska, jumping to her feet. She was halfway out of the room when Ash grabbed her arm. "Let me go."

"Hang on," said Ash.

"Why?" She looked at the hand. "Let me go I have to go to him."

"I thought you wanted to kill him? You can't do that if you're running into his arms, stressed out of your mind."

She opened her mouth and closed it again as Ash leaned in.

"I mean, he does deserve to suffer, so take a few minutes, calm down and bring on the pain. Make him suffer. No one else can, you know."

That might be the sweetest thing Ash had ever said to her and if circumstances were different she'd be touched.

Tamaska nodded and turned. Ash let her go and smiled.

"True. I'll be in the meeting room, and he can find me there," said Tamaska.

"I'm sure he will. Have fun...killing him?"

Tamaska walked off, angry, stressed, happy he was alive, embarrassed by Ash's parting words, and she stepped into the empty meeting room.

It was quiet. Too quiet in there and she didn't know what to do with herself.

What if he tried to find a way to tell her he'd made a mistake and his love was nothing more than a reaction to his imprisonment? What it—

Tamaska stopped. She'd send herself mad if she kept going.

Uncomfortable in the silence that would eat her sanity right up if she let it consume her, she turned on the television and cycled through its daytime programs to distract herself.

Footsteps in the hallway caught her attention, detected by hearing that was now better than ever before.

Great she was transforming, probably and he was going to kick her to the curb.

No, he wouldn't but the nerves still ate at her.

She sank into one of the lounge chairs and swung her legs over the arm, trying to look casual as Kodiak walled into the room.

"Where have you been?" she demanded. So much for casual. And murder. Although that last one was definitely on the table.

He looked tired, like he was struggling to stand. And her heart went out to him. It was such a traitor.

"I had to do something, Tamaska. And I needed to do it then."

"Not without fucking telling me first." Tamaska sat upright in the chair and frowned at him. "I had no idea what happened to you. What if the vampires had gotten you?"

"Not in the daytime." He moved closer to her. They don't have the Blood Opal anymore."

Good point—she'd forgotten about that. Still, she wasn't about to let him off the hook so easily.

"I was worried about you." She pointed an accusing finger

at him. Her anger had no visible effect on him, which only made her even more furious as he came even closer. "I love you and I was scared."

"I'm sorry—you…you do?" he asked softly.

She shot him an irritated look. "Well of course I do, what do you think I'm doing here?"

"I love you, too, you know."

"You're an ass."

A small smile bloomed briefly. "I wanted to get you something."

She was about to yell at him again, not because she wanted to but because it was better than losing her shit and falling apart, a complete blubbering mess, but his words gave her pause. She swallowed hard, trying to be patient.

"I…I'm listening."

Kodiak knelt beside her. And her heart started to thump madly, sending her pulse spinning. "Things haven't been smooth between us, not since the moment we met."

"That's for sure." But she smiled. Just a little.

"I want that to change." He looked nervous, unsure and she fell in love with him even more. "I want for us to be a team, officially. I want for you—officially—to be my mate."

Her pulse spiraled completely out of control. "You want to marry me?"

Kodiak hesitated. "We don't marry. But we choose our mates, which is sort of the same thing when we do it officially. We mate for life."

Tamaska didn't even have to think about it. Earlier he'd asked her to be his mate, but not like this, not…officially as he put it. "Yes." She clutched her chest. "I told you that last night, but yes, yes, yes."

His eyes widened. "You will?"

"No." She rolled her eyes. "Of course it's a big, fat yes. But don't fucking run off like that again."

Kodiak took something out of his pocket. "I got this for you." And he held it out.

Tamaska leaned forward as he unwrapped white velvet material. She gasped. Two pendants lay inside, bound with fine chains of gold.

They were beautiful. And she wanted to cry.

He lifted the larger pendant. "Since the opal doesn't work anymore, and belongs to you by birthright, I thought this would be a good reminder of how we met. A reminder of how we worked to fight the vampires, and how you became part of the pack."

He clasped the necklace around her, and the pendant settled above her breasts.

"I don't know what to say." Her fingers moved to touch it. The pendant felt like a gem, but it meant so much more to her. Them. It meant them. Her history she didn't know about, but that was just a tiny part, something to tell their children if they had them, but as she touched it, she knew.

The pendant was them, their bond.

As binding as a wedding ring. And more precious.

"Thank you would be enough." Kodiak laughed.

"Thanks." She kissed him gently. "You don't think I should return it?"

"The opal? Fuck, no. It's yours forever."

"What about the other pendant?" asked Tamaska. Pointing to the other.

"If you're all right with it, I plan to wear that one as a reminder for me. I'm a shard broken off from you, but together we're whole."

Emotion caught in her throat. With trembling fingers, she put the necklace on Kodiak. The Blood Opal had been set beautifully into rose gold, the metal adorning its natural luster.

This…this was a real bond. Perfection.

She kissed him long and hard, and desire flamed inside of Tamaska as her need for him flared into life.

"Breaking news," the presenter announced on the television, ending their kiss.

"There's been a string of unusual murders around the city. While the police have declined to comment…"

They looked at each other.

Vampires.

"They're up to something," said Kodiak. And he glared at the screen.

A normal woman, a human woman, would tell him to forget it. Tell him that the thoughts of revenge and destruction were where madness lay and he needed to just leave it alone.

Tamaska was not that kind of fucking woman.

"Hey, Kodiak?"

"Yeah?"

"How about I help you find out what?"

He looked at her a slow, sexy grin spreading on his handsome face. "Yeah?"

"Definitely."

"Are you ready?"

She laughed. "I'm your mate, Kodiak. I was born ready. Question is are you?"

His grin started to widen. "Absofuckinglutely, but…well, you know, after what you've gone through these last few days, you deserve a break."

"Not now." Her grin burst into life. "I know too much."

He kissed her deeply and said, "Well, let's go kick some vampire ass."

"I can't wait."

The End ~ for now!
Can't get enough of Tamaska and Kodiak?

Look out for Bk 4 Cursed Wolf.
Like witches and wolf shifters?
Check out my series Bk 1 Dark Moon Secrets here.
Keep up with Lilliana Rose's new releases by joining her
newsletter here.

ACKNOWLEDGMENTS

Big thanks to DJ for helping bring Rogue Wolf into the world and your long hours to help bring the ms into the world with me. Thanks to Ember and Rebecca for your super support and patience. Thanks to my creative friend Marianne, who is always there to boost me up during the journey. Thank you to Susan who patiently reads through my work and encourages me to keep writing.

Of course, thanks to my dogs, Kimba and Sprinkles, who are always at my feet being the quiet support I need. I miss you Kimba, but know you're with Astro running around up there and having fun.

ABOUT THE AUTHOR

Lilliana Rose is a bestselling author who writes romance in the subgenres of contemporary, paranormal, urban, and fantasy. She enjoys helping characters overcome problems or issues and the misunderstandings that often plague relationships to help them fall in love. Whether its city heels being replaced with country work boots, or some magic beyond this world, each story shows how love can prevail. She has over fifteen years of experience in various education systems as a teacher, a skip, and a jump from starting out in genetics research. It is all helpful for inspiring her writing. She has poetry, middle grade, picture book, novellas, and novels published under various pen names.

http://www.lillianarose.com/

Keep up to date with Lilliana on social media
Facebook, Twitter, Pinterest, Goodreads, Instagram